BABY BANK

A Lesbian Romantic Comedy

Sarah Robinson

To Baby Emery, whose existence sparked the idea for this entire story. Your moms are cool, too.

Chapter One

"I caught your show the other night," my gynecologist said from between my legs as he cranked open the speculum.

I kept my eyes glued to the ceiling tile above me, which had an informative list of the symptoms of herpes. Casual reading, I assumed. "At the Comedy Loft?"

I lowered my gaze when Dr. Nicholas Allen's head popped up above the sheet draped across my knees. "That's the one. You know, I loved your set on being bisexual and how that meant twice the rejection instead of twice the dates. My wife and I laughed and laughed. Really great stuff."

I gave him a tight-lipped grin and bob of my head. "Thanks. Always nice to meet a fan. It's pansexual, by the way."

"Of course. Right. So, how'd you come up with your stage name?" he asked.

"It's a play on my name. Tori Miles, Mila Torres." I didn't usually answer questions like that, but since he *was* inside me... "With my day job, it's easier to have some distance between that and my comedy."

"Makes total sense. You know what you should add to your next set?" I could feel the giant cotton swab making crampy friends with my cervix as he chatted away like he wasn't basically breathing into my bearded clam. "Vagina jokes. I've got tons of them."

Definitely something I wanted to hear from my gynecologist.

"For example," he continued. "Did you know that in older literature, the labia are referred to as meat curtains? Or the wooly beaver. Or a pink taco. Honestly, there's so much material there you could write a whole set on it."

"I think vaginas already have a monopoly on monologues," I replied.

He snorted and I swear to God I felt a spray. "That's clever. See, Mila? You're a great comedian!"

I hadn't asked for his validation, but this wasn't an uncommon conversation with the male species these days.

"You can go ahead and sit up now," he said after another minute. "All finished."

I shimmied my butt farther back onto the table and closed my legs. "All look good down there?"

"The nurse will call you if the results come back as abnormal, but I'm sure you're fine. It would be good to start thinking about your reproductive future though." He was pulling his gloves off with a snap and depositing them in a red biohazard box. "At thirty-four, you're considered almost an advanced age for pregnancy, and every year that goes by, your eggs will continue to degrade. Freezing them now could give you more options in the future for having children later in life. Have you considered having a family?"

"You know, strangely, no one has ever asked me when I'm going to settle down and have kids," I replied, tapping a finger to my chin to highlight the sarcasm dripping from my words.

But my sarcasm went directly past Dr. Allen. "Really? Well, you're lucky. Most women are hounded about that kind of thing. I'll give you a few pamphlets on fertility specialists that we work with often. Great people. Give them a call and get a consultation if you're interested. Certainly, no need to sign on the dotted line just yet, but good to get the information, right?"

"Right." I hugged the thin paper gown tighter around me and focused my gaze on the diagram against the window of an IUD plugging up a uterus.

"Unless you're thinking about having kids soon?" Dr. Allen looked up from the small computer he was working on off the small countertop next to the sink. "Single women have kids all the time lately. Not much you need a man for these days."

He chuckled at that last line, and I bet he thought he was clever. He wasn't entirely wrong though.

"If—and it's a big *if*—I were thinking about having kids on my own, what would the process be?" The question came out of my mouth before I could fully form a thought around it. "You know, out of curiosity. Not saying I'm actually considering it."

He didn't seem as shocked by my question as I was. "Well, right now, there's no reason to suspect that you couldn't carry a healthy pregnancy. An intrauterine insemination procedure could place the sperm and then you'd wait until a missed period to pee on a stick and see if it worked. There are even do-it-at-home kits, but I'd recommend going through a fertility clinic rather than the turkey baster route for better chances."

I nodded as if I was actually considering his words. It kind of scared me to realize that...I actually was. Was I having a stroke? Was this some sort of belated quarter-century crisis? "And what about...sperm? Can you just go to a sperm bank and ask for sperm?"

"Not without a credit card," he teased. "But seriously,

you're probably looking at twelve hundred dollars a pop on average. Though some places offer a discount for military or Costco memberships."

Discount sperm was *not* on my to-procreate list.

"Twelve hundred dollars?" My brows lifted as I tried to remember how much my former law school roommate used to get for his donations to a sperm bank. "I thought guys only got fifty bucks a deposit or something like that?"

"Oh, they do." Dr. Allen shrugged his shoulders. "Markups are second nature in this industry. The sample goes through rigorous testing, but also, the bank wants to make a profit to keep the doors open."

"The way of the world," I replied, the familiar disillusionment with capitalism in my tone.

He nodded as he finished up his notes and then stood. "Well, go ahead and get dressed, and I'll leave the paperwork and pamphlets at the front desk for you."

"Thank you." I shed the paper gown the moment he closed the door behind him. As quickly as possible, I grabbed my clothes that were folded neatly on the chair to my right—my underwear discreetly tucked into the pocket of my jeans. Heaven forbid my gynecologist find out what type of underwear I wear.

Moments later, I stepped out into the hallway and walked past Dr. Allen, who was typing away at some sort of makeshift computer station between two exam rooms.

"Good to see you!" he called out when he spotted me. The man actually waved vigorously as if I might not see him.

I smiled tightly and nodded my head, hoping that was enough to get me out of there unscathed.

"Mila Torres?" the receptionist called out to me as I tried to make it through the waiting room inconspicuously.

I turned and gave her my most innocent smile, pretending I hadn't noticed her there. "Oh, that's me."

"We don't have a card on file for you. How would you like to pay?" she asked as I stepped closer to the front desk, still trying to stay out of the line of sight of literally anyone possible.

I'd like to not pay, to be honest. "Is my insurance not covering the visit? It was just an annual."

She looked back at her computer screen and then back to me. "You haven't hit your deductible for the year yet."

That was basically gibberish to me, but I handed over my debit card anyway. If anyone had asked me in law school if being an attorney at a prominent law firm that handled all the politicians' divorces in Washington, DC, would mean I'd be bathing in money, I would have absolutely said, "Dollar, dollar bill, baby." Instead, I make six figures and can barely afford the mortgage on a narrow, two-bedroom row home in Capitol Hill that, for the same price, would buy a ten-bedroom McMansion in Ohio.

My cell phone began vibrating in my pocket as I left the office and made my way to the dingy parking garage to find the puke-green 2005 Ford Taurus I'd inherited from my grandfather. I'd used Band-Aids—yes, literal Band-Aids from the first aid kit in the glove box—to hold down the paint on the hood of the car that kept flapping up and hitting my windshield, but the clunky machine still worked fine, so I didn't care. It wasn't like I needed a car that often in the district and paying for a monthly parking spot wasn't my favorite budgeting expense, so I was just planning on letting this one ride out into the sunset.

"Hello?" I clicked the speakerphone button and placed my phone in its holder on the dashboard as I turned the car's engine on.

It connected to the small Bluetooth device I'd attached to

the old car's visor just as my best friend's voice blared through the speakers. "You're not even going to believe this shit, Mila."

"What?" I turned toward the exit and signaled my intent.

"Do you remember the Jolly Green Giant?" Isa Reyes had been one of my best friends since our undergraduate years and —like me—had been perpetually single. Except—unlike me— she nicknamed all her Tinder matches and had a steady rotation of dates every Thursday through Saturday night. "He called me *Tuesday*."

"Tuesday? Like via text?" I asked further, super confused.

She laughed, but it sounded bitter and like the type of laugh that, if I had been standing next to her, I would have had to start thinking about alibis for the both of us. "I wish. No! Mid act! My legs were straight up in the air and he was saying how good I felt, 'Tuesday.' I go, 'Who?' He says, 'You know, because we matched on a Tuesday.' It's how he keeps track of his dates! So, anyway, he's over."

"Yikes," I commented, definitely not mentioning that she also uses made-up names for her dates. This wasn't a *hold-me-accountable* moment. This was a *burn-the-patriarchy-to-the-ground* moment, and I was always on board for that. "I'm sorry, Isa. I know you really liked him."

"I liked his height." I could hear her tapping away on a keyboard in the background. She worked full-time as a public relations executive for a crisis management firm and multi-tasking was her bread and butter. There was a briskness about her, but being her friend all these years, I knew her soft underbelly. She sent most of her paycheck home to her parents in the Philippines every month and lived off the rest. Her heart was bigger than anyone I'd ever met, but so was her libido. "What about you? How was the gyno? They toss in a free happy ending this time? I recently saw this show on Netflix, and you won't believe what they did with a transvaginal wand—"

"He told me I should think about freezing my eggs." I cut her off quickly as I narrowly avoided running into the car in front of me when it randomly slammed on its brakes. I gritted my teeth. "The drivers in this town, I swear."

"I was thinking about doing that, but then I realized I don't want children." Isa laughed through the phone. "Can you imagine me as a mom?"

I wasn't about to walk into that trap, so I shifted the focus back to me. "Actually, I've been considering it."

"Freezing your eggs?"

I shook my head even though she couldn't see me. "No, having a kid."

There was silence for a moment and then a forced laugh. "Uh, Mila...what?"

"I'm serious," I continued. "I'm thirty-four years old and there's no ring on my finger. Hell, there isn't even a date on my calendar. But I've *always* wanted to be a mother. You know that. I've been talking about it since I got my first baby doll at age four. It has sucked waiting all this time for *the one* so that I can be the person I've always wanted to be. Why do I have to wait until I find the perfect partner? I can be a mom right here and now, thanks to science."

The idea had crept into my mind more than a few times before today's doctor visit. I loved my career and my social life and everything that made me who I am today, but there had never been a doubt in my mind that I was meant to be a mother one day. Maybe it was because my own mother was such a pivotal part of my life. She had also been a single mother, raising me completely alone. I know it could be done because I'd seen her do it—and excel at it, if I may brag on her behalf for a moment.

I wanted the chance to give that experience to the next

generation—an adoring, devoted mother. Was that really too much to ask? Was it really a two-person job?

Isa laughed again, and I could practically hear her shaking her head. "I can't imagine telling my parents I was buying sperm. They'd ask why I wasn't sending more money back to them if I was that rich."

I opened my car window and slid my credit card into the parking meter. "How much does sperm cost in the Philippines?"

"It doesn't," Isa continued. "You can't buy sperm. You can do IVF treatments, but that's like two-hundred-and-fifty-thousand Philippine pesos or more. So, maybe six thousand US dollars. It would be cheaper to adopt a baby than to make one over there."

I cringed at the thought of the cost it might be stateside. "The doctor told me it would be twelve hundred dollars to buy sperm here."

"What?" Isa all but shrieked through the phone. "No, that's ridiculous. Men do that for free in a sock. You can find that on Tinder with one swipe."

"It's insane, right?" I thought back to the few drunken one-night stands I'd had where my priority had been *not* getting pregnant. Hell, I'd paid fifty dollars over the counter at the pharmacy the next day for a morning-after pill twice in my life —all in an effort to make sure I wasn't signing a lifetime contract with some random dick.

And now I was considering *buying* sperm.

"Why not just get a friend to give you his for free?" Isa asked. I could still hear her typing on her computer in the background and what sounded like a work video call in progress. God, I hoped she was on mute. "Who do we know that would be a hands-off dad?"

I shook my head. "Absolutely not. I don't want any complications or strings tied. That's way too much pressure for a friendship. It definitely needs to be a stranger. If I go this route, it needs to be no strings tied, completely free of drama."

"Hmm." Isa paused, seeming to think about it for a minute. "Oh! I know. Use Baby Bank!"

"What's Baby Bank?" I turned my car down the block and scanned for an open parking spot on the street in front of my townhouse—a hit-or-miss situation most days. And by that, I mean almost always miss. "Do you mean a sperm bank?"

"No. Remember my lesbian neighbors, Jamie and Amy?"

I was friends with both women on Facebook after having met them at Isa's housewarming party, and I'd recently seen a pregnancy announcement on Jamie's page. "Yeah, Jamie's pregnant, right? I think I saw the announcement not too long ago."

"Fourteen weeks," Isa confirmed. "They used Baby Bank to get pregnant. You can download it in the app store."

"It's an app?" I maneuvered into a free spot against the curb a block from my townhouse and turned off my car, switching the call back to handheld. "What the heck are you talking about? You can't get pregnant by an app!"

"Have you seen the world we live in recently? Of course you can." She spit out another laugh, then I heard the crackling sound of a bag of chips being opened on the other end. "It's like Tinder, but for free sperm. Guys have profiles on there and you swipe until you find the sperm you want and then see if you match."

"That is *not* really a thing." But I was already opening the app store on my phone and typing the name in the search bar. Sure enough, Baby Bank popped up immediately. "Holy shit, it *is* a thing!"

"It's actually legit," Isa continued in between crunching and swallowing her snack. If I had to guess, knowing her, I'd say Cool Ranch Doritos. "Lots of couples use it when they're

9

trying to have a kid. Doesn't cost anything. All arrangements are worked out individually with the guy. Oh, but don't swipe on the profiles that say *NI only*."

I frowned. "What's *NI* mean?"

"Natural insemination only. It's just dudes trying to get laid."

I was already halfway through signing up for my own account, and of course, the first profile that popped up said NI ONLY. "Wow...why do men even sign up for this? What do they get out of it?"

"I don't know. Spread their seed?" Isa remarked, seemingly unfazed by the entire thing.

I grimaced as I closed out of the app and stepped out of my car. "I just got home. I'll talk to you later, okay?"

"Okay, but I'm coming over later tonight for some booze-induced swiping," she replied. "I want to pick a baby daddy with you!"

I grinned and shook my head. "I didn't say I'm going to do it!"

She laughed, then all I heard was what sounded like a chip going down the wrong pipe. She coughed and sputtered for a moment before returning to the phone. "But you didn't say no!"

I said goodbye and hung up the phone, then stuck it in my pocket while I finagled my keys into the lock on my front door. My orange-and-black-striped cat Macavity was primed and ready to shoot out between my legs and onto the street, but I blocked the old man with my bag and pushed him back inside. "Hey! No! Get back inside. Stop trying to leave me."

"Did he get out?" my roommate's voice called out from the other room. "That fucking cat tore up my Tieks this morning. I'm absolutely not speaking to him."

I locked the door behind me and wagged a finger at Macavity, lowering my voice to a harsh whisper. "You're causing trouble again."

With his escape to freedom shut down, he slinked away from me without a second look. I followed him into the kitchen where my roommate and friend Yasmeen Kiani was sitting on a stool at the counter in front of her computer—her usual work-from-home spot as a flailing serial entrepreneur who I'd met in law school before she dropped out to pursue business. And then another business. And another. At this point, I had no idea how she was paying her part of the rent, but the check kept coming, so I kept my nose out of it.

"How badly damaged are they?" I asked.

She pointed to the trash can in the corner of the kitchen where a tattered pair of expensive black and teal shoes lay on top. "El fin."

"I'll buy you a new pair," I assured her, mentally calculating an extra two hundred dollars (yes, it's ridiculous) into this month's budget. "How's work going?"

She didn't look up but pushed a plate of biscuits toward me that she'd made. We'd been friends since law school, but I would be lying if I didn't admit that her incredible cooking was the biggest reason I still lived here with her and our other roommate, Rachel Blumenthal—also an attorney we met in our law school days, except Rachel had actually completed law school and was now in environmental law with the EPA. "This big retailer is on their usual power trip. It makes no sense why they can't add a nonbinary or androgynous category to the gender section in their clothing store. My line would be absolutely perfect for their shelves, but they've got too many Karens who shop there apparently."

Sounded about white. "So, margaritas tonight?"

She glanced up at me as if I was crazy to even ask. Taco Tuesdays with the perfect margarita were as close to religion as we came at our home. "Of course. I bought more coarse salt this weekend for the rim."

"That's all you." I was an on-the-rocks, no-salt type of girl. I grabbed a cup of black coffee from our Keurig and then headed up the stairs to my bedroom. My desk was against the bay window facing the front of the house and gave me a lovely view of the homeless guy on the corner peeing into a trash can while I worked.

I looked around my bedroom and pictured myself as a mother. I couldn't keep living in Capitol Hill the way we were now, that was for sure. I loved the location, and the mortgage was easy to afford, with Rachel paying rent for living in the den and Yasmeen paying for the other bedroom. But could they still live here if I brought a baby into the mix?

Right now, we had a *Golden Girls* style living concept that had been working well for all of us over the last decade. Originally, we'd all been focused on law school and then beginning our careers, and now we were all in our mid-thirties, and I realized that...maybe I wanted other parts of life instead of just the career.

I splayed out across the bed and propped myself up on my elbows as I began scrolling through my phone. The Baby Bank app was calling to me, but I didn't give in to the temptation. Instead, I opened up my email—my first mistake—and groaned at the familiar name at the top of my inbox.

From: Arielle Elliot, aelliot@washingtontimes.com
Re: Respond for Comment - URGENT

Ms. Torres,

. . .

I've attempted to reach you through your office on multiple occasions and have only received the usual "no comment" statement from your receptionist and marketing team. As you know, however, Senator Murphy's possible affair and impregnation of his campaign intern leading to the current divorce proceedings with his wife has major implications on current political agendas given his stance on women's reproductive rights and the bill he's currently championing in the Senate. It is very important that I confirm the details of this case with you in order to properly inform the voting public with regard to who they are supporting.

My contact information is below. Please follow up as soon as possible.

Kindly,
   Ari Elliot
   Lead Reporter, Washington Times
   Email: aelliot@washingtontimes.com
   Phone: 202-555-6969

I immediately hit delete on her email. A hazard of my job had always been reporters, and I had been trained well in how to artfully dodge them, but Arielle Elliot was like a dog with a bone. We had yet to meet—which was by sheer skill on my part, thank you very much—since I evaded her as swiftly and skillfully as a deadbeat dad who doesn't want to pay child support. I wasn't even the primary counsel on the case she was referencing, so I sure as hell wasn't about to tie my name to it in the papers.

Although, that was kind of true about all my clients. It was pretty rare that I had a redeemable client who was actually a good person in their day-to-day life and not just a scheming hopeful politician trying to destitute their wife. This job required some depersonalization on my part—trying to keep my own morals and feelings out of the picture so that I could actually do the work...and well.

I let go of my phone and let it fall to the bed as I rolled over and stared up at the ceiling. Macavity came and joined me, sitting in a round pile of fur by my head and purring so loudly that he vibrated the entire bed. My hand drifted down to my stomach, and I closed my eyes, imagining a baby kicking inside one day. A little cherub with pudgy cheeks calling me *mama* and running around like a toddler gymnast climbing the walls of this house. The smile spread over my face before I could overthink it.

I wanted to be a mother. And I didn't want to wait.

Chapter Two

I an, 24. *Capitol Hill Staffer. These swimmers deserve to swim the entire ocean. I'm ready to populate the sea! Message me if you'd like to get good and pregnant as soon as possible.*

"Absolutely not." I swiped left immediately. *Sorry, Ian.*

Yasmeen pointed to the profile that popped up next. "What about Garrett?"

We had cast my phone screen to our Apple TV so Yasmeen, Rachel, Isa, and I were all swiping on potential baby daddies in my living room while stuffing ourselves with Taco Bell delivery from DoorDash and homemade margaritas.

"He says he's a lobbyist for Walgreens," I replied, frowning as I tucked my legs beneath me on the couch and reached for another sip of my on-the-rocks margarita. "Anything remotely related to Big Pharma is out."

I swiped past three natural-insemination-only profiles before stopping on *Rashaad, 23.* "A creative looking to get creative with my legacy. I have twenty-twenty vision and never needed braces, but I do have seasonal allergies to pollen. I do not want to co-parent, so the kid is all yours. I wouldn't mind the occasional picture or update though." I read his bio out loud to my friends. "This guy has some potential. He's really cute."

"Oh, but he's in Woodbridge, though." Isa pointed at the screen where his location was displayed. She was sitting on the floor cross-legged with a plate of tacos in front of her and at least three pieces of shredded lettuce and cheese dropped on the front of her shirt.

Automatic swipe left. "Yeah, sorry. Northern Virginia is out, too."

Rachel laughed and propped her feet up on our coffee table. She was on her latest round of the keto diet, so her margarita was basically tequila and water. Her blonde hair was pulled back into a loose French braid and her blue eyes sparkled whenever she smiled. How she was still single, I would never understand. "Guys, Virginia is literally like a mile away. Less, even."

"But you have to cross a bridge," Yasmeen pointed out. "We don't do that. And Woodbridge is like a lot of bridges."

"What about Cliff?" Rachel gestured to the screen when the next profile popped up. "He's got a man bun *and* a caveman beard."

"In DC? That means he is probably a mixologist and talks about *his craft* way too much," I replied, only partially joking. "I don't know what he's hiding under that beard, but he's not bad looking. Oh, wait, that last line—looking to provide natural insemination only with no desire for co-parenting, etc. Next. Wait, what's PI mean?"

I pointed at the next profile that stated it was open to AI, PI, and NI.

Yasmeen typed something into her phone, then looked at me. "Partial insemination."

I scrunched up my face. "What the heck does that mean? How do you get partially pregnant?"

"Just the tip!" Isa raised her hand and pretended like she was cheering.

Yasmeen laughed. "Or maybe he just tries to aim close and then the swimmers have to battle it out to see who wins."

"I honestly can't even believe we're doing this," Rachel responded as I continued to swipe through more profiles. "You do realize that pregnancy means like ten months without margaritas, right? Or soft cheeses! What about eggs benedict? You love runny eggs."

"Not to mention she's going to be kicking us out." Yasmeen looked over at Rachel. "Unless she wants free childcare."

"Absolutely yes to free childcare," I joked. "I mean, I think until the baby is toddler age, they don't take up a lot of space. So, we have time to figure all that out. Right?"

Isa didn't look so sure. "The only people I know with kids seem to always be outgrowing their spaces. It's like plastic toys and baby gear expand and explode with no warning."

"Stop!" Yasmeen suddenly called out as she pointed to the profile on the screen. "Oh. My. God."

We all went quiet as we read the bio in front of us. *Hi, I'm Aston Li and I'm 27 years old. I have no desire to have a family of my own, but I love helping people in need and figure this is a way I can do it. I have a clean bill of health and I've worked with four couples and two single women successfully already. In fact, we have a Facebook group called Pieces of Aston where all the new parents can get to know each other and meet their child's half siblings. I work in IT and keep my head down, but I've got an impressive list of graduate degrees that are guaranteed to deliver you a smart kiddo.*

I swear my breath caught in my throat as I read, then I looked at his pictures and I was signed, sealed, delivered. "He's gorgeous *and* smart! Plus, he actually sounds like he's doing this for the right reasons."

"Okay, but a Facebook group for his sperm demons?" Isa wrinkled her nose. "And it's called Pieces of Aston? I might gag."

That was a little weird but also...really practical? "I'm on the fence with how I feel about that one."

"You should swipe right on him. Message him!" Yasmeen was clearly Team Aston as she leaned forward and clapped her hands to her knees. "I would absolutely make a baby with him as long as I didn't have to touch a penis."

"Do *you* want his information?" I laughed, offering her my phone. She shook her head, and it was a good thing she did because I wasn't about to let this one pass. I swiped right and clicked the message button. "What do I say to someone I want to make a baby with?"

We all paused on that one, since most of our dating experience had been quite the opposite.

"I don't think my normal openers on Bumble will work here," Rachel finally said. "I always ask if they were a steak, how would they want to be cooked? And I only date women, so..."

I grimaced. "Yeah, I'm definitely not opening with a line about meat."

"Just be genuine," Isa offered, actually sounding like the reasonable one for once. "Tell him you liked his profile and you'd like to talk further in person or on the phone."

"Zoom a baby daddy?" I laughed at the idea, even though all of this seemed crazy and far-fetched. "How's this sound?"

I typed up a quick greeting about myself and that I was interested in his profile. The girls all nodded and agreed that it was simple and no-nonsense, so I hit send.

"Now we wait," Isa announced, pushing herself up onto her feet. "Another round for anyone?"

We all downed the rest of our margs. Not even two seconds after the last sip, my phone pinged loudly with a new notification.

"Oh, my God, he responded." My breath caught in my throat. "What do I do?"

"You read it." Yasmeen grabbed my phone out of my hands and clicked on the notification. Aston's message pulled up on the Apple TV for all to read.

Great to meet you, Mila. I'd be more than happy to chat via phone or video call. I'm currently at a work conference in Colorado, but I'll be back home in Washington, DC, this weekend. In the meantime, I'd be happy to provide you with some references to other new moms I've worked with.

"He comes with references!" Rachel clapped her hands. "Yes, let's background check him for sure. I'll ask my friend in Metro PD to run his name."

I quickly wrote back to Aston that I'd love to speak to his references and that I was wondering how the process worked. He responded just as quickly the second time.

The way I've found most comfortable in the past is that the mom (or moms) books a hotel room for the exchange to occur. I'll leave my sample in the bathroom alone in a collection kit— you'll need to buy a home insemination kit for this—while you wait in the lobby and then I will leave the room so that you and your partner can do the rest in privacy.

He also included a few names and phone numbers beneath.

"That actually doesn't sound too creepy," Isa commented. "Sounds like a professional service, to be honest. Can you buy a home insemination kit off Amazon? Prime Now delivers in two hours, so you could be pregnant by tonight."

"He's still in Colorado," I reminded her. "I'd have to wait until this weekend, at least. Which is a good thing because it gives us time to check him out and make sure he's legit."

Yasmeen finished mixing up the next round of cocktails and passed one out to each of us. "Ask him if he's willing to send medical records and a recent physical."

Absolutely. I have a packet ready for any prospective moms that I can email you tonight. It will have my family medical history with names redacted, my own medical history, and a recent physical from the last year including a full blood panel. It will also have recent STD test results and my college and graduate school transcripts.

I immediately responded back to him with my email address and thanked him for his candor and openness. "I have a really good feeling about this guy."

Another notification popped up at the top of my screen, but this time, it was a motion detection alert from my Ring doorbell.

"Is someone here?" Yasmeen turned to look toward the front door seconds before someone knocked loudly on it. "Are we expecting someone else? Did they text first?"

I shook my head and pulled up the Ring app on my phone to look at the camera. Whoever it was, was standing too close to the camera for me to see their face. I got up and walked over to the front door, glancing through the peephole as I called out. "Who's there?"

"Is this the residence of Mila Torres, Esquire?" A woman's voice came from the other side of the door. She stepped back and I could now see her on the Ring camera—she was tall with sharp, yet somehow delicate, features and a brown leather coat that made her look like she was involved in espionage or intrigue.

I was certainly intrigued.

"Who's asking?" I replied, still not opening the door.

The woman checked her Apple Watch and seemed exasperated. "I'm a reporter from the *Washington Times*—Ari Elliot. I have a few questions I need to get answered tonight. Is she here?"

How did she find my address? I cleared my throat and quickly tried to think of a response. This chick was clearly determined, but I wasn't about to become her next source. I looked toward my friends, panic probably written all over my face.

"There's no one by that name who lives here," Isa answered for me, shouting through the door. "Sorry!"

"Ms. Torres, I just need a few minutes of your time. We can keep it entirely anonymous," the woman on the other side of the door continued.

"We'd love to help, but we don't know her!" Isa shot back, just as stubbornly.

I watched on the camera as the woman threw up her hands and sighed. She shook her head and pulled out her phone, tapping on it for a few moments.

Suddenly, the camera view disappeared on my phone and a new call came through. The caller ID only said *Washington, DC.* My phone loudly began ringing and I immediately regretted the ringtone I'd chosen. It sounded like an egg timer, and I couldn't hit decline fast enough.

"Oh my God, is she calling me?" I whispered to Isa.

Isa's eyes were wide. "That's her?"

I shrugged because I had no idea, but then the same number called again.

"Ms. Torres, I can hear your phone ringing. I know you're in there," the woman called through the door. "Can we please talk? I've done my research on you, and there's no way you support Senator Murphy's actions in this upcoming bill he's trying to pass limiting women's reproductive rights. You can help me expose him."

I don't know why, but I hit the floor the moment she said that. As if ducking down was going to be helpful at all since Ari Elliot certainly couldn't see through my wooden front door. Isa crouched down, too, and both Rachel and Yasmeen were watching wide-eyed from the couch.

Yasmeen leaned over and turned off the lamp that was on the end table. "Turn the lights off!"

Isa hit the light switch by the front door and the entire room went dark. She giggled as she called out again. "No one is home!"

"Are you drunk?" I angry-whispered at her. "Just tell her to go away. Tell her we called the cops."

"Good thinking." Isa nodded seriously, then snorted and laughed again. She cleared her throat when I glared at her and took a deep breath. "We're calling the police if you don't leave now!"

I opened the Ring app on my phone again and watched on the camera as Ari shook her head.

"I'm leaving my card in the mailbox," Ari let me know through the door. She seemed to look directly into the camera, and I felt a small tremor of excitement pass through me at that. Her eyes were intense and piercing, and her lips were full. If we'd met under different circumstances and she hadn't been a crazed stalker, I'd probably have flirted with her. "Please reach out, Ms. Torres."

I watched her pull her card out of her wallet and slip it through the mail slot, where it dropped right into my lap. She waited another moment as if hoping that was going to change my mind. There was a fierceness in her expression, and I doubted that this would be my last run-in with her... For some reason, that idea was giving me tingles up the back of my spine.

In truth, Ari wasn't wrong. I hated Senator Murphy, and I loathed that he'd secretly impregnated a campaign intern, coerced and paid for her to have an abortion and that he was now trying to pass legislation in his home state to limit women's rights to contraceptives and abortion procedures. It was the typical *do as I say, not as I do* white male politician approach, and it made me feel murderous.

But I was only one lawyer out of several on his divorce case with his wife, including my boss, one of the partners. I didn't have the option of whether or not to take him on as a client, but I did have a responsibility to him now that he was my client. It was the job—even if it made me feel sick to my stomach whenever he'd come by the offices and hit on the younger paralegals brazenly.

God, I hated when people thought they were above the law. Yet, here I was, helping him do just that. College me would have burned my bra at the very thought.

"She's gone." Isa was holding my phone now and watching the camera as I fingered the glossy business card in my hands that she'd left behind. Her name was even embossed. "Wow. That was crazy. It's like you've got your own paparazzi. And she's totally your type, too."

I tried to ignore Isa's commentary, even if I was thinking the same thing.

"I hate that you're working for him," Yasmeen added as she flicked the light back on. "He's absolute pond scum."

"I know, I know." I groaned as I pushed up to my feet and slid the business card into my back pocket. I joined them on the couch and downed more than half of my second margarita in two gulps. "We're close to a mediation, though. I'm pushing hard to make sure his wife gets everything she's owed. Poor woman was married to a complete pig."

"Hey, Aston emailed you back—there are two attachments!" Isa handed me my phone. "Let's read his transcripts. Also, you can't have anyone's baby who didn't graduate at least summa cum laude."

"As long as he has over a 3.0 GPA, I'll have his baby." I laughed but immediately downloaded the files he'd sent in his email. "This might be our strangest Taco Tuesday yet."

"Wait 'til next week when you're knocked up with a stranger's baby," Rachel replied. "Speaking of, when are you going to tell your mom about this plan?"

"How about after I give birth?" I loved my mom more than life itself, but the idea of telling her that I was choosing to follow in her footsteps when she'd spent a lifetime hammering into me that she never wanted me to make the "mistakes" she had made...thank you, but no. Not that I considered myself a mistake—and she certainly didn't either—but I knew she wanted more for me than the hard times she'd faced. But there was a big difference between her as a young pregnant college drop-out who worked at a nail salon and me as a thirty-four-year-old lawyer who owned her own row house a few blocks from one of the most powerful buildings in the country.

"She will find out," Rachel cautioned, letting out a low whistle. "You can't hide anything from Chicky."

"The moment the egg fertilizes, she's going to have some sort of sixth sense and come banging on this door just like that hot reporter did," Isa added. "You're going to have to tell her."

"That's a problem for another day," I replied, wondering how I'd get through our usual mother-daughter Sunday dinner this week without mentioning anything or without her guessing that I was holding something back. I held up my phone to show the transcript I had opened. "Tonight's problem is that Aston got a C in his human sexuality class. What if my baby ends up single and impregnating strangers on an app? I can't be a grandmother to eighty-seven grand-sperm-babies."

The girls laughed and we scanned through the rest of the transcript, all of which was pretty uneventful. He was clearly intelligent and probably a bit nerdy, but he seemed like a straight shooter.

At least, that's what I was hoping he'd be for me.

Chapter Three

"A better flow for your precious cargo," I read the words on the website out loud as I sat in front of my laptop at the kitchen table. "It has an angular opening. Do penises have angular openings?"

Rachel shrugged as she spooned a scoop of low-carb Greek yogurt into her mouth across from me. "I've never been that close to one to see."

"Fair," I said with a laugh. Rachel had come out in middle school to her family and by the time I met her in law school, she was one of the most secure lesbians I'd ever met. The rest of us all seemed to be figuring it out as we went, but Rachel knew with confidence who she was and what she wanted. It was one of the things I loved and admired most about her. "I've got to be honest. I thought a home insemination kit would be more expensive."

I had a few more minutes before I had to finish getting ready for work, but I'd promised myself I'd order the kit this morning. I'd already peed on a couple of ovulation sticks over the last few days and based on my period tracker app, I should be primed and ready on Monday or Tuesday. Thankfully, Aston would be back in town by that point, so this all could really happen a lot sooner than I had thought.

"It's basically just a medical-grade turkey baster," Rachel commented. "Order a couple in case the first one doesn't take."

"The package comes with two already, but there is a monthly subscription option," I noted. "How likely is it that I'd get pregnant on the first try?"

She finished her yogurt and tossed it in a perfect arc into the trash can. "Your mom did with you."

Fair. "But she was twenty years old when she conceived me. According to the research I've done, I'll be considered a geriatric pregnancy."

Rachel scrunched up her face. "At thirty-four?"

"Well, I'll probably turn thirty-five before I give birth." I clicked on an Insemination 101 video on the website I was perusing. An animated image of a woman inserting a syringe into her vagina popped up on my screen with elevator music in the background. "Oh, yikes. Okay, so she just shoves it all up there like one and done."

Rachel leaned over to see my screen. "It seems pretty easy. You just have to get it right up next to the cervix."

"It says that they recommend I have an orgasm once it is in to pull up the sperm." That didn't seem particularly difficult, but not sure I'd be in the mood at that particular moment.

"I've heard that before, too," Rachel agreed. She grabbed her side bag that lay on the credenza by the front door. "Plus, you have to put your legs up for like half an hour or something after. Anyway, I'm headed to work. See you tonight?"

I nodded, not looking up as I clicked *Add to cart*. Delivery time was only two days. Something about hitting *Place your order* made all of this feel very real. Not that it wasn't before, because I was not going into this with any illusions this would be easy. But, still, the idea of having a little human around that I could help learn and grow and become part of the world sounded fulfilling in a way that divorce law certainly didn't.

I pulled up Aston's email and looked through the list of names and numbers he'd sent me as references. The first one had the same last name as him, and I guessed it must be a relative. Hopefully he had not impregnated her, and she was more of a character witness. Either way, I tapped her number into my phone and hit send.

"Hi, I'm trying to reach Nomi Li?" I said when a woman's voice answered on the other end.

"This is she. Who is calling?"

"Hi, Ms. Li," I began, suddenly unsure of how to introduce myself in this scenario. "Uh, Aston Li gave me your information as a reference. I just wanted to call and see if you knew him, and if he, uh, well, I guess if he was a good guy? Healthy?"

"Christ, is this another call about his sperm?" The woman sighed and she sounded like she was a bit older than me. "I swear to God, that kid. Yes, Aston is healthy and he's a good boy. He doesn't listen to his mother, who would prefer he not populate half of Washington, DC with her grandchildren, but other than that, he's reliable."

"Oh, uh," I paused. "Are you his mother?"

"For the time being," she replied. "Listen, he's a little eccentric, but he's smart, very healthy, and we have good genes. No heart disease in the family. No cancer. And I haven't seen his penis in twenty years, but I remember it was always quite large when I was changing his diapers. All the things you'd want in a sperm donor."

Ashton Kutcher was about to jump out with a camera crew and tell me I was being punked...and how old I am based on that reference. "Thanks. That's, uh, that's really helpful and a lot...well, *a lot* of information. I appreciate you answering my call."

"No problem, honey. Just promise me you'll be great to my grandkid."

"I promise," I replied, because I was not sure there was anything else I could say. This was all around weird as hell. "Goodbye."

I hung up the phone and took a few calming breaths before texting Isa a summary of what had just happened. She responded back instantly with only laughing and shocked face emojis. Then I looked back at the list and called the next number he'd provided, Emily Hamilton.

"Hamilton residence," the woman answered after the third ring just as I was beginning to chicken out and wonder if I should just hang up.

"Hi, this is Mila Torres. I got your number from Aston Li as a reference."

"Oh!" She seemed to move away from the phone for a moment and shouted to someone in the background to stop climbing on the coffee table. "Are you looking to become a mom? Aston is incredible. We have two children through him, and he's been nothing but kind and respectful."

"Really? Two?" My interest was definitely piqued. "Like twins?"

"Nope. Max is almost three years old, and Lily will be six months next week. Are you in his Facebook group yet? You've got to join." She chuckled, then lowered her voice. "Listen, I know that sounds weird. Before I had Max, I thought this was the most insane thing I'd ever heard of, too."

I laughed lightly. "Yeah, I'm still trying to wrap my mind around all of it. How much contact does your family have with Aston now?"

"He doesn't co-parent if that's what you're worried about.

However, he's open to being in their life, so he really has more of a fun uncle role. My wife and I have actually gotten to know his family a bit. We love his sister, and his mother is quite a hoot. Have you talked to her yet?"

"I just did a few minutes ago," I admitted. "I can't imagine how she feels about all of this."

"I think she's just happy one of her kids finally reproduced," she joked. "And despite her sass, she loves being a grandma to the kids—plus all their half sibs. She's not pushy or anything like that, though. Very open to respecting your wishes if you don't want them around at all."

"That's great to hear." I asked her a little bit more about her life and her interactions through the Baby Bank app before thanking her and hanging up the phone. I called two more mothers on the list, and everyone said basically the same things. Aston was a good guy, and the kids he helped make were all healthy, smart, and spunky little personalities.

I closed my computer and shoved my phone in my pocket. All in all, I felt really good about everything. This felt like the right thing to do. Even if it was so, so freaking weird.

Glancing at the clock, I realized I was running behind, and I had a briefing today that I couldn't miss. An alert came through on my phone that was vibrating in my pocket, but I glanced down at my Apple Watch to see the summary from CNN instead.

A hacker released Senator Chris Murphy's financial records on the dark web and a scandal has ensued.

Shit. I quickly pulled out my phone and saw my boss's number pop up as he called. *Right on time.* Clearly, he had the same alerts set up that I did, not that I was surprised.

"I just saw the news," I answered, quickly shoving my feet in some cute flats and straightening my unruly hair in the mirror by the front door. "I'm on my way to the office now. The metro was delayed."

An easy excuse that was hard to disprove since the metro was always running behind, or on fire, or God knows what else.

"Torres, this is becoming a bigger issue than we planned for," Michael Abbot launched into his usual rant. "The fucker paid for his intern's abortion with his credit card."

"He...what?" I scoffed. "What, like how Jerry Springer paid his hookers with a personal check? Are you serious?"

"Yep. May Jerry rest in peace." I could practically hear him shaking his head from the other end of the line. "This is why they hired us, though. We've got to find a way to spin this to not only keep it from becoming fodder in the divorce but also to make it irrelevant for the legislation he's currently trying to push through."

"You mean the one to defund organizations that focus on women's reproductive rights?" The irony was thick. "Please tell me that's not where they went to have the abortion."

"The charge is to one of the biggest organizations in that field," my boss confirmed. "Everyone's speculating on what the charge is for, and thankfully the records released in the hack don't specify. Still, this is a shit show. Unless we can pretend it was a tax-deductible donation. Not that that would make any more sense, given his political stances."

"Okay, well, we've gotten out of worse messes." I hurried down the steps of my building and into my waiting Lyft since my Ford Taurus had decided it wasn't starting today. "Remember Congressman Lipowitz and his kid's overdose? Or Member Jackston and the breast implants for his staffer?"

"God, you're making it hard for me to pretend that I like this job when you sum it all up like that," Abbot joked, though I knew he was a DC lifer if ever there was one. The man had zero morals and scruples left thanks, to an unhealthy daily dose of Xanax, Ambien, and the occasional bump of cocaine. Yet somehow, he was still one of the most respected partners in Washington, DC and working for him was going to put me on the map one day. Supposedly. Or at least, that's what I had been telling myself to do this job.

"Let's not have this one end up like the Lipowitz case, okay?"

"Got it." I hung up the phone and scanned through the rest of my work emails, as well as a quick glance at trending topics on Twitter. I still had a few minutes to spare after and took a moment to watch the green National Mall whiz by the car window.

Seriously, though...why do I work this job? It was moments like this that made me feel absolutely gross and dirty, and with the possibility of becoming a mother in the very near future, I was viewing Senator Murphy in a whole new light.

It hadn't always been like this, of course. I'd originally chosen divorce law because of my own mother's history, not because I wanted to live in the scumbag lane. My father—who we didn't ever speak about—had raked her heart over the coals and left her with nothing. They had never been married, but she'd thought they would be one day. She'd been so head over heels that she hadn't even seen it as a possibility that he'd up and run the moment she revealed her pregnancy status. But he'd been gone almost instantly and took any child support (financial and emotional) with him.

I'd watched my mother struggle and build her way up in her hourly paying nail salon job until she'd been able to purchase the entire salon for herself. Now she was the boss and had turned a small hole-in-the-wall manicure place into a thriving business with over a dozen estheticians on staff and a glass of champagne in every client's perfectly coiffed hands.

That's why I'd started in the business of divorce law—to give women a chance to fight back in a way my mom had never gotten the chance to. But then I actually started working in the field and the money tended to flow in one direction, and that was rarely toward the wife being left behind. It hadn't been too scandalous at first—a businessman here, a campaign staffer there during internship days. All had generally practical reasons for wanting to divorce their wives and my firm had insisted I take the case to expand my clientele as I moved up to junior associate and then associate. I'd been good at my job and won them what they were looking for, and through word of mouth, my company kept funneling richer and more influential men my way. All wanting to divorce their wives and not pay a dime for it. Except to me. They paid me a lot of dimes, and I appreciated that a lot. I donated as much as I could to the local domestic violence shelter, Planned Parenthood, and tons of other female-driven charities in the metropolitan area. But none of that lifted the stench of guilt off of me for sitting next to those men at the mediation table.

I opened my email app on my phone and scrolled through my trash box, locating the email from Ari Elliot. I still had her business card sitting at home on my nightstand. The truth was that I loved everything that Ari stood for—except how it would definitely affect my job and bank account.

But maybe that was the right thing to do. Maybe I was tired of working for a paycheck instead of a cause. Maybe that's why comedy had been calling to me so strongly recently.

I placed a hand on my stomach and imagined my future child and the life I wanted to give him or her. Money was a big part of that. I wanted to pay for the kid's college and graduate school—if that's what they wanted to do—and I wanted to make sure that they had everything I hadn't. But I also wanted to give them a mother who was happy and living life as authentically as possible, setting an example of who they could be one day.

Losing my job and getting pregnant at the same time didn't

go hand in hand from any practical standpoint. But maybe Ari was serious when she said she'd keep her source confidential...I hit reply.

Can we talk?

Send.

Chapter Four

There were very few things that would make me come to Northern Virginia, but trying out some new comedy on a lower-stakes market was one of them. And by that, I meant Open Mic Night at the Arlington Drafthouse. But hold your applause. Despite the big names in comedy that, for some inexplicable reason, continued to grace its stage, the building was one thunderstorm away from complete collapse. It was originally a bowling alley in the 1940s, and I think every owner since must have decided that spending money on renovations and decor was pointless.

"I mean, what are those on the walls?" I pointed to the peeling, padded felt artwork on both sides of the theater as I stared out at the crowd listening to my five minutes. "Palm trees? This is Virginia. Where the fuck are we getting palm trees? And why do they all look like they just went through a century-long hurricane?"

The crowd laughed politely and shook their heads. I wasn't landing them yet. I decided to double down.

"And the seating? I mean, you guys are basically sitting in

the old computer chairs from the nineties that we all caught our older brothers whacking it on," I continued, even though I didn't even have an older brother. Facts weren't important in comedy. "Where are the theater seats? Or, just the seats that won't give you a staph infection?"

More polite laughter. *Come on, Mila. You're losing them.*

"So, I was swiping for sperm the other day..." I walked across the stage nonchalantly, sticking one hand in my pocket and eyeing the crowd out of the corner of my eye. Scattered laughter—more confused than amused. "Did you guys know that was a thing?"

Someone shouted *"no"* from one of the middle aisles and someone else told him to shut up.

"Well, it is. In fact, they recently signed a partnership deal with DoorDash—buy twenty dollars' worth of Five Guys and get your sixth half off." I shrugged my shoulders like it was no big deal, the laughter in the room increasing around me. "I mean, I think it's pretty nice that they are at least packaging it separately now. It was always iffy when they'd ask if you wanted nuts on the side."

The crowd was leaning in now, and I saw several people put their phones down and focus on what I was saying for the first time in my entire set. Someone in the front row picked up the pitcher of beer in front of him and just started chugging the whole thing right from the side. *I think that's a compliment?* Either way, they were finally on the hook, and I wanted to reel them in.

"But seriously, the truth is that I'm single and I'm trying to get pregnant and I'm not sure how to break it to my mother, you know?" I cleared my throat, scanning the crowd again. "I haven't even told my mother that I do comedy part time. How do I also slide in, '*Oh, I'm having a stranger's baby*' on top of that? She's going to think it's a bit. Then I'll try to

36

convince her that it's real by telling her I met the man on a sperm app when I swiped right on him. She'll laugh harder and tell me I've really got a future in this comedy thing. Such a supportive mother. She's really so great. But then I'll have to double down and show her his Facebook group for all his baby mamas—real thing, by the way. That's not even a bit. And then I'll tell her that I just have to meet him at a hotel, and she'll have her first grandbaby by the time my next period doesn't show."

I was speaking quicker now, and the crowd was roaring with laughter.

"At that point, she'll either pee herself from laughing so hard—then, of course, be mad at me for that because thirty-four years later and it's still my fault for wrecking her pelvic floor—or she'll realize I'm being dead serious about this baby thing *and* the comedy thing and have me involuntarily committed." I shook my head dramatically for the crowd. "Either way, I'm pregnant and fucked, and I never even got fucked. Now *that* is a modern-day tragedy."

Cackles and gasping laughter from the audience fed my soul. I beamed at the crowd and offered them a wink. "I'm Tori Miles. Find me next month at Bier Baron Tavern in Washington, DC. Thanks for an incredible night, folks! You've been great!"

With that, I walked off the side of the stage where several other performers all offered me congratulations and high fives. One guy even randomly handed me a cigarette, which I tucked behind my ear, because I don't smoke but fuck it. I wasn't pregnant yet.

"That was wild," one of the male comedians going on later in the night said to me as he shook my hand. He held on a little tighter than I'd prefer, his eyes dropping to my chest before returning to my face. "But I'm going to need to know the name of that app. I've got swimmers just begging to meet their egg. Hook a friend up!"

I grimaced, surveying him with an exaggerated judgmental eye—just to make sure he clearly understood—and dramatically huffing my breath. "Uh, maybe give the next generation a break and not pass on your genes."

He laughed and nudged me with his elbow. "I can always expect the best zingers from you."

I dropped my serious expression and laughed in response. He assumed I was joking. For some reason I didn't fully understand comedians mostly networked by insulting each other. If I wanted another comedian to take me seriously, I'd realized that the quickest options were to roast them, drug them, or offer to get on my knees. The last option was clearly out—unless it was Iliza Shlesinger—but it was never Iliza. *Sigh.* Drugs were expensive, so that was out too, but it only cost my morals to eviscerate a funny man's fragile ego, so ding ding ding—we have a winner.

"Tori Miles?" Another man's voice called out to me from farther back in the wings of the stage. He was walking toward me, and I tried to place his face from another showcase or open mic night, but I couldn't remember who he was.

"Are you Tori Miles?" he repeated, coming to a stop in front of me.

"I am," I replied, reluctantly slowing my stride to accommodate him.

He began walking beside me as I headed behind the stage to the bar area. "I'm Mitchell Davros, and I'm a talent agent with the Comedic Talent Agency."

I immediately stopped walking and turned to look at him. "You're from CTA?"

I'd heard of them more than a few times and had almost

sent in a few clips of one of my shows at the Bier Baron before I'd chickened out at the last minute.

"I am. I was wondering if you had a minute to talk about representation or your plan for your career going forward." Mitchell had a suit jacket draped over one arm, and his other hand was in the pocket of the matching slacks. He looked like he'd already been at work all day, and this was as casual as it got for him. "We've been following your views on YouTube, and you're getting pretty popular. Plus, I liked your set out there, and we're looking for diverse female talent. Have you considered representation?"

"I have," I replied, straightening my shoulders. There was zero chance I was about to let this man know that my insides were jumping up and down, squealing like a schoolgirl. *Holy shit, they want to rep me? What is life! Shut it down, Mila.* I put on my most polite smile. "Do you have a business card? I'd be open to setting up a lunch and seeing what your organization can offer."

He lifted one brow, clearly surprised at my nonchalant response. "I do."

I took the business card he offered me and glanced over it for two seconds—long enough to seem interested but hopefully short enough to appear like I had other options. Which I most definitely did not. "Great. You can find me on Instagram at @torimilescomedy. DM me about lunch, and I'll see what I can do."

With that, I turned on my heels and walked up to the bar as if I didn't expect him to follow me. *Deep breaths, Mila.* I was close to hyperventilating but managed to calm myself down by the time I got to the bar. "Hey, Eddy. Can I have a Blue Moon?"

"The usual way?" the bartender asked.

"You know it. No orange slice and just a splash of orange

juice on top," I replied. That had been my go-to order at most bars since I was a server at a restaurant back in the day. After seeing how many unwashed hands chop up the fruit slices and garnishes and then going through a never-ending worldwide pandemic, there was zero chance I'd be freeballing it in the future with a rogue orange slice.

Eddy dropped off a frosty mug of the Belgian wheat ale in front of me.

"Thanks." I immediately downed half of it in a few gulps. I was slated to go back on stage later this evening for the late-night crowd, and my first performance had only snaked out a happy ending in the final stretch.

My phone vibrated in my pocket, and I pulled it out.

I'm here.

Never has a text made me both simultaneously excited and terrified, all in the same moment, but seeing Ari's message had my skin prickling into goose bumps. I quickly texted her to meet me out back before downing the rest of my beer and heading for the side hallway.

When I got outside, it was pitch black and all I could see were the lights in neighboring houses that were still on and the neon sign for the sushi restaurant next door. There's an area off the back door where the talent is directed to enter that most people hang out and smoke cigarettes—fun fact, the first time I ever tried marijuana was back here after opening for Brian Posehn once. He definitely has the best weed, but I quickly learned that that stuff was not for me after I spent the rest of the evening on the edge of a panic attack for funsies.

Turns out I'm too high-strung for anything to mellow me out. Damn my mother for being right about that, too.

"Over here," someone called out, and I immediately recognized the voice from the other side of the front door on Taco Tuesday. Her speech was softer this time than I expected and the way my spine tingled at the sound was definitely something I was trying to ignore.

"Thanks for coming out to Virginia," I said as I ushered the two of us over to an even darker corner off to the side. I surreptitiously glanced around to make sure we weren't in the line of any security cameras or passersby.

"Not many people I'd cross that bridge for," Ari replied.

She was wearing a frayed jean vest with cutoff sleeves over a dark-red camisole that was tucked into high-waisted pants, and I suddenly felt shlumpy in my wide-legged slacks and yellow-and-red-striped T-shirt. Ari just looked effortlessly cool. One side of her head was shaved close in an undercut, and the rest of her hair was a natural black and long with the occasional dark-green streak through it. When she moved, her hair would fall over one way or the other, and I wanted to pretend that my body wasn't reacting when she ran her hand through it...but that would be a lie. Meanwhile, my hair was haphazardly back in a messy bun and unwashed, and *that* was my performer look —like I'd actually tried today.

"I can't risk people seeing us together. So, I appreciate you coming to the back like this." I reached into the front of my shirt and pulled out the SD memory card tucked between the lining of my bra and my side boob. "Here. This is everything you'll need to decipher the financial records from the hack."

Her gaze stayed on my breasts a moment longer before shifting to the memory card in my hands. Almond-shaped, dark-brown eyes met mine with the same fierceness I'd seen through the Ring doorbell camera. *Did she always look at people like this? Or is this for me?*

I almost kicked myself for how much I wanted to feel like it was all for me. Christ, maybe I really did need to get laid. Even my inner monologue was getting desperate.

She took the memory card from me and slid it into the front

chest pocket of her vest. "You're doing the right thing. These will prove everything."

"All it will prove is he paid for a staffer's abortion," I replied. "Half the members and senators have a fund for that shit already set aside. It's not breaking news."

"To us in the district, sure," Ari countered. "But Middle America Karen is going to be shocked at what her representative is actually doing out here. I'm curious though...what are *you* doing out here?"

"In Virginia?" I looked away as if I could feign a way out of not understanding her question.

Ari shook her head and motioned to the building. "*Here,* here."

"I can have a creative side, too, you know." I'm not sure why I was suddenly getting defensive since she hadn't seen the show and didn't know the comedian side of me. "Law doesn't have to be more than a nine-to-five for me."

One corner of her lip lifted into a smirk. Shit, she knew she got to me. "Did I say it did?"

"No." I crossed my arms over my chest now and let out a huff. Well, now I just wanted to prove her wrong. "I just...I like to do open mic nights sometimes, okay? An agent even gave me his card tonight."

"For comedy?" Ari asked, one brow lifting higher than the other.

I nodded. "I can be funny."

"I have yet to see that side of you," Ari replied in a deadpan voice, but the smile on her face told me she was trying to push my buttons. "Thanks for the records. I'll see you around."

"Better if you don't," I responded to her back as she walked away.

She paused for half a second in her steps but didn't look back. Then she was gone around the side of the building, and I was standing there alone contemplating every life decision I'd ever made.

Law. Comedy. Motherhood. Throw the dice and pick one —or could I actually have all three?

One of the other comedians stuck his head out the back door. "What are you doing out here? You have to do the closing remarks after the headliner, remember?"

I nearly jumped out of my skin. "Uh...just catching my breath."

He furrowed his brow. "Hey, if you're smoking, you're supposed to share."

"I'm not!" I insisted, putting my hands up defensively even though he clearly had not seen Ari or had any actual clue what I'd been doing. Still, my nerves were on edge and it all just felt like too close of a call. "And I'm coming. Jesus Christ, it's like the fucking Secret Service runs this place."

He grinned and then pushed the door open wider for me. "You seem fidgety. You were definitely smoking something. Or snorting?"

"So was your mom throughout her entire pregnancy with you," I replied back, walking past him and toward the backstage area.

"Bazinga!" He laughed, then paused. "Hey, do people still say that?"

I didn't even bother answering him.

Chapter Five

"It's time to get knocked up!" Isa walked into my front entryway with so much gusto that the door actually slammed against the wall behind her.

"Christ, Isa!" My eyes widened as I went to check the wall behind the door for any damage. "You're going to knock a hole in my wall."

"You're about to have a baby," she countered, checking her reflection in the hall mirror and reapplying her lip color. She was wearing a little black cocktail dress and supersharp heels as if we were about to go out to a club—not impregnate me in a random hotel. I wasn't surprised. "Those become toddlers and then kids, you know. This place will be leveled by the time your spawn is done with it."

She wasn't wrong, but I still hadn't decided if I'd stay in this place post-baby or not. "Did you call a Lyft?"

"Three minutes away," she confirmed. "Where's Rachel and Yasmeen?"

"Only Rachel is coming." I turned toward the interior of the house and called out. I'd invited Yasmeen as well, but she had said that there were some limits in friendship she wasn't willing to cross, and insemination was one of them. Fair. "Rachel, we have to go!"

I pushed Macavity away from the door where he was already beginning to patrol half circles, sensing that his next opening to freedom might be soon.

Rachel flounced into the hallway a moment later, looking comfortable in light-wash jeans and a graphic T-shirt before she slipped on her TOMS shoes by the front door. "I still cannot believe we're actually doing this."

"You can't?" I was the one who should be freaking out right now, yet I honestly felt a strange sense of calm—or maybe it was numbness—that I had not expected. "Imagine how I feel."

We piled into the Lyft as soon as it pulled up, squishing all three of us into the back of the sedan. There wasn't enough money in the world to get me to sit in the front seat of a rideshare and I have no explanation for that other than crippling social anxiety at the idea of small talk with someone I don't know who was then going to rate me at the end of the ride.

"You have everything?" Rachel asked before closing the door to the car behind her.

I lifted the large tote bag in my lap and lightly shook it. "Gang's all here."

Isa laughed and peeked inside my bag which was full of two insemination kits, a vanilla-scented candle for mood lighting, and a rosary for my mother's sake. "Ooh, this is going to be *so* weird."

"I can't wait," I replied with a small laugh.

Twenty minutes later, we were pulling up outside the Moxy Hotel by the convention center and shuffling out of the back of the Lyft. Isa and Rachel stood behind me as I awkwardly checked in with the front desk and got two room keys. We glanced at each other surreptitiously as if we were on some type of covert mission before heading to the elevator bay. The ride up to the fourth floor was silent, and my nerves doubled the moment the key card beeped us into my room.

The suite itself was beautiful—an exposed brick wall, soft sheets on a large bed, fake plants in the corner, and a great view of...the building next to us. It would work just fine for my purposes. I placed the tote bag on the corner of the bed and pulled out the slender box holding the first insemination kit.

"So, I guess we just set everything up and then go down and wait?" I said, glancing toward my friends.

They both gave me the deer in the headlights look, as if they hadn't thought that far ahead. *I mean, I'm the one actually doing this.* I'm literally holding an insemination kit in my hands.

"Do you want us to wait outside?" Rachel asked, fidgeting with the ends of her hair sticking out of the bottom of her braid. She walked over to the window and pulled the blinds closed.

"Should one of us offer to stay up here to help him out?" Isa always knew how to break the tension in anything with a sexual joke.

I shot her a look and we both laughed before I headed into the bathroom. The instructions were all listed clearly in the box, but I figured it would be nice to at least set everything up for him. I'd even brought some extra supplies with me for comfort, so hopefully my sperm daddy would appreciate that.

Collection cup. *Check.*

Fertility-safe lube. *Check.*

Baby wipes. *Check.*

A Post-It with the Wi-Fi information. *Check.*

I'd looked to see if Playboy still made magazines or anything like that, but apparently not. So, I figured he would have to make do with the Internet like the rest of Gen Z.

I surveyed the makeshift masturbation station before calling out to the girls. "Am I forgetting anything?"

Isa stepped into the bathroom and looked over my shoulder. "I don't think so. What else do men need to jerk it?"

That was a question I'd never actually asked a man before. "Uh...a towel? Or tissues? A stale gym sock?"

Isa grimaced. "Remind me again why I date men?"

"I've been wondering the same thing for myself." I put both a hand towel and a box of tissues at the end of the counter, just in case.

This would probably be considered a weird moment to think of Ari if I really reflected on the nuances of it, but her face came to mind anyway. It had been a while since I'd gone on a date, and a few nights ago, behind the drafthouse, certainly didn't count as a date. But part of me still wished I'd asked her to come inside and have a drink with me if we'd been in some sort of alternate universe. Instead, we were still in the universe where being seen together would potentially lose me my job, my license, and my entire career.

"So, do we wait here?" Rachel asked as I walked back into the bedroom. "Or hang out in the lobby? What's the protocol for a dick-and-dash situation?"

I laughed. "I told Aston that we'd meet him in the bar downstairs to give him the key card."

Rachel scrunched up her nose, her brows pinched. "And then he'll just come up here and do his thing?"

"Pretty much," I confirmed. I glanced back toward the bathroom, but I couldn't think of anything else we needed to do beforehand. I surveyed the room for privacy and comfort, but I hoped he didn't need the bed since I'm guessing that's where I'd be after to do my thing. "I guess we should just go down and wait?"

"I need a drink," Isa confirmed, staring down at her phone.

Her finger was swiping across the screen quickly, then came to a pause. "Oh, look. The League says this guy is fifty feet away. I bet he's in the bar downstairs."

Rachel peered over her shoulder. "He could be a guest staying here. What's the League? Is that a dating app?"

"Yeah, but it's for, like, high-profile people only," Isa explained. "It took me six months to get off the waiting list. You basically have to be Ivy League or working on the Hill, or you can't get in."

I rolled my eyes. "That's gross."

"Super gross," Isa agreed but then sighed and shook her head. "I hate that staffers and interns are my types. But give me a former frat boy, a big man at Stanford who comes to Washington thinking he'll be hot shit here, and I melt. I can't wait for the Hill to level them when they find out they'll be getting a member coffee or buying cocaine off a tween at a prep school to slip to a chief of staff. That fall from glory is such a beautiful thing to witness and is the perfect moment to grab one before they become rich and jaded."

We moved out into the hallway, and I pressed the button for the elevator. "Did you tell that to your therapist?"

"Oh, no." Isa shook her head. "She would not approve. She keeps telling me I have attachment issues."

"I wonder what makes her think that?" I walk onto the elevator as they pile in behind me.

Isa shoots me an exasperated look over her smirk. "Judge all you want, honey, but I'm not the one currently waiting on a man to jack it in a hotel room for me."

I laughed as the elevator doors opened in the lobby. "Touché."

"I feel like we should ride the mechanical horse," Rachel said, changing topics as she pointed toward the bar area that was littered with game tables and random, eclectic furniture, including a carousel horse that promised a good ride for twenty-five cents.

"Oh shit, look!" Isa's voice dropped lower, and she held her phone up to both Rachel and me.

The dating profile of a man with a lumberjack-style beard wearing all plaid stared back at me, but then I followed Isa's not-so-subtle nod toward the bar in front of us. Mr. Lumberjack was spinning a cocktail mixer behind the bar like an expert. He caught a bottle of vodka behind his back without even looking and even I paused for a second to admire him.

I nudged her side. "Now is your chance, Isa. Swipe right. Rachel and I are going to play foosball."

She was already walking in his direction like I was a distant thought.

"Guess it's just us." Rachel pointed at the foosball table. "Should we bet on a game? Stakes are loser gets pregnant."

I laughed. "You know I'm terrible at this game."

"And you're about to get pregnant, so it all works out." Rachel was already in position and dropped the ball in the center.

I quickly tried to catch up, but she beat me in record time. I threw my hands up and stepped back from the table. "This game is rigged!"

"Mila?" A man's voice called out somewhere behind me, and I whirled around to see a young Asian man walking up to me. "Hey, I'm Aston."

"Aston Li?" I asked, even though I'd never met anyone else with that name.

He was taller than I'd expected based on his photographs, and his frame was thin but athletic. I gave him the full once-over—literally looked him up and down like I was about to buy a piece of him. Except he was donating it to me for free.

"Good to finally meet you," he said as he stuck out a hand

toward me.

I shook his hand and appreciated that his grip was firm. "You, too. Uh, I have to admit...I don't really know what we do next."

"Did you get a room upstairs?" he asked, pointing toward the ceiling.

I nodded. "Room four-oh-seven."

"Is there a collection cup up there?" He sounded like he was checking boxes off a list.

I nodded again. "It came with the insemination kit."

I felt my face flush at having explained that piece—I mean, obviously the kit is where it came from. It's not like I'm walking around with extra collection cups for jizz and giggles.

"Great, then give me the key card, and I'll go do what I need to do," he explained as he stuck out his hand. "My sister is picking me up in a few minutes, so it shouldn't take long. Ten, fifteen minutes tops."

That seemed like an odd brag, but okay. I pulled the key card from my pocket and placed it in his open palm. "It's four-oh-seven," I repeated, nerves swarming my belly.

"Got it." He saluted me like he was in the military and then headed for the elevators.

"Hey, Aston?" I called out after him.

He turned and looked at me, lifting one brow higher than the other.

I couldn't find the words for a moment. I just had so many questions and there was no way he could answer all of them, but maybe one. "I...uh, well...why?"

Aston turned fully now to face me, and then he shrugged his shoulders lightly. His hand ran through his thick, straight black hair as he let out a slow exhale. "Family is the best thing I have in my life. I want more people to have that in whatever way they want."

That was as good a reason as any, but for some reason, there was suddenly a lump in my throat. "Thanks," I squeaked out.

He nodded and then was gone behind closed elevator doors.

"He's really doing it," Rachel said, coming to stand beside me. "Mila, you're about to become a mom. Also, he's tall and that has to be a good sign."

My heart was pounding so hard in my chest that I felt like my rib cage might break open and set it free. "Holy freaking shit. It's really happening."

"Mila?"

I turned to face the voice calling out to me from the front entrance of Bar Moxy.

Ari Elliot was standing in the doorway, her brows furrowed. She walked toward me with a hesitancy that made my heart sink into my stomach as if I'd done something wrong. It's like she caught me, and I was suddenly a deer in headlights and completely unsure if I was okay with being run over. Spoiler alert: I was.

"This is unexpected. What are you doing here?" she asked when she reached me.

It didn't sound like an accusation, but I still took a step back as if it was.

Rachel elbowed me, probably to get me out of my silent stupor.

"Uh..." I was not prepared with a response to that question, but my lawyer mode turned on for emotional distance and self-preservation. "Well, what are *you* doing here?"

The corners of her lips turned upward and the tenseness I'd felt in her approach seemed to ease...but only barely. "They make a really great Moxy Mule here. Want one?"

Rachel turned away from Ari and whispered in my ear. "Get it, girl. Go, go, go!"

Say no. Absolutely say no. My inner voice got shoved into a back closet and completely ignored, but the esquire label on my business card was desperately trying to remind me of the stakes. I surveyed the room for a moment, but I didn't see anyone I recognized. Safe enough, right? There was only one security camera in the corner, and if I kept my head down, I was pretty sure I'd be unrecognizable on it.

"I could try one," I replied, my voice barely above a whisper and my sphincter tighter than a Catholic nun preaching abstinence to fifth graders. *A lot of people had a drink or two on the night they were inseminated, right?* "But just one."

I walked over to the bar with Ari, and we took a set of barstools next to one another on the corner where I could angle my back to the security camera. "Maybe we should sit like one stool apart," I said. "Just to make it look like we're not together."

"There's like four people here, but sure," Ari commented, spacing our seating so that there was an empty barstool between us.

She ordered two Moxy Mules from Mr. Lumberjack, and I shot a wink to Isa on the other end, still pining away after her League swipe. She'd been in conversation with him before Ari had called him over, and it seemed like she was doing well.

"I'm surprised you said yes at all," Ari said as she turned to me after she'd placed the order. "To a drink, I mean."

"Who turns down a free drink?" I shrugged my shoulders like I was normally that casual and breezy. Totally chill. "You're buying, I'm drinking. Wait, you are buying, right?"

Ari laughed and her head tipped back just enough for me to gaze at her throat and collarbone. Don't judge me, but the intersection of a woman's throat dipping into her collarbone is one of the most sensual things in existence, and I knew from personal experience that a delicate kiss placed there was undeniably delicious and led to all kinds of yummy tingling.

"I meant, I'm surprised you're willing to be seen with me in public," Ari continued, and my attention returned to her eyes.

"Oh, right. That. Well, the empty stool..." I nodded toward the space between us, but my body returned to its previous rigidity as my inner voice popped back out of the closet and screamed at me. *We are not in Northern Virginia anymore! People might actually know me here. Calm down, toots,* I tried to remind myself. I had surveyed the room already and saw no one familiar. Plus, the old folks I work with would definitely not frequent a place like this. "I have so much going on today that I don't have time to worry about work right now."

"That's disconcerting." Ari lifted one brow again, and concern appeared on her face. "What's going on?"

"It's unrelated," I assured her because impregnating myself was not a topic I was ready to discuss—let alone, know *how* to discuss it with a woman who could both end my career and make my stomach flip-flop all in the same sentence.

Ari frowned, still eyeing me suspiciously. "Well, if you want to talk about it, I'm happy to listen."

Mr. Lumberjack chose that moment to return to us and pointed a finger with way too long of a fingernail at Ari. "Washington Times?"

She looked a bit surprised at his question but then nodded. "I do work for them, yes."

"Did you write the article about how men are lonelier than ever and need to go to therapy if they want to get a date?" Mr. Lumberjack was grinning now, leaning his elbows against the bar. "Because I'll tell you, the moment I put that I was going to therapy on my Hinge profile, my matches blew up."

Hinge and The League. This guy was multitasking.

Ari glanced sideways at me, but I did nothing to save her from this interview. She narrowed her eyes at me for a brief second as if accusing me of exactly what I was doing.

"Uh, well...I cowrote that article with another reporter," Ari confirmed, returning her gaze to him. I didn't miss the way her foot was tapping against the barstool leg. "I'm glad it got you into therapy. Always a great move for everyone."

Mr. Lumberjack shook his head, stepping back like she'd slapped him. "Hell, no. I didn't go. That's for pussies. I just put it on my profile as chick bait and it worked like a charm."

Okay, I should probably text Isa right now to never speak to this asshole. I tried to catch her eye over his shoulder, but she was looking down at her phone.

"What about you? You a writer as well?" He turned his gaze to me and crossed his arms over his chest, clearly trying to puff himself up a bit with the air of male mediocrity. "I haven't seen you around here before."

Isa was off her phone and now shooting me daggers from the other end of the bar, but she didn't have to worry one bit about me stealing her man.

"Yes, I actually write the obituaries. It's really fun, and you never know when you're going to meet the next person you'll write about. Keeps it an adventure, you know?" I shrugged my shoulders. "Like they could be serving my drink one day and then I'm writing about their tragic death in a Segway accident a week later. This world is crazy, right?"

He blinked a few extra times than seemed necessary. "Uh... right. Okay. I'm going to, uh, go clean some glasses."

"Have fun!" I waved to him and put on a too-cheery expression before leaning back and looking over at Ari. "Sorry."

"At least *you* didn't get recognized, Ms. Obits." Ari was grinning and shaking her head. "You got off scot-free on that one."

I lifted my brows with a scoff. "If *that* tragic display of toxic masculinity is what scot-free looks like, then clearly you never spend much time in Navy Yard."

"I think the last time I was around frat bros was when I covered a Booz Allen press conference," she joked back. "Not my people, and not my scene."

She reached into the back pocket of her jeans and pulled out a wallet, sifting through until she found a credit card. She slid it out of the slot and placed it on the edge of the bar in front of her for Mr. Lumberjack whenever he dared to wander back this way.

A different bartender swiped it from her instead and I saw Mr. Lumberjack nod his thanks. Typical.

"Going already?" I asked. Not that I was expecting her to float me drinks all night or anything, but it just felt...abrupt. The conversation had felt like it was going somewhere, and then, bam, I was staring at a stop sign.

"I have another commitment," she said, but this time she spoke slower, and she let her gaze fall down my body in the obvious, sexy kind of way that made every part of me clench up. "But I'd like to do this again sometime. Not on official business. Just for pleasure. Maybe somewhere both of us can stay anonymous."

Breathe, Mila. I straightened my shoulders. "I guess that would be okay, you know...like privately. Privately is good."

"Sure, privately," she repeated, her eyes narrowing and her smile widening. "For now. Not forever."

I didn't have a response for that, but I was interrupted before I could come up with one.

"Hey, Ari. Thanks for the ride." Aston walked up between the two of us and presented me with the key card I'd given to him maybe ten minutes ago. "Here's your key card back, Mila. Hope it all works out."

On autopilot, I took the key card from him with two fingers, trying to touch as little of it as possible.

Ari's eyes widened as she turned to look at me, and her

mouth fell open. I'm pretty sure my expression was the exact same because there was absolutely zero chance that the girl I was flirting with somehow knew the man who was impregnating me.

"Wait, um..." I cleared my throat as I looked at the key card between my fingers and tried to make sense of the situation unfolding in front of me. "You two know each other?"

Aston frowned and then looked between Ari and me. "Wait...*you two* know each other?"

"Uhh." Ari finally seemed to be the one stumped for words now. It was actually kind of cute to see if I wasn't about to shit bricks in a panic. "Mila, are you...wait, Aston, is this...?"

"Yeah, I met Mila on the Baby Bank app," Aston filled her in, but then he turned to me and said the worst thing I could ever have imagined. "Mila, how do you know my sister?"

My sister. Holy guacamole, am I about to conceive a child with my crush's brother? Wait, is Ari even my crush? The feeling in my core right now would seem to suggest yes...and very much yes. This is a clusterfuck worse than Congress in a filibuster.

"*Sister?* Like, as in...biological sister?" I repeated the word again as if maybe I'd suddenly forgotten how to speak English and *sister* actually meant a distant friend he'd never see again. "Uh, you guys have very different last names."

Aston nodded. "Ari used to be a Li also, but she got married and divorced in her twenties."

"It was too much of a hassle to change it once." Ari shrugged, and she seemed way too cool, calm, and collected in this moment. My eyes tried to bore into her as if begging her to freak the fuck out like I was, but she seemed to look everywhere but me. "Didn't feel like going through the whole name change process again."

Okay, there was definitely more to *that* story, but my

shocked self couldn't even process this moment, let alone the untangling of that juicy bit of history Aston had just dropped in my lap.

I put my Moxy Mule down hard on the bar top and it made a clattering sound as I stood up from my seat. "Well, this has been lovely, but I should go. Things to do, people to make, you know. That sort of thing. Thanks for the drink, Ari. And, Aston, of course...thank you for the, um, stuff you donated. I mean, were you able to... uh, you know, finish? Or whatever?"

Aston looked down at the key card in my hand then back at me like he was second-guessing his decision to procreate with me. "It's on the counter in the collection cup. But...should we discuss this?"

He pointed between me and Ari, concern clearly etched on his face.

"There's nothing going on here," I promised him, hoping he wouldn't ask me to prove the validity of that statement. "Ari and I met on a work project. It was brief and I had no idea you two were related. I'm so sorry, it's definitely a little weird, but we're just acquaintances."

For someone who had been looking everywhere but me a moment ago, Ari now didn't take her eyes off me, and I swear to God they were trying to burn through me. Successfully, I might add. "Yeah, Mila has been helpful with an article I'm working on. That's it."

Everything I'd ever heard out of her mouth before this very moment had always sounded true, except that last sentence. A liar can spot a liar.

Aston seemed to pick up on it, too. "Listen, if this is too complicated..."

"It's not," I assured him, panic suddenly filling my chest at the thought of losing it all. The girl and the boy...and the boy's sperm. I was not historically great at relationships. That much I knew with certainty. So, anything with Ari was nothing more than a fantasy or my next breakup. But motherhood? I was ready for that. Now that I'd done the research, I realized that it was possible...I was invested. I *really*, really wanted this baby. "I promise, Aston. I'm all in."

He looked at me carefully a moment longer. "Okay. Well, good luck. If you need anything else, let me know."

I nodded my head, and reluctantly he turned back toward his sister. When he was looking at her, the similarity was obvious. Same hair, same eyes, same nose, same chin—how had I not seen that earlier? I swallowed hard and tried to convince myself that I hadn't accidentally picked a sperm donor based on a reporter I thought was cute.

"Yeah," Ari echoed, though her tone was slower and more nuanced. "Good luck, Mila."

I waved the key card between us because I had no idea how to move my muscles like a normal human being right then. "Yeah, thanks. Uh, good night. Get home safe."

Rachel was watching me from the foosball table and her eyes were as big as dinner plates, but she didn't move to join me, and I had no idea how much of that conversation she had just heard. I headed for the elevator bank as fast as my legs could carry me and punched the button for it to open. It didn't respond, so I hit it again, then a third time. I turned to look back at everyone and gave them an awkward grin and wave—or maybe it was a complete seizure, I didn't know at this point.

The elevator doors closed, and I hit the number four and then leaned back against the wall and tried to steady my breathing. There was no way I was going to do this, right? No way. Absolutely insane. Completely impossible.

The elevator opened on the fourth floor, and I stepped out. *But am I?*

Chapter Six

So, are you pregnant yet? A text message from Isa popped up on the lock screen of my cell phone as I held the phone above my face and looked up at the ceiling.

I exited my messages and turned on the camera app to take a picture of my feet propped up against the headboard of the hotel bed. *Still letting it settle.*

Isa just sent back a vomiting-face green emoji.

You asked, I wrote back.

Not that I was going to give her more information than that anyway. I understood why she was asking though, because I'd been up here a lot longer than I'd originally stated I'd be. Not that the process itself had taken very long, but the emotional spiral and panic attack over trying to decide if I would actually go through with this entire weird-ass situation had added a minimum of forty-five more minutes to the start.

Everything after I'd finally said "fuck it" had gone very much according to plan, but honestly, it all felt so clinical. I didn't feel overly emotionally weepy or suddenly touched by

Mother Goose. Anxiety—yes. Sentimentality? Nope. Honestly, it wasn't all that dissimilar to putting in a tampon—except maybe longer and skinnier and farther north. It actually made me think of this pencil dick I once found myself in bed with when I was in college, who used to brag at every party about how *big* he was. Turns out, length literally means nothing when it comes to female pleasure—it's all about girth.

That was around the time I started dating women.

Hey, do you think Bernard can hitch a ride back to our place in our Lyft? Isa was already on the next topic in her message back to me. *He's almost off his shift.*

Is that the bartender? I shifted my legs against the wall, trying to get a little more comfortable as I let a stranger's baby serum ruminate in my cervix for the suggested thirty minutes. One person told me it only takes four seconds for the sperm to reach the egg, but then that same person told me that ovaries aren't even actually attached to our fallopian tubes and it's basically a catch-and-grab situation. So, who the hell knows what actually happens down there?

Yeah, Bernard, the bartender. Is that weird? I thought he was hitting on you for a second back there, but he's been in full-on charm mode with me for the last hour and I'm digging it.

I rolled my eyes, annoyed already at the thought of sharing a Lyft with his beard or that Isa continued to have the worst romance picker of anyone I knew. *I'll catch my own Lyft home. You might want to avoid him though. He came across as a major asshole when I talked to him. Red flags on fire.*

She was unfazed. *Hey, as long as the dick is good.*

Isa didn't write more after that, and I knew from experience that there was no point in continuing to argue with her about her hookup choices. I wasn't even sure why I was annoyed, but I just was. It felt like out of all the nights that could be about hooking up, maybe tonight would just be about me? It's not like there was clearly understood etiquette for how to act when your friend is impregnating herself upstairs. Still, I wouldn't have minded a little more attention in that moment since I was one syringe of baby batter away from an existential crisis right then.

Literally, everything might be about to change in my life.

The thought was sobering, but the reality was that I did need to make some changes. Not just for this potential, hopeful baby but for me. My career, my friendships, my home...something was going to have to give.

That's an uncomfy thought. Just as I was about to place my phone down on the sheets next to me, however, it began ringing loudly.

I swiped to answer the call as soon as I saw my mother's face pop up on the screen. "Hello?"

"Do you want to hear some absolute bullshit?" Chicky said through the phone, not bothering with greetings. That was Chicky—always to the point and didn't give two shits who knew it.

"What?" I placed the call on speakerphone and laid it on the sheets next to my head.

"*Mija*, remember that retail space off of *H* Street by Gallery Place that I was looking at for a second location?" she began.

I knew what she was talking about but didn't respond since I also knew it was a rhetorical question.

She kept going without a pause, "Well, Sweet Feet is offering the owner twenty percent over asking in an attempt to outbid me, which would be fine if that's all they were doing."

"But it's not?"

"Hell no," Chicky practically shrieked into the phone. "Linda got the owner's son a summer internship at Deloitte through one of her customers. It's complete bribery."

I wrinkled my nose. "Why does he want to work at Deloitte?"

"Probably an aspiring frat boy for their date rape division or a hopeful alcoholic. Who knows?" my mother replied with a loud sigh. "Either way, they're giving them the space. And you know that Linda is just sitting over there on her Sweet Feet throne laughing her *culo* off at me."

"Mom, I really think Linda is just running her own business and not thinking about The Gel Bar." That was the name of my mother's nail salon, which I thought was pretty fitting since they also had a liquor license and offered drinks to their customers while they had their mani-pedis. I felt like that made Chicky's business more specialized and boutique compared to a cut-and-paste chain like Sweet Feet Nails. "Plus, you guys have pretty different business models. It's not really like Sweet Feet is competition."

"Thank you, baby," she replied, her voice a bit softer now. "I know you're right, but the way Linda sits across the aisle from me at church, looking so goddamn smug, I swear I just want to rub her nose in it one time. Oh, speaking of that..."

"God, Mother, what did you do?" I asked, my tone already one of dread.

"So, you know how Linda fawns all over Reverend Wilson like he's God's gift to the DMV?" I immediately felt a pit in my stomach at the idea of where this story was going. "I got to chatting with Reverend Wilson, and wouldn't you know it...he's single."

"Mom, no." If I had to throw my half-inseminated self off this bed to chase her out of the church's coffers and get her a refund on this one-way ticket to hell, I would absolutely do it. "You cannot date the reverend to get back at Linda."

"It might have started that way," Chicky replied, and I groaned loud enough to ensure she heard me over the little growling sound she was making. "But Steve is actually quite the *caballero.*"

Her voice went up an octave at the end there, almost like she was being shy. If there was one thing to know about my mother, shyness was *not* it.

"I was thinking it might be nice if you met him," Chicky continued. "So, I invited him to our dinner on Sunday."

The irony was not lost on me that I was currently trying to knock myself up with a potential bastard baby while my mother was bragging to me about her new religious love interest.

"Mom, I've met Reverend Wilson tons of times. At church." Not that I actually went that often because I tended to be more of the Christmas and Easter type. But it was important to my mother, and I wasn't opposed to religion entirely. "You know this."

"You've met Reverend Wilson," she agreed. "But I want you to meet Steve. He's...well, he's just dreamy." She actually sighed dramatically at that last line. "I really think you'll like him, Mila."

"Linda is going to be really upset about this," I replied.

I could hear my mother smiling as she answered. "If that is the Lord's will, then who am I to say differently?"

Now I was laughing. "Fine, Mom. I'll meet him on Sunday. Again."

"That's all I ask. Now, tell me what you've been up to. I feel like I haven't seen you in years."

I rolled my eyes at the ceiling. "We literally have dinner every Sunday together. It's been like two days."

Chicky chuckled. "Sure, but a lot could happen in two days!"

I glanced around, grateful that she couldn't see the expression on my face right now because, yes...a lot *could* happen in two days. "Uh...I mean, nothing much. I'm just really busy at work. That senator case is...it's just a mess and I'm billing over-time on it."

"Well, don't work too hard, darling," Chicky replied. "You really need to get out there and meet someone. I don't like the idea of you being home alone every night and working all day. That's no way to live."

Note to self, I should probably tell her I do stand-up comedy several nights a week at some point. There really was no good reason I hadn't told her yet, except that my mother was already incredibly enmeshed in my life. My therapist had encouraged me to practice boundary setting and what was mine versus what was ours. I'd decided that seeing how I liked comedy could just be mine for a while...eventually, I'd tell her. Though, I would probably leave out the part that half my mate-rial is based on her.

Oh, and the baby thing, too. I guess I also need to tell her that at some point.

"I mean, I still have roommates," I steered the conversation far away. "It's not like I'm actually home alone."

"Yes, yes. They're perfectly fine, but they won't be there forever. Just like I won't be here forever, and I'd like to see the next generation of Torres women, you know." Chicky was a dog with a bone when it came to my reproductive rights. "Is there anyone who you've been talking to lately?"

Yes, my sperm donor's sister.

Nope. Absolutely could not say that.

"Uh, you know, it's just been so busy. Not really easy to find the time for dating," I stalled. My mother was well-versed in my tactics by now.

"Mila, what are you not telling me?" And there it was.

"Nothing!" My voice was way too high-pitched to be truth-ful. I cleared my throat and tried to lower it an octave. "Hey, listen, I have got to go, Mom. I've got a call on the other line. I'll see you Sunday!"

"Mila—"

"Bye!" I clicked end on the call and let out a loud exhale. Obviously, avoidance was only going to buy me so much time with my mother, but that was a bridge for another day.

The thirty-minute timer I'd set on my phone started beeping, signaling its end. *Thank God.* I sat up and swung my legs around the side of the bed, shimmying myself into a standing position. I could immediately feel the seepage—sorry, I really don't know how else to describe it—and quickly crab-walked to the bathroom to clean up.

If a swimmer hadn't already found my egg, I'd just have to try again next month because there was zero chance in hell I was sitting in this sperm bath another minute.

After a waist-down shower with some hotel soap—an abridged version of my go-to daily wash of pits, tits, and slits—I pulled my panties and jeans back on and began to clean up the bathroom. I'm sure hotel cleaning staff saw enough crap in their jobs, so I wasn't about to leave half a cup of sperm sitting out for the next shift to stumble across.

As I went to pick up the collection cup and walk it over to the trash, my hands fumbled with it just enough for the container to tip sideways. In a panic, I grabbed at it with my other hand to keep it from falling, but all that accomplished was my palm over the collection cup opening as the cup spilled upside down.

Now, listen, it's not like we're talking about a hugely full cup of baby juice here. Plus, I had already used two syringes full, but there were still some...leftovers.

And I was now holding those leftovers in my open palm.

I could feel the Moxy Mule I'd had earlier threatening to rebel as I involuntarily dry-heaved and ran for the sink. It took at least twenty seconds for the water to become scalding enough to make me feel any sort of clean as I attempted to boil off at least two layers of skin from my palm.

I promise I will never understand when people say sexuality is a choice. If I could stop being occasionally attracted to men, I certainly would have chosen that by now. There were honestly so few upsides to the entire Y chromosome.

Suddenly the thought hit me...what if I gave birth to a son?

I stared in the mirror as I dried my bright-red hand off on the towel hanging off the wall. *Was the skin peeling?* Well, good. I honestly hadn't considered the possibility before of having a son. Not that I really cared one way or the other because gender is a social construct. But I wouldn't know the first thing about cleaning a penis as a single mother. Is that even a thing? Or are penises self-cleaning like vaginas?

Maybe Reverend Wilson will have some tips if he becomes the grandfather.

All right, that one went too far, even for me. Apologies.

I quickly rushed around the hotel room and finished throwing away the conception evidence, righting my clothes, and straightening my hair before grabbing my purse and leaving the room. One elevator ride down later, and I was walking into the Moxy lobby.

Rachel was sitting at one of the corner barstools, looking down at her phone, but I didn't see Isa around.

"Where's Isa?" I asked Rachel when I reached her.

Rachel grinned and wiggled her brows at me. "How'd it go?"

"Fine." I shrugged. "I mean, I guess we'll find out in two weeks. Did Isa leave?"

"No, but she said to go home without her. She and the beard went out back for a smoke break like ten minutes ago, and I haven't seen her since." Rachel was not Isa's biggest fan, and I was fully aware of the tension between them. I knew she tolerated Isa because I loved her, but Rachel considered herself fiercely loyal to her friends and Isa tended to think about herself first...like always. But that's also probably why we worked out because I wasn't too far off of that selfish mark myself. "I mean, are you really surprised? It's Isa."

I chuckled, partially from the discomfort of the moment. "No, she is who she is. Straight women are their own brand of crazy. You want another drink here, or should we head home?"

"Home," Rachel confirmed. "There's a new documentary on Netflix I've been wanting to see about a fertility doctor who impregnates like fifty of his clients unknowingly with his own sperm when they think it was actually an anonymous donor and now he's got like eighty-seven children."

I blinked slowly, turning to look at her as we stepped out onto the curb to wait for our Lyft. "Yeah, that totally seems on brand with the activities of the night. What a great selection."

My voice was dripping in sarcasm, but Rachel didn't pick up on it.

"My thoughts exactly," she agreed.

Fantastic.

Chapter Seven

Y*ou have got to be freaking kidding me.*

I scrolled through the other rideshare apps on my phone, but there would have to be dire circumstances for me to take anything other than a Lyft. And meeting my mother's new romantic interest was not so dire I'd risk my life with Uber, whose only driver requirements were being a *breathing human* and having *no recent murder record.* But seeing as how the closest option available on Lyft right now was a shared ride...

Almost qualified as dire.

I decided to suck it up and just book it since there was no way my car was going to make it that far or I was going to risk the prime parking spot I'd found several days ago. So Lyft it was. Lukas and his shared ride would be arriving in four minutes to take me to Chicky's townhouse in Germantown, MD, but the chances of another rider needing to leave Washington, DC, to go to the far reaches of Southern Maryland seemed unlikely.

An older model Prius pulled up silently where I was

standing on the sidewalk in front of my house. I checked the license plate on the back of the car briefly to make sure I wasn't about to be kidnapped, then slid into the back seat.

"Mila?" A younger male voice called out from the front seat to confirm the passenger's name.

"Yes. Are you Lukas?" I asked as I closed the door beside me and began putting on my seat belt, dropping my purse on the floor of the car between my legs.

"I am, and guess what?" the young man replied.

As I lifted my head back up while the car was pulling away from the curb, the sound of bells and clanging filled the interior of the car. Neon strip lights lining the car's roof lit up in a bright, strobe-light fashion. *What the hell?*

"Welcome to *Take a Lyft, Win a Gift!*" The young man driving had now turned around to smile at me since he had pulled up to a stop sign. He looked like he was just shy of twenty-five years old and clearly had other plans for me than a peaceful ride to Germantown. "Are you ready for the ride of your—"

Suddenly a woman's face came into view from the front passenger seat, turning to look back at me. "Wait...Mila?"

Ari Elliot was sitting in the front seat of my Lyft.

Because of course she is.

"Uh..." I tried to form words, but this situation had completely escaped my realm of understanding.

"Ari, you ruined my intro," Lukas scoffed in a mildly annoyed fashion and looked back at the road in front of him as he pulled through the intersection. I now noticed that there was a camera attached to the dashboard of the car that was pointing directly back at me. "We're going to need to start over. Can we run that from the top one more time, ma'am?"

Ma'am? Christ, now I really was feeling geriatric.

"I'm a little confused here..." I responded instead because if

Ari hadn't been there, I'm pretty sure this was the beginning plot of how I'd be sold into human trafficking. "What the hell is happening right now?"

"It's for TikTok," Ari responded, her body still turned to look back at where I was sitting. "Lukas does videos of unsuspecting people playing his Lyft game show and posts them to TikTok. He goes to graduate school in the evenings for communications, and it's part of his capstone project."

I blinked slowly, trying to process. "Uh...okay...and you're on the game show?"

"Hell no," Ari replied, shooting a grin at Lukas. "No offense, son. I'm just here to supervise so his father feels better about Lukas using his car to do this."

Son? Acca-scuse me?

"Like he needs a guard for a freaking Prius. Wait, so how do you guys know each other?" Lukas asked after rolling his eyes about his father.

Ari shrugged her shoulders loosely. "She might be pregnant with my brother's baby."

Lukas glanced back at me in the rearview mirror. "You're one of Uncle Aston's customers?"

"I don't think I'd refer to myself as his customer exactly," I replied, though I didn't have better verbiage to throw out there. "But I'm confused...Ari, Lukas is your son? I would have thought you were in your thirties, like me."

"Oh!" Ari's eyes lit up like she just realized that none of this was known to me. "That probably sounded weird to you without context. But, yeah. I was married to his dad in my twenties. Hence the last name Elliott. Lukas is my stepson."

"Ah." I would not have guessed that sequence of events in a million years. "I didn't know you were ever married to a man."

"*Man* is a stretch when talking about my dad," Lukas piped

in. "Incapable of minding his own business would be a better descriptor."

Ari rolled her eyes dramatically and then winked at me. "Kids. So dramatic sometimes. Well, you'll find out soon enough about that, I'm sure."

Maybe I had blacked out and was dreaming right now, but either way, I was definitely going to have more questions about all of this later.

"So, are you in?" Lukas cut Ari off and looked back at me in the rearview mirror. "If you sign this release form, we can start filming. I'll pull over and pretend to pick you up again since Ari ruined our initial take."

He shot Ari an annoyed look, and she grinned.

My brows furrowed. "What's in this for me again?"

"Five hundred dollars and some Internet fame," Lukas responded. "Also, my undying love and affection."

"Well, when you put it that way." I had no interest in Internet fame, but the kid seemed genuine and something about his connection to Ari made me feel a bit more comfortable. Plus, it couldn't hurt my comedy career to get a little publicity. "I guess we can, but can you call me Tori? That's my stage name."

"Ooh, a second name. The intrigue! I like it. I'm on board." Lukas pumped his fist in the air and then pulled over to the side of the road. "Now get out."

"Lukas, have some tact. Christ," Ari told him as I stepped out of the car and closed the door behind me.

I waited a full ten seconds before opening the car door and sliding back into my seat.

"Are you Tori?" Lukas asked.

I said that I was as I pulled on my seat belt.

"Welcome to *Take a Lyft, Win a Gift!*" Lukas announced as

the lights in the car all began flashing once again. I pretended to be surprised. "Are you ready for the ride of your life, Tori?"

"Anytime a man has asked me that before, I've been disappointed," I replied with a noncommittal shrug. "But, sure. Let's do it."

Lukas looked straight at the camera and wiggled his brows. "Don't worry, Tori. I aim to please in ten minutes or less."

"Not the flex you think it is," I replied.

"You're going to get a series of five tough trivia questions as I transport you from your starting point to your destination, and if—*if*—you get all five correct, you will walk out of this Lyft with five hundred buckaroos. You will also be given one hint that you can use at any point—but once you use it, that's it. You're on your own! Are you game?"

"I'm ready!" I pumped both of my fists in the air and put on as perky of a smile as I could, mentally pretending I was on stage. Mila Torres wasn't super comfortable with the spotlight, but Tori Miles could win a crowd, so here we fucking go.

"Question number one," Lukas began as he looked forward and drove up the street. "The Loch Ness Monster has long been feared by seamen, but leading theories today state that the sea serpent most likely witnessed sticking out of the water was actually a...what?"

"Whale penis!" That was an easy one.

The lights in the cabin went crazy again, and Ari chuckled as she made every attempt to stay out of the camera frame.

"Ding ding ding!" Lukas cheered. "You're on to question number two! It's ninety-two degrees outside in the DC swamp weather, and someone tells you that you're sweating like a pig. What does that mean?"

"Pigs don't sweat, so...you're rolling around in mud to cool down?" I frowned, unsure.

"Also known as the cesspool on Capitol Hill," Lukas joked

as the lights went off again to signal success. "But correct again! It was a trick question because pigs do not sweat. Ready for question number three?"

"If it's not a trick," I replied.

"I'll keep this one simple for you," Lukas assured me, but more so the camera as he turned onto Highway 270 with ease. "Question number three, what television series showed the first interracial kiss on American network television?"

"Captain Kirk and Uhura on Star Trek!" I shouted my response back so fast even Lukas paused to look at me.

"Shit, I didn't think you'd get that one!" Lukas exclaimed, then clicked the button to make all the lights go off again.

Ari looked back at me, and her brows rose. "Good pull."

"Uhura could still get it." I shrugged, because I felt like that was a universal fact that most nerdy lesbians know, particularly with how sad we all were with her recent passing. "She was gorgeous."

"Okay, it's time to make things more difficult," Lukas says. "Question number four, what is Scotland's national animal?"

I chewed on the edge of my thumbnail for a moment, trying to place this fact. I'd heard it before—it was something nonsensical—but it felt just out of reach in my brain.

"Give me a hint," I finally replied.

Lukas grinned at me through the rearview mirror and then looked into the camera. "This national animal is particularly horny."

"Unicorn!" My mind connected the dots immediately, despite the fact that his hint was basically meant for an adolescent boy.

"Ladies and gentlemen, Tori is on fire!" Lukas called out. "We only have one more question before we arrive at your destination, and this one is for all the marbles. Are... you...ready?"

He was using his best game show voice-over as he dialed it up for the camera, and I couldn't help but laugh because it was a bit endearing how into this he was. I actually was kind of looking forward to watching his final TikTok video on the whole thing because I could see how his personality would make this an interesting watch.

"I'm ready!" I shouted back, trying to match his enthusiasm level.

Lukas did a drum roll on the steering wheel alongside a dramatic pause before beginning. "Question number five, for five hundred dollars, the very first winner of RuPaul's Drag Race on season one was...who?"

I grinned because that was just too easy. "Bebe Zahara Benet!"

Ari let out a loud laugh from the front seat. "I told you not to use that question! Every queer person knows that one!"

Lukas glanced back at me in the rearview mirror. "She doesn't look queer."

Ari smacked his upper arm with a firm clap. "What the hell, Lukas? You can't say stuff like that. There is no one way to look queer."

"What?" He shrugged his shoulders defensively and gave me a sheepish grin. "It's a fair thought!"

"It's a borderline homophobic thought," I added my two cents to the conversation. "But for Ari's son, I'll let it slide this one time."

"Wait, so are you guys..." Lukas was pulling over to the curb in front of my mother's townhouse, and he put the car into park. "Are you two together?"

"What? No!" I barked out my response to Lukas so quickly that Ari glanced back at me, her brows furrowed. She almost looked...disappointed? The expression disappeared immediately, though.

Ari cleared her throat and shook her head. "Lukas, I swear to God, I can't even with you sometimes. Just give the poor woman her money."

Lukas held up five crisp one-hundred-dollar bills and handed them to me. "Fair's fair. You won it. But, also, make sure to give me five stars on the Lyft app."

He also handed me a release to sign so that he could put the video up, and after a careful read over the terms and conditions —hello, I *was* a lawyer still—I signed my legal name on the bottom.

"Hi!" My mother's voice was beckoning to me from the front yard, and I glanced out the window to see her waving furtively at me as she briskly walked up to the car. "*Hola, mija!*"

I gave her a small wave and unbuckled my seat belt. "Well, I guess that's my cue to go..."

"It was really nice meeting you, Tori!" Lukas said.

"Her name is Mila," Ari corrected him. "Thanks for playing, Mila! I'll send you the link when it goes live."

"That sounds great." I opened the car door and stepped one foot out onto the pavement. "I'll see you guys later."

"Are these your friends?" My mother ducked her head down to look inside the car, waving at Ari and Lukas. "Oh, you both have to join us for dinner. There's plenty of food!"

"Mom! They're working," I told her, already feeling my cheeks heat. I don't know how it's possible that she can make me feel like I'm thirteen years old again so quickly, but here we are.

"I mean, I *am* hungry," Lukas called out, leaning down to look across Ari and out at my mother. "What are you serving?"

"Good Lord," Ari groaned under her breath, but I caught it.

"*Pozole,*" my mother told him. "You'll love it—lots of meat and veggies. Come in, come in. Call me Chicky and park in the driveway there."

Well, this is happening.

"Mom, they were *just* giving me a ride," I whispered to her as Lukas pulled his car into the driveway as instructed. "You didn't need to invite them in."

"*Ay, mija,* what kind of hospitality is that?" She frowned at me, and I was emotionally transported back to childhood with one disapproving look. "Go inside and set two extra plates at the table. Steve can show you where everything is."

"I used to live here, Mom," I reminded her with all the sass of the preteen I could feel myself reverting into. "I don't need your new boyfriend to show me around *my* house."

She wasn't listening anymore, though, as she was already walking over to Lukas's car and welcoming him and Ari to her home.

I groaned and stomped inside with every bit of teenage angst I could muster up in this thirtysomething, possibly pregnant body.

What are the chances that I'll get through this dinner without my comedy career or possible uterus guest being mentioned?

I'm guessing...not good.

Chapter Eight

"**H**ave you ever accidentally drowned someone you were trying to baptize?" Lukas shoved a spoonful of meat and veggies into his mouth as he looked across the dinner table at Reverend Steve.

Lord, please let this dinner go quickly. I closed my eyes and imagined that I wasn't currently sitting between the stepson of the woman I was having dirty dreams about and the man of God who was probably sinning with my mother. No, I was on the water somewhere in the Maldives in one of those over-the-water cabanas with the glass bottom cutouts and a diving board right off the bedroom.

Splash. Gone. My eyes opened again as my mother gave me an extra dinner roll.

"Here, Mila. You look like you're still hungry," she said, her tone matter of fact.

Reverend Steve cleared his throat roughly. I imagined he hadn't been asked that question before. "Uh, what?"

"Like when you're dunking someone underwater, do you ever drop them and then they drown? Is that like a straight ticket to heaven because you died during a baptism? Like a get-out-of-hell-free card?" Lukas's face was completely straight, and, good Lord, the kid was serious.

"No. No one has ever been injured during a baptism I've performed, nor have I ever heard of that happening. We are always very careful during baptisms, and there is other clergy nearby as well, in case I ever need help." To his credit, Reverend Steve seemed to have recovered from the surprise of the question and was now just speaking frankly. "Have you ever been baptized?"

"No." Lukas shook his head. "I can't swim."

Ari let out a low groan, and I glanced right to catch her eye. She offered me an apologetic look and mouthed *I'm sorry*. I shook my head like it was no big deal. I'm just super chill and laid back like that, you know?

"So, Ari, tell me how you met my Mila," my mother changes the topic unceremoniously as everyone at the table turns to look at Ari and me.

Motherfucking shit.

"Oh...I...uh, well, technically, I first met her at one of her shows." Ari smiled triumphantly as if she'd just found a loophole out of answering that question that was completely safe.

She was absolutely wrong.

"What show? You're in a show?" My mother's gaze now turned to me, and I felt my stomach drop into my rectum—if that's even possible.

Ari's eyes widened and she began to stammer. "Uh, I mean...like at *a* show. We were both at a show and ran into each other."

My mother's eyes narrowed on me. She wasn't fooled for even a second. "Mila Torres, you tell me what's going on right now."

Lukas let out a low whistle like the adolescent boy he was.

"Well, uh, it's not a big deal, Mom. Just, you know... remember how when I was younger, I talked about being a comedian one day?" I cleared my throat, but then quickly took a big bite of the roll on my plate and chewed it as slowly as I could manage.

"Yes?" Her eyes were still narrowed on me like lasers.

"I've been, uh...dabbling in it. Here and there, you know. For fun. Nothing serious."

"She's really good, though," Lukas interrupted, then held up his phone to my mother. I immediately recognized the video clip he was showing her and made a mental note to leave him a review with zero stars. "Look at her last clip on YouTube. She has like two hundred thousand views. And she's going to be on my TikTok channel, so she might be really famous after that."

My mother took the phone from Lukas and hit play. My voice immediately came over the speakers, and I cringed.

The thing about being an only child to a single mother is... there's never anyone else to blame. The plastic on the couch ripped? Mija, what did you do? There is a stray kitten hidden in the linen closet? We are not a hotel for fleas, mija!"

The crowd roared in the background for a split second before my mother hit pause and lifted her eyes to me in the most excruciatingly slow way possible.

"When is your next show?" she asked, her voice smooth as the ice over a frozen lake of underwater graves.

I swallowed the bread currently clogging my throat. "Uh...I might be opening for someone at the beginning of next month at this place in DC."

"What place?" Her response was so quick it almost cut me off.

"The Comedy Loft." I shoved the piece of bread that she'd offered me in my mouth.

My mother handed the phone back to Lukas and then

picked up her fork. "Well, I expect you'll get the reverend and me each a front-row ticket. That would be such a nice date night, right, honey?"

She looked at the reverend expectantly, and honestly, his expression looked as panicked as I felt.

He cleared his throat. "Uh, yeah. It's been a while since I've seen a good comedy show. Who are you opening for?"

I swallowed again. "Randy Feltface, the Purple Puppet."

"Did you hear that, Steve?" My mother's face split into a too-wide grin that reminded me of the Joker right before he blew up a hospital. "My daughter is a comedian, and she's opening for a puppet. I wonder what else we'll learn today."

God, please let that be it.

"You know, Randy is really fun—his style is considered biting wit, and he's from Australia," Lukas piped up. "Can I get tickets to come too?"

Ari elbowed him hard in the side.

"Ow! What? Do you want to go too?" Lukas rubbed his side and then looked back at me. "Can we both get tickets?"

"It'll be like a reunion," my mother added, now turning her deadly beaming smile toward me. "You can do that, right?"

"Sure," I ground out the words in a higher octave than I normally spoke in. "Sounds like a great time."

To be slaughtered by my mother.

Lukas kept talking about Randy Feltface and explaining some of his most popular jokes.

I finished everything on my plate as quickly as possible and stood up from the table. "Does anyone want a drink? I can go grab some sodas or beers from the fridge in the garage."

"I'll take a Coke," Reverend Steve said.

Lukas raised one hand. "Beer!"

"You know what, I'll help you. That's a lot to carry." Ari stood up as well and ushered me out of the room. We were completely silent as we walked through the kitchen, and I opened the side door that led to the garage. The moment the door closed behind us, the garage illuminated with automatic lighting and Ari let out a loud sigh. "Mila, I am *so* sorry."

I waved a hand like it was no big deal. "No need," I assured her. "Honestly, it's my fault. I really should have told her by now."

Ari was quiet for a moment and then opened the door to the old white fridge against the far wall. "I'm guessing she doesn't know about my brother either?"

I shook my head and took the can of orange soda she handed me. Cracking open the top, I took a long drink.

"You guys aren't very close?" Ari opened a can of Coke and took a sip, closing the fridge behind her as we both just stood there for a moment.

"The opposite," I replied. "Chicky is...she's incredible. We're beyond close. Sometimes so close that I forget where she ends and I begin."

"Oh." Ari nodded at that. "So, you wanted something of your own?"

I fidgeted with the edge of my soda can. "For a little bit. Not forever. I just wanted to see if this was ever going to be anything, you know? Comedy has been a whirlwind, but it was never meant to become anything other than fun. But that agent sent me a contract for representation that I'm strongly considering signing."

Ari's eyes widened. "Whoa. That's big time."

"It feels like it," I agreed, then took another gulp of orange soda. "But I have a job already. And it's a good job."

Something between a scoff and a laugh came out of Ari's mouth. Her brows rose almost to her hairline, and she ran a hand effortlessly through her black-and-green long hair. "Uh...

is it? I mean, not to pry, but you seem to have pretty different beliefs than some of the partners you work for."

"That is becoming more and more glaringly obvious," I replied with a sigh this time. "But for now, it paid for law school, and I've learned a lot during my time there and could be junior partner in a few years if I keep my caseload high. The connections they can make me are...invaluable."

"Like where to hide a senator's darkest secrets?" Ari took another sip of her soda, then cocked her head to the side. Her hair was a bit longer than when I'd first met her and when it fell over, it exposed the shaved part of her head. I noticed that there had once been a pattern shaved into it, though I couldn't tell what it was exactly since the undercut had grown out some.

Get it together, Mila, I reminded myself so I didn't reach out and trace a finger across the markings.

I quickly swallowed another swig of soda. "We should probably get back inside before my mother thinks I'm hiding something else out here."

"Like a baby?" Ari was grinning now, and I could tell she was joking, but yeah, that was exactly what I was worried about. "Any news on that front yet?"

"Still a little early to test." I turned my eyes down and could feel my cheeks heating. "This must be so weird for you. I'm sorry you got dragged into this dinner."

"Don't be." Ari shook her head, then her eyes found mine, and she held my gaze. "It's been fun. I like seeing where you came from. It's like getting a glimpse behind the curtain."

My chest felt tight like it was harder to take a breath. The way she was looking at me felt...heavy. I fumbled over my next sentence. "There's, uh, not much to see behind the curtain."

Ari stepped closer to me and lifted her hand to the side of my face. The tip of her finger touched just above my cheekbone, and she softly slid it down to my jaw in an excruciatingly wonderful, slow caress. "I really like what I see."

Holy shitballs. I'm pretty sure Tiffany's "I Think We're Alone Now" began playing in the background, or maybe just in my head, but I could hear it clear as day.

I had to remind myself to take in another breath, and then another, and another. When she moved her hand, letting it drop by her side, I felt the absence not just on my cheek but in my core.

Children, behave...

My voice was barely above a whisper. "Ari..."

Running just as fast as we can...what would they say if they ever knew?

Her gaze dropped to my mouth, and I couldn't stop myself from sliding my tongue across my bottom lip. God, I wanted her to kiss me right now. She wanted that, too. I could feel it in the way her eyelids seemed heavier than moments before or the way her gaze flickered down to my mouth for several long seconds.

I took half a step forward to close the distance between us but was met with...nothing.

She had stepped back and cleared her throat. "I...uh...sorry. That was...I don't know what that was."

"It felt like a movie moment," I replied, looking down at my feet and trying not to focus on the heat in my cheeks at her rejection.

"Except we're not in a movie, and you might be pregnant." Ari ran her hand through her hair again, and the distressed look on her face made my heart squeeze. "I just...I can't be involved with that, you know?"

I swallowed hard and turned on my practical, nonemotional side to try to get me through this moment. "It's too complicated. I mean, it's your brother. Of course."

"This isn't about Aston," she continued, then looked toward the fridge behind me as if to change the subject. "The reverend wanted a Coke, right? I know Lukas asked for a beer."

I nodded my head, feeling like a numbness was spreading across my skin and capturing my throat. I wanted to rewind the last thirty seconds and pretend none of that had just happened.

Ari handed me a cold can of Coke as she took out a bottle of Modelo Especial for Lukas. "Do you want another soda?"

I shook my head. "Ari, I..."

"Hey, it's nothing." She cut me off with a shake of her head, and why did her eyes look so damn sad right now? She looked like she didn't agree with anything she was saying, and yet...she was still saying it. "We don't have to make this a big deal. You've got a lot going on in your life right now that you need to focus on."

That's certainly an understatement.

"Come on." She motioned toward the house, her smile back like nothing had ever happened. "Let's go back in."

I followed her back inside with all the muster of a kicked puppy, but I barely made it over the threshold into the kitchen before my mother ushered me back into the garage.

Ari glanced at me over her shoulder, her expression seeming to ask if she should intervene. I shook my head because there was no hope for that.

Chicky pointed one finger, and I turned on my heels so automatically I could practically feel the angsty adolescent in me recoiling in fear. "*Mija*, outside."

She shut the door to the house behind us and I turned around slowly, sheepishly, shoulders down to face her.

"Mom, I know that that was a lot of news for you," I tried to detour her off the war path, but she put one hand up to silence me.

I silenced.

She was pacing back and forth across the garage floor now, wagging her finger at me. "I ask you to come home and meet my Steve for one normal dinner, and I find out—in front of him— that you're leading a secret life. What if he were to tell Linda about this?"

Ah, okay. So, this was about how I made her look in front of other people. I loved my mother, but her focus on how others perceived her was not one of the traits I wanted to pass down to the next generation.

"Obviously, that was not ideal, nor how I wanted that to happen," I replied. "But if I may remind you, you invited my Lyft drivers in for dinner against my will."

"Lyft drivers, my *culo*," Chicky scoffed. "You're dating that girl, aren't you?"

That was definitely more of a statement than a question.

"I am not!" My voice was a lot higher pitched than I'd intended it to be and Chicky caught that immediately as well. I tried to lower my octave. "I mean, Ari is a friend. A good friend. Just a friend."

Chicky rolled her eyes. "Oh, sure, and Reverend Steve only does missionary."

I grimaced. "Oh, God, that mental image will require at least three therapy sessions."

She didn't say anything back, but her expression seemed to deflate from angry to heartbroken, and I knew we were on the second part of the guilt journey now. "I just don't understand why you wouldn't tell me about your second career. Me? Your mother? What is there that you cannot tell me? What have I done to deserve this distance?"

Shit, the guilt angle worked like a charm, and she fucking knew it. "Mom, I promise I wasn't hiding it from you. I'm still figuring it out, you know? Law is my passion. This has just been fun—like kind of a dare to myself on if I could even do it or not."

That had been true when I started comedy, but now it felt like a lie as I was saying it out loud.

"Two hundred thousand views on YouTube, Mila," my mother reminded me, the tinge of pride in her voice not something I missed. "Clearly, you can do it."

That was the closest to a compliment I was going to get until her guilt trip was over.

"I'm starting to think that, too." I shrugged my shoulders and tried not to smile, but we were closing in on phase three of our usual mother-daughter fight, which was the lovey-dovey make up part. "It's...it's kind of wild, you know? Like, maybe I could actually be a comedian one day? In real life."

"*Ay, mija,* of course you can." Chicky was smiling sympathetically now, back in her position of power, comforting me. "I've been telling you since you were a baby that you were made for a stage. You're hilarious, and the world will find that out soon enough."

"Thanks, Mom." I smiled back at her, and the tension between us simmered away.

"But can you make me one promise?" Chicky asked, now lifting one finger in the air between us. "Keep your law license current. You never know when I may need legal counsel."

I laughed at that one because if that wasn't the goddamn truth, then maybe pigs could sweat. "Okay, Mom. I promise."

"See? It's not so hard to tell your mother things, right?" She held out her arms to me and I folded into them like a little kid. "Come on, now. Let's get back to dinner. We have guests to entertain."

Eye on the prize always, Chicky.

Chapter Nine

Today was the day.

I examined the sheet of paper that I'd taped all twelve pregnancy tests to so far—one for each day since insemination. I know I know—it was overkill, but I was sure that if I was pregnant, I'd be able to see some faintness of a line as the days passed.

So far, absolutely nothing but the damn control line. This, to be fair, should have been expected, but it was my first time, and I couldn't help but be eager to track the potential progress.

I was excited.

That might seem obvious, or like...I *should* be excited, you know? But reality is always two steps behind imagination, and when I imagined this moment, I hadn't pictured it happening this way. At least, not exactly. I'd pictured sitting with my partner, excited together. And yet, there was still something really special about being on this journey on my own. My mother had done it and I felt like I was carrying on the tradition in some way.

I scanned the paper full of negative pregnancy tests one more time and stopped on the empty thirteenth line. I jotted today's date next to it—the day my period tracker told me I was due to start shark week. And so far, there'd been no appearance of any ripped and shed uterine lining in my undies.

A good sign!

I tore open the packet that held the fresh pregnancy test stick and placed it between my legs as I awkwardly squat-hovered over my toilet. Thankfully, since I owned the place, I had the master bedroom and accompanying bathroom. It wasn't all that small, so I could spread out a bit without worrying about one of my roommates walking in and seeing me staring down the barrel of my vagina like a contortionist over the toilet.

I conjured images of rushing waterfalls and willed my early morning bladder to bring me a positive result. I stared forward in an attempt to concentrate, but my gaze caught on the illustrated photograph on my wall of an elephant sitting on and crushing a toilet seat with the sign next to it that read "5 stars, would poop here again."

I should probably get rid of some of my novelty decor if I bring a baby into this place.

Returning my concentration to between my legs, I pushed down and finally began peeing on the stick. Well, mostly on the stick, but also on my hand, the toilet seat, and the inside of my thighs.

Jesus, it was like a wonky faucet down there, spraying in every direction.

Once I figured I'd gotten enough on the stick for it to count, I Kegeled my stream to a stop and grimaced as I placed the wet stick down on the bathroom countertop, then emptied the rest of my bladder into the bowl and grabbed some toilet paper to clean up. After washing my hands, I picked up my cell phone and set a timer for five minutes.

And then I sat on the edge of the bathtub and waited.

And waited.

The longest five minutes I've ever fucking waited.

Okay, I'm exaggerating, but it might as well have felt like an hour.

My cell phone timer went off, and I bounced off the edge of the tub in one giant leap toward the sink counter, which resulted in nearly knocking the test strip into the sink. Grabbing it just in time, I held it up and examined the results.

Control line, check.

Pregnancy line? Holy blue balls, also check.

It was faint, but it was there. A second line. The only time I'd ever seen a second line was that one time in 2020—a year we do not ever speak of—when I got COVID-19, but this was so much freaking better than that nightmare.

Something wet hit my forearm, and I glanced at it to see a small puddle of clear liquid beading around one of the hair follicles on my arm. I am not a crier, okay? I don't cry, and it's not that I have anything against people who do, but crying is equivalent to a workout for me, and I also haven't been to a gym in five years.

But I *was* crying. Big, fat alligator tears were pouring down my cheeks in quicker and quicker succession and I didn't even care that I'd just peed on the damn thing—I kissed the beautiful second line.

I'm pregnant.

I'm going to be a mom.

Oh, sweet Bebe Bennet, I am going to be A MOTHER.

"Yasmeen!" I threw open the door to my bathroom and began screaming at the top of my lungs. "Rachel! Yasmeen, Rachel!"

There was a clatter in another room, and moments later, the door to my bedroom swung open as Yasmeen rushed inside.

"What's wrong?" Her eyes were darting around the room with her hands out in front of her like she was a boxer looking for an intruder that was currently attacking me. A boxer whose hair was in rollers tucked under a silk scarf with a few stragglers poking out and wearing only pajama shorts and a lacy camisole that was doing nothing to cover her nipples.

Rachel barreled into Yasmeen from behind seconds later. "Is Next Door Becky naked again?"

I laughed, shaking my head. "No, her blinds are closed," I said, referencing our nudist neighbor across the alleyway, who often treated us to free peep shows. Rachel wouldn't admit it, but I think there was a crush happening there because she seemed to always time her leaving for work at the same time as Becky. At some point, it's just no longer an accident.

"So, what's going on?" Rachel frowned, her shoulders sagging.

I held up the stick in front of me. "Look!"

"Oh my God, you have COVID?" Yasmeen's hand flew in front of her nose and mouth, immediately covering both. "Why did you call us in here? You have to quarantine! Girl, you know I've got my vacation next week—I swear to God, if I have to cancel it, then you're reimbursing me for everything I paid to Travelzoo."

"Yasmeen! I'm not sick! I'm pregnant," I clarified, holding up the instruction pamphlet with the guide. Good Lord, this pandemic was a never-ending post-traumatic flashback for everyone. "Look, it says I am *pregnant*!"

Rachel leaned in closer, narrowing her eyes. "Like...with a baby?"

I placed the stick down on the counter then placed both hands on my hips. "No, with a fucking octopus, like that documentary of the lady who went swimming in the ocean."

Rachel grimaced. "Don't remind me about that story. I still haven't been able to go swimming."

"Mila, you're pregnant!" Yasmeen was bouncing on the tips of her toes, her voice already a full octave higher than it was when she thought I was giving her the modern-day plague. "Holy crap, it worked! The Baby Bank worked!"

She grabbed my hands and now I was bouncing with her, and since when did my boobs suddenly get so sensitive?

"Ah, hold on," I told her, stopping the bouncing to wrap my arms around my achy chest. "The girls did not like that."

"Sore nips! That's a pregnancy sign!" Yasmeen clapped her hands. "We've got to celebrate. Shots? Let's do shots!"

"She's pregnant, dingbat," Rachel reminded Yasmeen. "She can't drink."

"Oh my God, no more margaritas on Tuesdays?" Yasmeen looked stricken, a hand on her chest. "Okay, it's going to be okay. We knew this might happen. Let's think about this—would a baby know if we took edibles instead?"

I pushed past Yasmeen and walked into my bedroom. "No drugs, no alcohol for the next nine months."

"And no soft cheeses," Rachel added, her eyes glued to her phone as she began reading off a list that she must have just Googled. "Also, deli meat. Sushi. Only one cup of coffee or less a day. Uncooked bean sprouts? I don't know what that is. If you have a steak, it has to be fully cooked—no more medium rare. Poached eggs are a no go, too, so that means no eggs benny at brunch. Firm yolks only."

"Oh, my God." Yasmeen walked out of the bathroom behind Rachel and began reading over her shoulder. "Damn, Mila...are you sure about this? It's like literally all your favorite things on here."

Well-done steak was not something I'd emotionally

prepared for, but I swallowed the lump in my throat. "It'll be worth it. It's only nine months. Anyone can do that, right?"

"Actually, it says here that pregnancy is ten months long—forty weeks. And that some of these restrictions also apply if you breastfeed the first year or two after as well," Rachel continued reading off whatever Satan-spawned website she'd found. "This one here says the World Health Organization recommends at least two years of breastfeeding. So, ten months plus two years...might as well round up to at least three years. And then what if you want the baby to have a sibling by then—two years seems like a good age gap for siblings—so you get pregnant again and now we're up to six years. You'll be in your forties. Might be pushing it to try for a third at that age."

I grabbed Rachel's phone from her and tossed it onto the bed. "Jesus, Rachel. You are *not* helping."

"But I'm sure a bouncing little baby totally makes up for all those years," Rachel added, trying to appease me as she went to collect her phone. "I was just saying what the website said."

"Wait, does this mean we have to change Macavity's litter box now?" Yasmeen's eyes suddenly went wide. "Rachel, look at the website. No litter boxes. Is that a thing?"

"No changing litter boxes if you're pregnant," Rachel confirmed, back on her phone. "I vote we start leaving the door open more often and then we might not have to deal with this at all."

I began pushing both women toward my bedroom door. "You all have been a fountain of joy. Thanks soooo much."

Sarcasm dripped from my tongue as they both stepped into the hallway and no, I was not going to let them give my cat away to the streets of his dreams.

"We are so excited for you!" Yasmeen grabbed my hands again. "We're totally going to celebrate. I'm throwing you an impromptu baby shower. Tonight!"

"Oh, we have to go to As You Are," Rachel added, looking at Yasmeen. "We can throw it there. I'll message Jo on Instagram and tell them to save us the couch."

"You guys go crazy. Give me a few minutes so I can call Aston and tell him the news," I was laughing now because the idea of having a way-too-early baby shower at a lesbian bar actually sounded pretty fun.

"Pieces of Aston!" Yasmeen shouted over her shoulder as she and Rachel walked away from me down the hallway. "You're in the baby mama Facebook group now!"

I rolled my eyes and closed my bedroom door with a loud thud. I scrolled through my recent calls until I found Aston's name, then hit the call button. He picked up on the third ring, and it sounded like his mouth was full.

"Hello?" he mumbled around whatever he'd stuffed in his face.

"Are you eating?" I asked.

There was a pause for a moment as I imagined he swallowed. "Yeah, steamed pork buns. Have you ever been to Joy Luck House? I'll take you some time because their food is incredible."

I pulled the phone away from my ear for a moment to check the time on my cell phone. "You're having steamed pork buns for breakfast?"

"Don't forget rice," he added, and now his mouth sounded full again. "Anyway, what's up?"

"I have news." I paused for a moment as I tried to figure out my next words. Macavity snaked around my feet, rubbing up against me nonchalantly and leaving tufts of orange fur against my pants. "I'm pregnant."

I guess it was easier to say than I thought.

"Congrats! That's amazing. I'm turning the video on." Suddenly the phone call turned into a FaceTime and Aston's face popped up in front of me...and then Ari's face. "Hey, Ari, did you hear that? Mila's pregnant."

"Ari's there?" Was that squeaky sound my voice?

Ari waved at me, in the same way one might wave to an old friend they see from a distance but don't actually want to stop and come talk to.

Aston returned to the center of the screen long enough to hand it off to his sister entirely. "Yeah, we're having breakfast together. Here, say hi!"

"So, uh, it worked?" Ari's face was now center screen, but she wasn't looking directly at me. Almost off to the side, but I wasn't sure. "You're pregnant?"

"Uh, yeah...well, I mean, that's what the stick says. I haven't gone to a doctor or anything yet." I was definitely fumbling with my words now. I walked into the bathroom and picked up the stick to show her. God, it was still wet. "Uh, hold on. Let me wipe it off. Look, here, I mean, it's still so early. Who knows what could happen? But it says 'pregnant.'"

It was not lost on me that one near kiss and subsequent rejection with my future baby aunt had made me lose all ability to form normal sentences or maintain regular eye contact, goddamn it.

"Well, that's great news!" Ari sounded congratulatory, but it was strained in the way her jaw was clenched. Or maybe I was just reading tension into her tone.

Stop overthinking everything, I mentally reminded myself.

"Thanks," I replied. "Uh, yeah. I'm excited."

"Let us know if you need anything." Aston was back on the screen now. "Mom's going to be so excited."

"Wait, you're going to tell your mom?" I was back to squeaking now. "I mean, I haven't even told my mom yet."

Ari's face was back on the screen now. "Yeah, about that...

don't you think that's a conversation you guys should have pretty soon?"

Her tone sounded like she was challenging me. Like it was a dare. I immediately felt defensive because I didn't want to think about that conversation right now. I just wanted to celebrate, and this had already gone way off the rails.

"You can add her to my Facebook group if you want," Aston offered, looking over Ari's shoulder. "She can meet all the other grandmothers."

The thought sank in my stomach like a pound of rocks. *Good Lord, can you imagine?* "Uh, Chicky isn't the Facebook type."

That was a lie. She posted regular Jesus memes and shared way too many mini-kitchen baking show videos on her feed. I'd literally had to mute her from my feed because if I saw one more pin-sized pavlova being made, I might delete my Facebook entirely. Also, she shared a photo of Jonathan Van Ness last week with a Bible verse as the caption, and I'm one-hundred-percent sure she thought that was a picture of Jesus. Close, but no.

"Well, the offer stands," Aston repeated. "But, hey, this is your journey, Mama. Do whatever you want!"

Hearing him call me Mama felt incredibly weird and exciting all at the same time. "Thanks, uh, yeah, it was nice talking to you both, but I'm going to go."

Aston waved at the screen. "Call us with updates if you want! Or not."

"Will do," I lied and hit the "end call" button.

Phone in one hand and pregnancy stick in the other, I walked to the edge of my bed, turned around, and let myself fall backward onto the comforter. Macavity hopped up and joined me, grooming himself with a ridiculous level of attention to detail. Holy shit, what a morning. I dropped the stick and phone on the bed and moved my hands to the lowest part of my stomach and just rested them there.

A tiny fetus, a soon-to-be mom, a sperm donor, and his sister all walk into a bar...the joke could practically write itself. I turn over and grab the notebook on my nightstand and begin jotting down some ideas for my next comedy set.

Hey, when inspiration strikes...

Chapter Ten

"Hers has to be a virgin pillow princess," Yasmeen clarified to the woman behind the bar with the most incredible dreadlocks tied together at the base of her neck.

"Is there such a thing?" the bartender shot back, a sly smile on her face.

Yasmeen grinned and wiggled her brows. "Hey, listen, I don't know what you're doing later, but—"

I yanked on Yasmeen's arm. "We're here to celebrate me, remember? Not for a hookup."

"A girl can multitask," she huffed but then winked at the bartender once more. "I'm actually really great at multitasking with my hands and my—"

I shot her a look. "Yasmeen, I swear to God, if you finish that sentence..."

"Fine, fine, I won't finish, but anyone I'm with absolutely will." Yasmeen grinned even wider now, but the bartender was just laughing.

She finished pouring out the shots but pulled one aside and

handed it directly to me. "Here's the one with no alcohol. Congratulations, by the way."

"Thank you." I was pretty sure she'd be able to see how hard I was blushing, but thankfully the lights were kind of dim. I turned to Yasmeen. "Did Rachel find a table?"

Yasmeen pointed toward the windows overlooking the patio then gathered up as many shots as she could from the bar. "Yeah, outside. It's a nice night, too."

"Great." I followed her out, grabbing the last few and making sure to keep them separate from my virgin shot, which was basically just grenadine and a dash of Sprite a la Shirley Temple style.

When we got out the door and onto the patio, I saw that Rachel had pushed several tables together and there were only two empty seats left around it after a lot of our friends had trickled in and filled it up. Yasmeen began passing out shots to everyone as I sat in the empty head-of-the-table seat she'd directed me toward.

Yasmeen held up her shot high in the air. "Okay, everyone —this is the world's earliest baby shower, so we're celebrating that Mila is our designated driver for the next nine months!"

"Technically ten," Rachel added, but I shot her a look and her grin faded.

Isa was sitting next to her, and I blew her a kiss because, of course, she'd be the first person there. Nothing about her was queer, but she fit in with my friends seamlessly. To her left was my friend Samira, an immigration lawyer during the week and pole dancing instructor on the weekends. I'd met her at work a few years ago, and we had become fast friends since. Across from her was Yas's friend Kari, who had blown up on TikTok doing transition videos from her usual masc style to lipstick lesbian set to whatever the latest popular sound was. Usually something by Lizzo, let's be honest. She now had over two million followers who wanted to sleep with both the male and female versions of her, and I really couldn't blame them one bit.

On the other side of the table by Yasmeen was Yasmeen's latest love—zero chance this one was going to last, and so I hadn't even bothered learning her name—and that chick's roommate, who I'm pretty sure I made out with once a few months ago in the bathroom here.

But that's another story for a never time.

"Cheers to Mila, everyone!" Yasmeen tapped the bottom of her shot glass on the tabletop. "And cheers to the Baby Bank app!"

I laughed and raised my virgin glass of cherry syrup to do the same. "Cheers to Baby Bank!"

Everyone tossed back their drinks with the ease of any professional drinker and wished me congratulations before launching off into their own stories and conversations.

"Isn't that Tori?" A male voice saying my stage name caught my ear above the story Rachel was currently telling of a new keto recipe she was planning to try—listen, we're a fun group, but we're still in our thirties. Most nights ended with exchanging a recipe or a complaint about a neighbor who was too loud after our bedtimes.

I glanced over and made eye contact with two men walking down the sidewalk past the patio—one was wearing a gray baseball cap that just said *not a contractor* on the front and the other was Lukas.

"Lukas?" I called out, surprised to see him again. I waved a hand at him and his friend. "Hey! Come join us."

He grinned, then pointed to his friend. "Can Phil come too? I promise he is semi-tolerable after a few drinks."

Yasmeen cackled from where she was sitting and waved them over. "The more, the merrier."

Lukas hopped over the fence that sectioned off the patio

area from the sidewalk and was laced with rainbow ribbons the entire way across, then pulled a chair from another table up next to me. His friend walked around the fence rather than jumping it, and I immediately liked him.

"Are you guys celebrating something?" Lukas lifted my shot glass to his nose and sniffed it. "This smells hella sweet."

"It's nonalcoholic," I clarified as I took it back from him and wiped the rim of the glass. His nose had gotten way too close to it for my comfort, and to be honest, I was probably going to need to ask for a new glass entirely.

"Ah, so that means..." Lukas lifted his brow and a huge grin split across his face. He wiggled his eyebrows suggestively. "Did the uncle's baby juice work?"

It may have been a mistake to invite this man-child to our table.

"Uh, I am pregnant, if that's what you mean." God, I hoped that was what he meant. "So, we're celebrating that."

"How do you guys know each other?" Rachel asked, leaning in and clearly giving Lukas and his friend the suspicious once-over. Always the no-nonsense one in our group, there was zero chance she wasn't going to vet them thoroughly.

"I'm the uncle!" Lukas grinned, then his smile dropped into a frown. "Wait...no. I'm the cousin? First cousin? First cousin once removed?"

I put my hand directly over his mouth to shut him up. "You're Lukas, and that's it."

Rachel's eyes were wider now. "I'm confused."

I removed my hand from Lukas's mouth and shot him a warning look. "Lukas is Ari's stepson."

"Ari, Ari? Like...your Ari?" Rachel sputtered the words and now the entire table was clueing in to the fact that this was a conversation they wanted to follow.

"She's not *my* Ari." *Please let a sinkhole open beneath my chair.* "She's...you know...Aston's sister and this is her stepson."

"Ari has an adult stepson?" Yasmeen was frowning now, then looked at Lukas. "How old are you, kid?"

"I'm twenty-five, thank you very much," he replied with an air of feigned indignation. "I was twelve though, when my dad married Ari. So, I've always called her my stepmom just for fun."

Yasmeen waved her hands across her body in the motion of a large *X*. "Time-out, time-out, time-the-fuck-out. I need to hear this entire goddamn story right now."

Lukas grinned, clearly excited to be center stage for the moment. His friend, Phil, was sitting slightly behind him but was watching a video on his phone and had his AirPods in his ears, so he had clearly chosen to tune out the entire party. Seemed like a douche now.

"What story?" Lukas held up his hands like he had no idea what people were referring to.

"Come with me to the bar." I was standing now and pulling Lukas to his feet because something felt wrong talking about Ari in front of everyone this way. I felt...protective. Maybe that's the new mother instinct in me? Or maybe it's the I almost kissed her and really wished I had part of me. Either way, Lukas had to go. "Let's go get you a drink."

"Hey, have you seen your TikTok yet?" Lukas asked as he walked alongside me. "You're one of the highest views I've had yet on my channel. We just passed five hundred thousand on it."

"Really?" My interest was definitely piqued by that. "I saw I was tagged a few times in the comments of something, but I've been a bit busy to explore it."

"Right, baby-making and all that. Congratulations, by the way." Lukas pointed toward my stomach. "It's really cool of you to go through all of this to become a mom. If you know our family, you know someone who is willing to bend over backward like that for something they believe in would fit right in."

"Speaking of family," I snagged the opportunity the moment he left that door open. "I really am confused about the whole Ari-is-your-stepmom thing."

"Who isn't?" he asked jokingly as we got up to the bar.

I turned to the bartender. "Can we get one Pride Pilsner and a glass of water, please? It's pretty hot in here—is the air conditioner not working?"

"The air conditioner broke this afternoon," one of the bartenders called back. "But hydration is my love language. Let me get you that water first. Kid, I need to see your ID."

I was a pregnant pansexual woman in a queer bar during the summer with no air conditioning, so I was basically experiencing my first hate crime.

"Shit, I swear this baby face is never going to go away," Lukas sighed under his breath but then pulled his wallet out of his back pocket.

"Aw, it's cute though," I told him, this time bucking his chin gently with my knuckles like I would a little kid. "Embrace the baby face."

The bartender handed us our drinks and we stepped over to the side where a wooden bar ran the whole length of the inside of the bottom floor. I swung myself up onto a stool, but Lukas just leaned against the bar as he cracked open his pilsner.

"So...Ari?" I prompted him.

He let out a loud burp after a huge chug. "Oh, yeah. Ari. What about her?"

"How did she end up with your dad? What happened there? Why did they get divorced?" The questions were tumbling out of me faster than my tongue could keep up with the syllables. "Are they still friends now? What's going on?"

Lukas grinned, and I knew in that moment that he realized he had the upper hand. "Holy shit, are you jealous, Baby Mama? You've got the hots for Ari, don't you? I fucking called it in the car, and you both acted like I was homophobic."

There was zero chance that my face hadn't tinged entirely hot pink in that moment. I looked away and took a quick sip of my water, only for it to get stuck halfway down my throat and cause me to sputter for a moment before I could find my words. "I didn't say any of that. I was just curious."

"Nah, I can tell a crush when I see one." Lukas shook his head. "And listen, I can't blame you. Ari is one of the best people I've ever met. Anyone would be lucky to lock that down."

I grimaced. "That's a weird thing to say about your stepmom."

He laughed, and it sounded halfway between schoolyard boy and Furby doll. "Maybe if she was a regular stepmom, but there was never anything romantic between Ari and my dad. My dad's still head over heels in love with my mom—always will be."

Acca-scuse me. I felt like someone had hit the brakes on a runaway train. "Where's your mom?"

"At home," he replied, then took a smaller sip of his beer this time. "On our mantel in a big ol' urn."

"Oh. Oh! Lukas, I'm so sorry." At any point, I could have just left well enough alone and not badgered a poor boy about his dead mother and fake replacement lesbian stepmom, but here we are. The damage was done. "I didn't know."

Lukas shrugged. "It's fine. It was a long time ago. So long that I barely remember her. A few glimpses here and there, but it's fuzzy. The stories about her and all the photos my dad keeps—that's probably my strongest memory. He still talks about her as if she's here, and that's actually been really nice. Kind of like she is sometimes, you know?"

I felt a lump in my throat and, goddamn, these pregnancy hormones. "That's really sweet."

"My father teaches in the journalism program at George Washington University, and that's how he met Ari. She was one of his students." Lukas looked away for a moment, and I saw him go somewhere in his mind with the way his face flinched. "It was confusing back then. I was still pretty young. Still grieving my mother. The whole situation was, I'll admit it, pretty weird. But after they did what they needed to do to help Ari's situation, they divorced, and we've stayed in contact ever since. She's like a big sister to me now, honestly. She's family."

I so badly wanted to ask what Ari's situation was and for more details. I wanted to peel back his forehead and climb into his brain and watch his memories like a drive-in movie theater with a bucket of popcorn, but I kept my mouth shut and just waited.

"I'm glad you like her," Lukas finally said, and for the first time, his voice sounded soft and vulnerable. "She's an amazing person. But I'd be a shit stepson if I didn't say that you better watch out. There's a lot of people willing to step in and fight for her if you were to ever hurt her."

His gaze finally rested on me, and there was nothing threatening about his expression—only honesty. He loved Ari clearly, very deeply. It was touching to see the impact she'd had on him, and not that it made any of it make more sense to me in that moment, but it certainly deepened my understanding of how she moved around in the world. Or maybe it deepened my lack of understanding of her.

Either way, I was pretty sure that I was going down a

perilous path that I wouldn't be able to come back from. And I wasn't sure I wanted to.

"Shit, did you see that?" Lukas's attention was diverted now, and he was pointing somewhere behind me. I turned to see the flat-screen television over the bar on the news.

Breaking News Alert: Leader of GOP bill to block abortion rights, Senator Murphy's secret dealings with pregnant campaign staffer have been leaked.

My phone was already buzzing in my pocket, and my stomach sank into my feet. Holy shit, the article was out.

I was definitely going to be fired.

Chapter Eleven

"Mr. Abbot?" I answered the phone immediately and put one finger to my lips to tell Lukas to be quiet as I made a dash for the exit.

"Torres, there is not enough Kaopectate in the world to handle the diarrhea we're about to be swimming in."

My upper lip curled in disgust at that image as I found a spot to stand on the sidewalk under a streetlight that was relatively deserted. "Uh, what's going on?"

My boss scoffed audibly. "Have you turned on the news recently, Torres? We're absolutely fucked."

I had two choices now—pretend to be bad at my job, which is to stay on top of things like this, or pretend I knew about it and potentially raise questions from him on how I knew about it so quickly. Either way, yes, absolutely fucked.

"The Murphy abortion hit Politico twenty minutes ago," my boss continued, thankfully taking the choice away from me. "The wife's attorney is already subpoenaing the records and filing a motion to revisit the split of assets."

"That is...pretty damning," I replied, actually being honest this time.

"Damning for who? Senator Murphy, of course. But also, our firm, Torres." I could hear the rattle of a bottle of pills in the background and then the sound of him swallowing some sort of liquid. "The only people who had those records were our team."

"And the campaign staffer who was pregnant," I quickly added. *Deny, deny, deny.* "And the clinic where she had the procedure. Maybe her friends and family. Possibly people on his staff as well. Has he let anyone go recently?"

At what point in my law career had lying become so easy? The words rolled off my tongue like nothing, and, honestly, I sounded so damn believable, I was almost fooling myself.

"That's a good point," Abbot replied pensively, and I could practically see him already planning the crisis management strategy. "Hmm, reach out to his team and get me a list of recent terminations—voluntary or involuntary."

I glanced behind me at my table of friends on the patio. Yasmeen was waving for me to come back, and I held up one finger to her to wait. "Sure thing. I'll do that first thing in the morning."

"Now, Torres."

I should have seen that one coming.

He continued, "If there are no leads on that list, we have to consider that the leak came from within our firm. We might have a mole."

My tongue clogged the back of my throat as I tried to respond to that with anything halfway decent.

"Have one of the paralegals send it over as soon as it's ready," Abbot finished. "I'll be waiting for it."

"Yes, sir." I hung up the phone quickly, just in case he might have considered extending the conversation further.

A deep breath escaped me, and despite how warm the night was outside, I shivered.

Instead of going back to my table, I picked my phone back up and shot off a quick internal message to our team of paralegals about the information needed and the deadline with an offer of overtime pay.

Hey, shit rolls downhill, but at least we'll pay them time and a half.

Just as I hit send, a text message notification popped up at the top of my screen. Ari's name was in bold above it.

Are you doing okay?

Damn my susceptible heart for feeling anything other than dread in this moment because there were those damn butterflies that had nearly floored me in the garage a few days ago. I knew she had said she didn't want to be involved, but checking in on me...was getting involved.

I opened Ari's text message and crafted a reply. And then I deleted it. One more time. It still didn't sound right. Delete again. Third time is the charm? Delete, delete, delete.

Mila, I can see you typing and stopping.

Ari's second text came through before I'd even sent one response back. *Shit.* This was stupid. I hit her contact information and pressed the call button instead, holding the phone up to my ear as I huddled back under the streetlight and turned away from the inquisitive looks of my friends at the table.

"Hey," she answered on the first ring.

"Sorry," I immediately blurted out. "I wasn't avoiding you or anything. I just wasn't sure how to respond."

She was quiet for a moment, then she sighed. "I'm guessing you've seen the news?"

"Yeah, I just got off the phone with my boss," I confirmed. "I think I might vomit, but I'm not sure if that's a pregnancy side effect or just pure anxiety."

Ari let out a halfhearted chuckle then paused. "Hey, I'm really sorry about the timing. This went to my editor almost a week ago, and I didn't know it was going to go live today. I didn't know you'd find out...you know, everything baby-related today. Totally shit timing."

"I mean, I didn't know either." I reverted to people-pleasing mode. Her discomfort was making me uncomfortable, and I just wanted it all to go away. Too many feelings, blech. "But, uh, listen, we're still...you know, confidential, right?"

"Mila, I'd never reveal a source," she confirmed. "Not to anyone—my editor included."

She sounded very truthful, and honestly, I had no reason not to believe her, but damn all these feelings. My skin felt like it was vibrating so hard it was going to slide right off my bones. Was this what a panic attack for two felt like? Because it felt like my body was reacting in double time.

"Where are you?" Ari asked after I didn't respond. "Do you need someone to come get you?"

I shook my head but then remembered she couldn't see me. "No, I'm out with friends right now. Actually, I'm out with Lukas."

"What?" Ari's voice squeaked slightly, or maybe squawk is a better way to describe it. "What are you doing with Lukas?"

"It was an accident. Just ran into him." Okay, why was I going off on this tangent? "But, yeah, I'm fine. We can meet up though."

"You want to meet up?" She sounded as surprised to hear that as I'd been hearing myself say it. "Like now?"

"Do you live near Barrack's Row?" I asked. "I can grab a Lyft and come to you."

"Not really. I'm in Dupont." She paused for a moment, and then her voice seemed to lower. "Are you sure, Mila? It's after ten."

I pulled the phone away from my face to glance at the time. "Oh, shit. I'm sorry. You don't want company this late."

She cut me off immediately. "I didn't say that."

"Okay." I paused again, this time looking down at my shoes as I rubbed the rubber edge against the concrete.

"I'll text you my address," she finally said. "See you soon."

What the hell am I doing?

"Great." And I hung up the phone.

I was clearly not okay. I was unwell. I was unhinged. I was completely hormonal. I didn't know what to call it, but someone needed to come do a welfare check on me because I was making really bad choices and just piling them up on my plate like it was a never-ending buffet.

My feet somehow carried me back to my table of friends. Lukas had joined them again and was regaling the group with a story about how he'd once been so drunk that he'd peed on a playground at two o'clock in the morning and had almost been placed on the sex offender registry for it.

Seriously—bad choices.

"Hey, guys, I'm going to close out my tab," I said to the table as a whole. "Going to catch a Lyft home."

"I'll go with you," Rachel said and then visibly yawned. "I don't have the stamina these kids do."

"Uh, right, okay, yes." I had not prepared for this scenario, but I wasn't about to say no in front of the entire group and have an interrogation started. "Let me just go close my tab."

I ran back inside as quickly as I could and paid the bartender for my two cherry syrup virgin shots and Lukas's beer.

"You okay, honey?" The bartender shot me an inquisitive look.

One of the reasons I loved this place is that the staff was

überprotective of patrons, and absolutely nothing was going to happen without them stepping in to help.

I grinned, though I felt more like puking. "Yeah, just trying to figure out how to get myself out of a mess I got myself into."

"Story of my life," the bartender replied as they handed me my receipt. "Let me know if you need a cover. Anyone here is happy to help."

"Thanks." God, I appreciated queer people. Walking into a lesbian bar was like walking into someone's living room and they'd already decided you are family and you need a good drink. The fact that there were less than twenty-five of them in the country just made me angrier at the patriarchy.

The moment I was back on the sidewalk, Rachel flagged me down.

"I just called a Lyft. It should be here in two minutes." She was staring down at her phone, zooming the map in on the car's location.

"Um, can we...uh..." I took a deep breath. "Can we add a stop on the way home?"

"Sure." She shrugged and clicked the "add stop" button. "Where do you want to stop? Are you craving something already? They say that happens when you're pregnant."

I recited off Ari's address that she'd texted me. Not that I'd memorized it by heart, but also that, yes, I'd memorized it by heart.

"What's there?" Rachel asked, squinting at her screen. "It just looks like residences."

Thankfully the Lyft was about half a block away from us and so it was easy to divert her attention when I spotted it down the street. "Oh, look! There it is! Come on, let's go."

I grabbed her arm and pulled her along with me, shoving her into the back seat of an old Toyota Corolla as fast as I could.

As soon as I was in, I shut the door behind me and pulled on my seat belt.

"Okay, so I'm going to get out at the first stop," I said casually like it was absolutely not a big deal. *Yes, it is.* "And you can keep going on home, and I'll see you later. Cool?"

Rachel's face went from confused to suspicious in a flash. "What's going on?"

"Nothing." I held both of my hands up as if that made me innocent.

"Then where are you going?" Rachel was absolutely going to keep interrogating me until I gave her *something*.

"It's not a big deal," I promised her. God, lying really was getting way too easy. "It's just a friend I'm going to see."

Rachel furrowed her brow. "You're going for a hookup the night you find out you're pregnant?"

The Lyft driver was clearly trying so hard not to stare at us in the rearview mirror. *Sir, you're failing.*

"Hey, I'm pregnant," I replied, "not dead. I'm allowed to still have fun and friends."

She regarded me for a moment like she wasn't sure what to do about that information. Finally, she shrugged her shoulders and looked forward. "Fine, but text me when you're coming home so I know you're safe. I'll feed Macavity for you."

"Deal." Thank fucking God. "I really appreciate it, and I'll be fine. I promise."

"Pregnancy has made you squirrelier than usual," she replied. "These next nine months are going to be interesting."

Understatement of the fucking century.

Chapter Twelve

"You're here," Ari said as she opened her front door. Her normally bright eyes were heavy, and I immediately felt guilty for keeping her up so late.

What the hell was I even doing here?

"Honestly, I half expected you'd not show," she continued.

I stood in the doorway and fumbled with my cell phone in my hands as if that might make me look busy or like I had any purpose in this moment. "Uh, well, you know...I'm here. I'm a person of my word, you know."

I mean, sometimes.

"I wasn't saying that." Ari was wearing a black, wifebeater-style tank top that left a gap, showing off her midriff above the looser pajama pants that were tied low on her hips. She looked ready for bed but stepped to the side and motioned for me to come in.

I did but only slowly, awkwardly, and with a minor shuffle-slash-trip over the threshold.

"You good?" she asked, her fingers wrapping around my forearm as she steadied me.

I glanced up at her and realized that this was the first time I'd seen her without makeup on. Not that she wore a heavy layer normally, but definitely eyeliner and mascara. Now, however, her face was fresh and clean, and there were little freckles across the bridge of her nose that I'd never seen before. Everything about her usual presence was strong and stoic, but here in front of me now, she seemed softer, more vulnerable. Like I was seeing behind a shield that she normally kept pretty close to the vest.

"Sorry." I straightened and then placed my phone and keys down on the small table by the front door where her wallet and keys were also sitting. There was a round mirror above the table and I tried not to focus on the way my hair was looking a bit unkempt or the smudge of mascara below my eye. Actually, I made quick work of wiping that away and pretending like it had never been there in the first place. "I, uh, it's just been a long day. You know?"

Ari nodded, then walked farther into her apartment as I hesitantly followed her. For what appeared to be a one-bedroom, one-bathroom apartment in the heart of Washington, DC, the layout was spacious. There was a giant—and I mean, *giant*—flat-screen television on one wall and a microsuede sectional on the other that actually looked pretty comfortable beneath the colorful throw blankets and pillows she'd decorated it with. Above the couch on the wall was a large mirror and someone had drawn little red hearts on one side of it with what looked like lipstick.

But it was the plants that captured and held my attention the longest. The wall with the windows bowed out in a semicircle as the bay window overlooked the street below. Instead of a bench or something like that, there was a short bookshelf built into the wall and topped with at least a dozen different potted plants—not like a small collection, but like a draping garden that scaled the windows and walls with ivy leaves and branches and greenery everywhere.

"Welcome to my urban jungle," Ari joked as she motioned toward the plants. "I have a thing for plants."

"No kidding," I commented as I walked over to them and gently fingered a green leaf that she'd obviously tended carefully. I felt a stirring in my chest at the thought of her nurturing each one carefully, knowing that that was a side to her that existed. When I turned around, Ari was seated on the couch with her knees about six inches apart, an elbow propped up on each. "They are beautiful, though. I've never been able to keep anything alive."

Her eyes darted down toward my stomach, and I remembered that I was pregnant.

"I mean, plant-wise. I hope children are different."

She smiled, and the tension in her body eased as she leaned back into the couch. "I would hope so."

I was maybe three or four feet away from her, just standing in the middle of her living room, trying to find anywhere to look but at her. My breath caught in my throat when I did, though, and I let out a slow exhale to try to calm myself.

"I'm not sure what I'm doing here," I finally said, quieter now and trailing off at the end.

"Do you want to come sit?" Ari asked, tilting her head to the side.

"Okay." I walked over to her and placed my knee on the couch next to her leg, straddling my other knee across her lap to the other side of the couch.

She leaned back farther to give me space on her lap and her hands gripped my hips to steady me. "I meant to come sit on the couch, but I'm not hating this."

"Oh, my God," I groaned and slid sideways off her lap in a

desperate attempt to run away. Why had I just assumed she meant her lap? "I should go—"

Ari's fingers dug into my hips, pulling me back onto her lap gently. "Don't."

When my eyes met hers, neither one of us was smiling...or frowning. We were just staring, and there was a darkness in her eyes that felt conflicted. The way her brows were ever so slightly furrowed, I could feel a tension battling it out in her brain. The same inner conflict was playing out in mine.

Slowly, I placed a hand on both of her shoulders and rested my weight on her lap as if testing the waters. Despite the million directions my mind was going in, I felt more than a little comfortable pressed against her. My gaze traveled south to her lips, and her tongue slid across the bottom, wetting it just enough to make my breath catch.

"We shouldn't..." I'm whispering now, and I don't even believe me.

"Definitely not," she agreed, her voice dipping into a low rumble that I could feel in my chest.

"We could..." I added, still whispering.

"We can," she agreed, and now her eyes were focused on my lips.

I parted my mouth just enough to breathe in, but the way her eyes flared at that felt like a fire had been set in my core. The tension in her expression seemed to settle on...something.

"I want to."

The words were barely out of my mouth when Ari's hand slid up my back and to the base of my neck. She guided me closer to her, my face mere centimeters from hers. My lips parted again, anticipating hers, but she paused.

I could feel her breath against my skin, and her mouth was so damn close but not close enough.

"We're crossing a line." She was the one whispering now

and her breath smelled like peppermint, as if she'd just brushed her teeth before I came over. "Tell me to stop, Mila. Tell me we shouldn't do this."

Any words felt lodged in my throat and like they were fighting their way to the surface, but I managed to get them out.

"I want this...I want tonight."

"Just tonight?" She brushed her knuckles across my cheek so gently.

"Just tonight," I confirmed, and that felt like the biggest lie I'd told in a while.

"I'll try," she whispered, and the strain was back in her voice, but I didn't have time to focus on it because then her lips were suddenly on mine.

I tilted my head to the side just enough to allow her more access to all of me and her tongue slid across my lower lip. She kissed my top lip with a softness that I could only describe as adoringly. This was the nurturing side of her—I could feel it in the way she touched me, the way she held me.

My hands slid from her shoulders to either side of her neck until I was cupping her face and pulling her closer to me. Our mouths were completely entangled and yet it didn't feel close enough. I needed more.

I needed her. Tonight. I could convince myself that it was just tonight.

"Mila." My name sounded like a prayer on her lips as she spoke between kisses and her hands moved back down to my hips and then rounded my ass. She pulled me tighter against her, and I couldn't help but rock forward, letting the friction between my jeans and her pajama pants further ignite the inferno happening inside me.

She was exploring my mouth now, cradling my head in her hands as she seemed to focus on me in a way I'd never experienced before. I felt like she was cherishing me with every touch, every brush of her lips, and every caress of her fingertips against my skin. God, is this how it's always supposed to feel? I'd had make-out sessions before, but this was not that.

I didn't know what the hell this was, but I couldn't let go of her.

Ari's hands were in the back pockets of my jeans now, and I never hated denim more than I did in that moment for separating us. I couldn't stop myself from moving against her, rubbing my body in a desperate attempt to find even the slightest relief. She didn't stop me—instead, she pulled me tighter against her and spread her legs wider to allow me more room.

A moan escaped my lips as I rocked against her. Who was I right now? "Ari...please...I need..."

I couldn't actually form the rest of that sentence, but she somehow heard me anyway as her hands left my back pockets and she unbuttoned the front of my jeans and slid down the zipper. She pushed me backward just enough so that I stood up off the couch, allowing her to shimmy the jeans down my legs entirely.

We were still kissing, and everything felt hurried and tangled and hot and immediate, and I needed those fucking jeans off right then.

The moment I stepped out of them, she pulled me back onto her lap and when I rocked my core against her again, the fire felt like I was about to lose control entirely.

I kissed her harder, as if anchoring myself to her mouth would keep me from complete implosion, but when her hand slid inside the front of my underwear—*God, what underwear am I even wearing today? Please let it not be something embarrassing like the cats in astronaut suits pair I wear all the time*—I nearly melted against her.

She moved against me like she'd been there before, and

when she dipped inside me, I lost the ability to breathe. I lost the ability to remember all the reasons why this was probably a bad idea or how she'd turned me down barely a week ago in my mother's garage and nothing had changed between then and now. Nothing except that her fingers were inside me and her lips were on me and I never wanted her to stop.

My face was buried into the side of her neck, clinging to her as she brought me to the edge of the cliff and threw me off without hesitation. I could hear her own labored breathing in my ear, and knowing that she was feeling the same heat as I was only brought me higher. My body bucked against her hand as she orchestrated my climax and hugged me closer until every muscle in my core finished tensing and pulsating.

"God, Mila…" Her voice was throaty and coarse and rumbled against my skin in the same rhythm my orgasm was vibrating through me.

I finally sagged against her in desperate need of air as my body drifted into a soft bliss. I tried to steady my breathing, and she removed her hand and wrapped it around my back, now fully embracing me in the tightest bear hug I never knew I needed until just then.

Completely encased by her, my head on her shoulder, we just stayed like that for several more moments. My breath finally slowed to match the steadiness of hers as I felt her chest rise and fall beneath mine. I couldn't remember the last time I'd even been held like this, but my brain wasn't easily forming thoughts right now as everything felt like delicious mush.

My eyes were closed when a yawn involuntarily escaped me.

"Let's get you in bed." Ari's voice was soothing now, the coarseness of a few minutes ago gone. I missed it, and I wanted it back, but when I glanced at her face, it was set. Whatever emotional opening I'd seen in her had sealed shut and she stood up from the couch, still holding me against her like it was the most natural thing in the world. My legs were wrapped around her center, and I clung to her like I was refusing to let her peel me off.

Thankfully, she wasn't asking me to.

She kicked open her bedroom door with one foot and bumped her shoulder against the light switch on the wall to make the room dark before she brought me over to the side of the bed and laid me down—not as smoothly as the carrying part had been because my back hit the mattress with an unromantic sort of thud. I yawned anyway because I didn't have time to sit in anxious thoughts of how I might have looked splayed across the bed like that or why she'd shut down when things had opened up so deeply.

Ari pulled the blanket up over my waist as she crawled in behind me. My back to her chest, she curled her body around mine and rested her arm across my torso. This didn't feel sealed shut. It felt like a crack in the facade, and I wanted to stay awake to remember this moment, to memorize everything I was feeling, but sleep was pulling me harder than I'd expected.

"I don't want just tonight," I whispered to her as my eyes fluttered to a close. I wasn't even sure why I was admitting that out loud, but I didn't have the brainpower right now to consider the consequences of my words.

She chuckled lightly, and her body tensed just a fraction against mine. "Get some sleep, Mila."

Her arm pulled tighter around me, and the last thing I remembered before sleep got a hold of me was that I'd be really, really happy if I fell asleep like this every night.

But she'd only given me tonight.

Chapter Thirteen

I was alone in Ari's bed when I woke up the next morning, and my first impulse was to run.

Just leave. Get out. Run far away and pretend none of this had ever happened. Instead, I lay on my side, staring out the window that was only partially shaded and replayed every moment from the previous evening in my head. One perspective was that I had come over here, thrown myself at Ari, begged her to make me come, and then fell asleep on top of her.

That didn't make me sound great.

The other perspective was that we actually connected, and she wanted me as badly as I wanted her in that moment despite how she'd previously told me she couldn't...wouldn't. But maybe that's all it was...just a moment. A moment where her guard lowered and she gave in to what she was feeling instead of what she really wanted. And maybe this was the first time in my life that I'd felt absolute peace in a partner's arms, and I didn't want to walk away from that. Maybe I wanted to cling to that even tighter and never let her go.

I wasn't sure I would even get that choice.

I rolled over onto my back and surveyed her bedroom in the morning light. It was minimally decorated with the exception of two things—art and plants. On every wall was at least one colorful painting that somehow depicted a woman's body but in delicate, intricate, and unobtrusive ways. The one to the right of the flat screen in the corner was shades of blue and beige, and just the back of a woman turned away from the viewer, her head tucked into her knees. It felt heavy, sad but deeply beautiful. I wondered why Ari had bought it, and what it meant to her.

There were also, yet again, at least a dozen plants in various spots in the room. Both nightstands had terracotta pots—also, as an aside, one nightstand had a pair of nail clippers on it, which I appreciated—the dresser had a whole terrarium of succulents on the top, and there was a large potted tree in the corner that looked like it might take over the entire room at some point if left unchecked. It somehow matched the artwork, though. As if the plants had been chosen to match the theme of each piece of art. It was all carefully thought of and orchestrated, but in a way that you'd have to pay attention to notice.

That was a theme about Ari I'd begun to see—this secret depth to her that was blatantly on display but hidden all the same. I felt like I'd only just begun to peel back the layers of what she kept close because there was still so much I didn't know. I didn't know her favorite color or what she thought about before she fell asleep at night. I didn't know what made her heart race, her skin prickle with fear, what—or who—made tears form in her eyes, or what she wanted out of her life.

And I was pregnant with her niece or nephew.

I'm pregnant. I rubbed a hand across my lower stomach, wondering if I'd done the right thing. I had wanted this. I had desperately, soul-achingly, wanted this baby. And now, I might have exactly that. I knew it was early and there was no reason to get ahead of myself just yet, but I was already imagining holding a little cherub-cheeked child in my arms.

And Ari wasn't in that image. She had been clear—she didn't want to be.

It was just me and the baby. The way I'd planned it. The way I'd wanted it to be.

I swallowed hard and pushed up to a seated position, glancing toward the nightstand for my cell phone. It wasn't there, and I vaguely remembered leaving it by the front door when I came in last night.

Shuffling off the bed, I realized my jeans were still in the living room. It seemed kind of strange to walk out of her bedroom without pants—like maybe that would be implying something more than this was. We'd agreed...just last night. That didn't mean naked time this morning as well...at least, I didn't think it did. I definitely wouldn't say no though...

The only other option was to check in her dresser for something to wear, but that also felt like it could carry some sort of message.

I stood staring at the dresser for thirty more seconds, then down at my bare legs, before finally deciding to see what she had. I pulled open the bottom drawer first, expecting to find pants down there. Instead, I was staring at her underwear and socks—half of which were TomboyX briefs or Bombas socks.

What kind of psychopath puts their underwear and socks in the bottom drawer?

I opened the drawer above that one and it was full of plain white tank tops. The one above that graphic T-shirts, and the one above that... hoodies. Just a lot of hoodies. The top drawer was her jeans and way too many basketball shorts. The woman had organized her entire dresser backward. *Well, clearly, it was a good thing she didn't want to be with me because I can't raise a child around someone this unhinged.*

I couldn't help but chuckle.

I grabbed one of those pairs of shorts and shuffled my legs into them as quickly as I could. They were a bit bigger on me, so I tied them tighter with the drawstring and then headed for the door to the living room.

The main room was also empty when I stepped into it, and I made a beeline for my jeans that lay in a crumpled-up ball on the floor by the couch. As I straightened and shook them out, the front door of the apartment opened behind me.

"You're awake," Ari said as she walked in.

I turned to look at her. "Oh, hi. Hello. Uh, good morning, I mean."

"I didn't know what you normally like to eat for breakfast, so I tried to pick a variety." She was placing a brown paper bag on the kitchen counter and pulling out various items. "We've got chocolate chip bagels and cream cheese. Cereal and milk—I assume you like Golden Grahams because who doesn't? A six-pack of glazed donuts. And some bread and eggs if you want me to make you some French toast—I'm an expert French toast maker." Ari looked around for a moment like she'd lost something, then picked up a paper coffee cup she'd set down behind the bag. "Oh, and coffee, of course."

I was trying not to smile as I walked over to the counter, but this was...something. "Do you normally eat a pound of sugar for breakfast, or is this just a special occasion?"

Ari looked at me like she had no idea what I was talking about. "What do you mean? Look, this cereal has great fiber. And eggs are protein."

"Okay, between this and your upside-down clothes drawers, I'm beginning to worry about the genetics I've bestowed upon my future child," I said, but then took a donut from the sleeve for a quick bite.

"Can't a girl have a sweet tooth?" Ari grinned as she

watched me eat, and I couldn't help but notice the way her gaze paused on my mouth as my tongue licked the sugar off my top lip.

"I'm generally an 'eggs and toast,' or maybe 'overnight oats' person for breakfast. Sometimes I even just eat an avocado with lemon juice or some everything bagel seasoning." I polished off the donut like an expert and sucked the sticky sugar off of my fingertips.

"That sounds boring," Ari replied, grabbing a donut for herself.

I shrugged. "Some of us aren't blessed with your clearly high-powered metabolism."

She grinned and smacked a hand against her flat stomach. "You didn't get to see it last night, but I'm *this* close to a six-pack. Few more weeks, and I might get there."

I tried not to let my gaze follow her motions or notice the fact that she was wearing almost identical shorts to the ones I'd stolen out of her drawer. I definitely wasn't paying attention to the way the fitted T-shirt she was wearing hugged her body. And no part of me was watching how her hair fell against her shoulder when she looked at me, the green streaks more prominent from this angle.

"Oh..." That was literally all I could manage to say.

Ari reached out a hand to me and wrapped it around my wrist, gently tugging me toward her. Her voice was quieter, questioning as her other hand grazed my jawline. "I had fun last night."

The coarseness was back in her voice, and I shivered under her touch, leaning forward just enough to ask her to kiss me.

But then there was a knock on the door, and I sprang back from her like I'd just been caught red-handed committing a crime.

Ari blinked, clearly surprised by my sudden movement

away, then glanced toward the door. "Uh, I'm not expecting anyone."

"I'll go in the bedroom," I said even quieter than a whisper, almost just mouthing the words as I pointed toward her room and scurried over to hide inside.

Christ, I was hiding in her apartment now.

Better believe my ear was plastered to the other side of her bedroom door, though, as I tried to listen to who was there.

"Arielle Elliot?" the voice was low and threatening, like how you'd expect a drill sergeant to sound. "Secret Service. We need to ask you a few questions."

Fuck.

That's it. I was going to jail. I was going to give birth in a prison infirmary and never see my baby. My stomach felt like it had joined my heart in my chest and was beating frantically against my rib cage so loudly that I had to strain even harder to hear over the sound of rushing blood in my ears.

Ari responded to them, saying...something. I couldn't make out her response.

The deep voice was back. "That is your right."

What was her right? Why were they telling her her rights?

I suddenly remembered my phone and keys were on the table next to the front door and probably within eyeshot of the agent. What was the minimum sentence for leaking confidential documents? Or was that considered treason? I didn't think it rose to that level, but I was pretty sure I was about to be behind bars anyway.

Ari was speaking again, and then I heard the front door shut. Oh, God, they were in the apartment. They were coming to get me.

I backed away from the bedroom door and glanced around for a better place to hide. Closet seemed obvious. Everyone would look there. So, under the bed it was. I scurried under there so fucking fast I almost lost the shorts I was wearing, and my nose immediately began to seize up at the amount of dust that Ari clearly never vacuumed under here.

The bedroom door opened, and I held my breath. The scene from *Taken* was playing out in my mind, and I wished Liam Neeson was real because I could really use him right about now.

"Mila?" Ari's voice broke the silence, and it didn't seem to be followed by anything—or anyone—else. "Where did you go?"

The jig was up. I stuck one hand out from under the bed and tentatively waved. "Is it safe?"

She laughed. "Why are you under the bed? Of course it's safe."

I scooted far enough to get my head and shoulders out and look at her. "I heard them say Secret Service."

"Yeah, I have to go in and talk with them. They're giving me time to call the paper's lawyer first to meet me at their offices." Ari crossed her arms over her chest and looked down at me. "We're already prepared for this. We knew publishing that article would bring heat."

I pushed myself the rest of the way out from under the bed and brushed the dust bunnies off my clothes, trying to smooth my hair. I couldn't meet her eyes and my entire body felt on high alert. "Right. Right, that makes sense. I...I need to find my phone."

I headed for the table by the front door, with Ari following behind at a slower pace, carefully looking around the corner first before walking out into the main area. I lifted my iPhone, clicking on the screen only to see dozens of missed notifications —text messages, breaking news alerts from CNN, and at least a hundred new emails.

Shit.

"Is everything okay? You seem really spooked." Ari's hand touched my arm and I pulled away automatically.

"Yeah, yeah, it's fine. It's just...you know, I said we shouldn't be seen together. The Secret Service can definitely not see us together." I was rambling, but I didn't miss the hurt in her eyes at my words, and yet, I couldn't stop them. "I just need to catch up on whatever I missed and head to work as quickly as possible."

She put her hands up and walked into the kitchen, leaving me alone.

I checked my texts first, quickly responding to Rachel's worried message with an apology for not having texted her that I was safe last night and thanking her for feeding Macavity for me. She replied back almost immediately with an angry face emoji followed by an eye-rolling face emoji, then just said, *Hope you had fun with Ari.*

Busted. I glanced at Ari in my peripheral vision as she poured herself a bowl of cereal. Fun was certainly an accurate description, and somehow not enough.

The emails were next—several from my boss, a few from the paralegals who'd probably worked through the night, and then a super stark, short email from Senator Murphy's Chief of Staff that simply read *Call me.*

Ominous.

Lastly, I checked Politico and CNN, and thankfully, it seemed like no further news had gotten out past what I'd already seen last night. So far. I'd given the public enough to taste that someone was going to dig up the rest—it was only a matter of time.

Ari was scooping a spoonful of cereal into her mouth when I turned around to face her. I cleared my throat. "Um, I am going to go."

She placed the cereal bowl down on the counter. "You don't have to rush out."

That wasn't what the anxiety demon in my chest was screaming at me right now—*run, run, run!* I headed for her bedroom and closed myself in there long enough to change from her shorts back into my jeans, then returned to the living room.

"Is there a back way out of this building?" I asked her as I scooped up the rest of my belongings.

A flash of hurt crossed Ari's expression again, but she wiped it away just as quickly as she had before. She nodded and cleared her throat. "Yeah, if you go down the stairs at the end of the hallway, there's an exit into the alleyway. You can skip the lobby entirely."

"Great," I said, one hand on the front door. I paused before turning the knob and looked back over my shoulder at Ari. "I... uh, I had a great time."

Her lips lifted into a smile that didn't reach her eyes. "Me, too."

"Good. Okay. That was good. This is good." I sounded like I was trying to convince the both of us. My mouth was dry. "Well, okay then. Bye."

I opened the front door and glanced down both directions of the hallway to assure it was empty—it was—and then stepped out, closing the door quickly behind me. I didn't move away from the door yet, though. Instead, I just stood there wishing I could turn around and walk right back in.

Which I probably could. But I wasn't going to. I couldn't. I *shouldn't*.

I could hear my therapist's voice in the back of my head asking me what I was afraid of. My entire career crashing and burning. That whole potential jail thing. Making things complicated with my future baby daddy. Messing up my child's future family. Getting my heart broken.

That last one resonated hard.

I heard the door open behind me, but I didn't turn around right away. Ari's hand intertwined with mine and she tugged me to face her. When I did, I kept my eyes down at my feet because I was pretty sure if she looked at me, she'd see tears were already beginning to form. I wasn't about to be that girl who cries after a one-night stand. I cannot be *that* lesbian.

Ari's knuckles gently pressed under my chin, encouraging me to look at her anyway. She leaned in and pressed her lips to mine with a softness I didn't feel like I deserved.

"Mila, everything is going to be okay. You did the right thing. We're going to figure this out, and...you're welcome back anytime." Her voice was even softer than her touch, and I leaned in to kiss her again—harder this time.

When I finally pulled away, her lips were darker and slightly swollen from the franticness of the last few moments. I *had* to go. If I stayed, I wasn't sure I'd leave and that was not an option if I wanted to keep my life remotely intact.

I loosened my grip on her hand and stepped backward. "I have to go."

She didn't say anything, her eyes still trained on mine. But I couldn't stay there, and so I turned on my heels and headed down the hall toward the sign marked "stairs" at the end. I didn't hear Ari's door close behind me and I imagined she was still standing there watching me walk away, but I didn't look back once. I took the stairs two at a time while requesting a Lyft to come pick me up, and then burst into the alleyway like an escaped convict on the lam.

The Lyft arrived seconds after I got to the sidewalk on the opposite end of the alley, a different street than her building was on, and I slid in so quickly that I didn't even do my normal safety check of the license plate number.

"Mila?" the driver asked, looking in the rearview mirror at me.

"Yes, that's me." I sank down as low in the seat as I could, hoping not to be spotted by anyone with a badge.

My cell phone buzzed in my hand and a text message from Abbot popped on the screen.

The moment you get to the office today, come straight to my office. The Secret Service wants to talk to you.

I rested my head against the back of the seat and groaned. I was utterly and completely fucked. I was literally running away from the Secret Service just to run back into them. Yep, this was how I would end up in jail. All the reasons for why I'd gone down this path suddenly seemed hard to grasp, and I had to mentally pause and remind myself—I gave Ari that information because Senator Murphy was awful, and his constituents deserved to know the type of man they were supporting. The women who he was trying to take away access to birth control and reproductive rights all deserved to know what a vile and disgusting hypocrite he was. That was worth whatever might happen—the cause was important enough to make this worth it.

At least, I badly, badly wanted to believe that. I just wasn't sure if I'd made that decision to appease my own conscience when, in reality, I should have been thinking about my future child instead. That they mattered more than the principal— that's what parents were supposed to feel, right?

I'm doing this all wrong.

Chapter Fourteen

The Secret Service had gone through literally every file in our office—drawers and hard drives—by the time lunch rolled around. I was seated at my desk, pretending to be busy with work but really watching them out of the corner of my eye. Any minute, someone was going to walk up to me and slap cuffs on me and haul me off to jail.

I mean, not really. My initial reaction had been all panic and no legal thought because this certainly wasn't considered treason. It wasn't even like I'd broken a criminal law. Civil, sure. Ethical, definitely. The contract with my employer? Also, check. Okay, maybe that did involve some laws.

My desk phone rang, and I grabbed it quickly. "Hello?"

"Hi, this is Dr. Allen's office returning your phone call. You left a message saying you wanted to schedule an appointment?"

The knot in my throat loosened, and I let out an exhale. "Yes, uh, please, can I schedule a first...pregnancy appointment?"

Suddenly I realized I had no idea what it was supposed to

be called or what I was asking for, or if I'd even be able to make the appointment and not be behind bars.

"A what?" the receptionist asked.

"I mean, like a blood test? Or baby check?" I was stammering now. "To check if there is a baby in there."

The receptionist on the other end chuckled. "Did you get a positive pregnancy stick, ma'am?"

"Yes, I peed on it." That seemed like more information than she'd asked, but it was out there now. "Uh, yes. I think I'm pregnant."

"Your first, I'm guessing?" she asked. "When was the first day of your last period?"

I picked up my cell phone and glanced through my tracking app for all things shark week related and read her off the date.

"So, generally, we don't have moms come in until the eighth week. Before then, it's just too early to hear or see much," she explained to me, but I was having a hard time following her after the word *mom*. "So, let's get you booked for that week and just make sure to come in with a full bladder for a urine test. We'll do some blood work, and the doctor will do your first transvaginal ultrasound."

The only experience I had with transvaginal ultrasounds was the Canadian Netflix show Isa had forced me to watch, where one of the women had orgasmed during her transvaginal ultrasound and honestly, I wasn't sure I'd ever be able to think of anything else.

Definitely not something I wanted to happen in front of Dr. Allen.

"Okay," I squeaked out, not fully registering the date and times she began listing off until I finally opened my calendar and verified when I could come in. Assuming I was still a free woman. Finally, having settled on a date, I said goodbye.

The moment I hung up the phone, my cell phone rang, and Isa's name appeared on the screen.

"Hey," I said, lifting it to my ear. "Are you okay?"

"Am *I* okay? You're the one who is pregnant!" Isa's voice was like a boom box through the speaker. "Are you feeling anything yet? Sore boobs? Pukey tummy? Hair on your nipples?"

"What?" My face twisted in confusion. "Why would there be hair?"

"I don't know," Isa replied nonchalantly. "My aunt said that happened when she was pregnant. And her areolas got, like, super dark. She said they never went back to their original color even after the baby."

It was clearly a mistake to be the first one of my friend group to get pregnant because everything these women didn't know was terrifying me for what might actually be coming.

"I'm fine right now—not hairy," I clarified. "Work is just really stressful at the moment."

"Okay, I won't bother you," Isa responded. "But I wanted to ask if you could ask your mom to squeeze me in for a pedicure at the salon. My feet are busted looking."

"Sure, I'll text her now." There was zero chance my mother would say no. Out of all my friends, I think Isa was her favorite. Not that I'd tell Yasmeen or Rachel that because they all had their own feelings about Isa already.

"Come with me?" she asked. "Wait, can pregnant women get pedicures? Is it, like, toxic to the baby or something?"

"I can get a pedicure," I replied, although I jotted a note to myself on the Post-it notes in front of me to double-check WebMD. "It would be nice, actually. I really need to relax."

Another understatement. I was wound tighter than a tangled kitchen phone cord from the late nineties.

"Cool. Text me the appointment time, and I'll see you

there." Isa hung up before I could say anything else, and I quickly pulled up Google to see if I was allowed to go to a nail salon.

Seriously, why is half the world off-limits to pregnant people? It's a bit ridiculous. WebMD wasn't particularly helpful, just saying that I should ask my doctor but that it's generally considered safe. *Generally.* What the hell does that even mean? When is it not generally safe? Fuck it. I was barely pregnant. It couldn't do any harm this early—at least not any more harm than spending my pregnancy in jail might be.

At least, that's what I was going to tell myself.

I texted my mother with the request, and she responded in less than twenty seconds with a time later that afternoon, which I quickly forwarded to Isa. She confirmed that she would be there, and I put my phone back down on my desk. At least I had something to look forward to today—something to keep my mind off everything happening at my office.

My cell phone rang again, though, and this time it was not a number I had saved to my contacts. Normally, I'd let it go to voice mail because it was probably spam, but I was fine with any possible distraction today, and it couldn't be the Secret Service since they were already right here.

"Hello?" I answered on the second ring.

"Is this Tori Miles?"

I'd never gotten a spam call to my stage name before. "Speaking."

"Hi, Tori, this is Mitchell Davros. We met briefly at your show at the Arlington Drafthouse a few weeks ago, and I wanted to follow up on the email I sent you with our contract."

I gripped the phone tighter. "Mr. Davros, of course."

"Fantastic," he continued. "Listen, I'm not going to beat around the bush. The Comedic Talent Agency wants to represent you. We're currently working on a package for a Netflix comedy special for underrated voices, and I think you'd be perfect in the ensemble."

Abso-fucking-lutely I would be. Could I do comedy behind bars? I mean, with Zoom, why not? Anything was possible.

"Interesting," I replied with as much nonchalance as I could gather. Apparently, lying didn't just extend to my lawyer side. "I'd be open to hearing more about the package, but the current contract you sent had a few things in it I didn't love. I'll email it back to you with notes. Then, can you send me back a revised contract to review?"

"I can do that." He recited my email address for confirmation, and I told him that it was correct. "I'll look it over this afternoon. I'd also love to set up a time when I can take you out to lunch with the team and get you familiar with how we work. We're looking forward to working with you."

"Okay, I'll look at my calendar. I'm sure I could fit that in in the next few weeks if the contract seems of interest." Maybe I should actually have been an actor instead because my cool-as-a-cucumber performance right now was Oscar-worthy. "Thanks for the information, and I look forward to talking further."

"Have a great afternoon, Tori." He hung up the phone and I calmly placed my cell phone down on the desk.

Then I just stared at it.

For at least five whole minutes.

Because I was so freaking excited—and terrified—that I only wanted to call one person and tell her. But that wasn't really an option at this point.

"Torres." My boss stuck his head through my office door, pulling me from my do-I-or-don't-I thoughts. "Come to my office. Senator Murphy is on his way up."

"He's *here* here?" I squeaked, standing up so quickly that

my office chair toppled over behind me. I quickly grabbed it to put it back upright.

Abbot frowned at me. "Get it together, Torres. We need to be emulating confidence right now, given this entire shitstorm that might be about to rain down on us. Look around. We're under investigation."

Key word: we. The firm was under investigation—not me specifically. Despite my twice-in-a-day run-in with the Secret Service, it did appear that I was still off their radar. And thank hallelujah for that.

Though my nerves felt no less tense at that knowledge.

"Yes, sir," I responded with everything short of a military salute before following him out of my office and down the hall to his.

Being the managing partner, he had the corner office that was really more like a living room, conference room, office, and bar all in one. With two walls of windows overlooking the Potomac River, there was more than enough space to host the senator and his entire staff if he wanted to.

I surveyed the seating options and opted for an armchair next to the couch so that I wouldn't have to bump elbows with anyone. Abbot's secretary brought me an in-house tablet that we used for confidential files only, and I began searching through the senator's paperwork to see how far the paralegals had gotten with the most recent draft of the divorce filings.

Secret Service entered the office first, stationing two officers in far corners of the room and drawing the blinds on all of the windows. A few minutes later, Senator Murphy walked in with a frazzled-looking staffer next to him.

"Abbot, let's talk." The man was every bit as gruff in person as he was on the news, and though this was my third time meeting him face to face, I didn't feel any more comfortable. In

137

fact, I felt a churning in my gut the moment I saw him, and I had to exhale slowly to allow the wave of nausea to pass.

Murphy went straight to the couch next to me and sat smack-dab in the middle of it, his knees spread wide in the worst manspreading incident I'd ever witnessed. So much so that the staffer literally didn't have enough room to sit next to him on the three-person couch. So, he just stood next to the couch, nervously fiddling with one of his three cell phones.

Abbot took the other armchair on the opposite side of the couch from me, leaning forward with his elbows on his knees. "Senator Murphy, my team has been working all night on this news leak. We've compiled a list of potential suspects who might have benefited from this situation."

"I don't give a shit about that." Murphy waved his hand in the air noncommittally, and his suit jacket fell open, revealing one side of his shirt wasn't actually fully tucked into his pants. That did not bode well for wherever he'd been right before this. "Everyone hates me, so that list would probably take a decade to get through. What I care about is that bitch now knowing about it and wanting to renegotiate assets. I'm not giving her a dime more than I already agreed to."

My nausea was returning with every word that came out of his vile, thin-lipped mouth. Was this morning sickness or unadulterated feminist rage? I couldn't tell the difference in that moment.

"That's definitely an area we can discuss," Abbot agreed but then pursed his lips. "We have another issue, however. The press has found out the name of the staffer who had the procedure and she's decided to launch a civil suit against you."

"A civil suit?" Murphy's face twisted into a snarl. "What the hell for? I paid for everything she needed to get rid of the kid. Even got her another job on the hill for a member. That's above and beyond already. I was a goddamn gentleman."

Do not say anything, Mila. Do not tell him that a gentleman wouldn't have had an affair with a staffer, to begin with, and then insist she get an abortion despite the fact that reports indicate she had wanted to keep the baby. Definitely do not say any of that out loud.

"Your actions were beyond admirable," Abbot chimed in, and that statement alone almost made me blow chunks.

My stomach was no longer just a little nauseous—I was on a goddamn boat rocking back and forth and if I so much as breathed wrong, the donuts I'd had for breakfast would be reappearing very soon.

"Still, however, we do have to address the suit," Abbot continued. "She's claiming violation of privacy, coercion of a medical procedure, and sexual harassment. Her lawyer put a two-million-dollar settlement figure on it and states that they won't negotiate lower because if we don't settle, she's going to take the book deal offered to her by Simon & Schuster."

Murphy stood up from the couch and began pacing back and forth in front of it. "Are you married, Abbot?"

"I am," my boss replied.

Murphy frowned. "You have kids?"

"Two," Abbot replied. "They're both in college and beyond at this point, though."

"What about you?" Murphy turned to look at me—actually acknowledging me for the first time today. "You look like you're still in your fertile years or close to it. You a mother yet, sweetheart?"

Do not call me sweetheart, Tiny Dick Man. "I am not."

I'm allowed this lie. No qualms attached. There was zero chance I was telling this man anything about my uterus.

The senator nodded slowly then turned to his staffer. "Get me a water. Sparkling."

The staffer scurried away with ease thanks to his lack of

backbone, and I heard him mumble something under his breath about having gone to Stanford for this. I made a mental note to try to get his number for Isa.

"It's all so twisted if you really think about it," Murphy continued, still pacing. "She decides to get pregnant, and suddenly I'm to blame. She could have said no. She could have asked for a rubber. She could have stopped it from implanting. That bitch wanted this—she knew she could milk me for my seed and then for my wallet after."

And it was in that moment that the donuts from earlier decided to reappear.

With a suddenness I had not expected, my entire torso lurched forward, almost carrying me off the armchair I was sitting in, and I emptied the contents of my stomach onto the office floor...and Senator Murphy.

"What the fuck!" Senator Murphy jumped back away from me, but not fast enough. His shoes and pants were splattered with stomach bile and pieces of glazed bread—oh, and there was the prenatal vitamin I'd taken earlier, too.

Immediately, strong hands were on both of my upper arms and yanked me back away from the senator. The Secret Service officers had jumped in and pulled me away, and I realized that they actually saw *me* as a threat. In that room, I was the threat in that moment—not his toxic masculinity.

"Get her out of here," the senator shouted.

Secret Service was dragging me backward, and it was hard to keep my feet underneath me to steady myself.

"Senator Murphy, I am so sorry," Abbot was saying as I was dragged out into the hallway.

"Ma'am, do you need a bathroom?" One of the officers asked me as they let go of me in the hallway.

"Uh, yes." I put a hand to my mouth, feeling warm guck stuck to my chin. "I need to clean up. I'm sorry about that."

"Officer Sanchez will escort you to the bathroom, then pack your bag and head home." The male officer motioned to the female officer, who had been standing in the hallway this entire time. "We're going to ask that you not return to the office today, but do not leave the district anytime soon."

I put my hands up defensively. "Fine. Whatever."

Officer Sanchez pointed me toward the bathroom, and I plodded along beside her. I went straight to the sink and began rinsing out my mouth and washing my face. There was some vomit on my shirt as well, but I didn't have an extra one, so I just tried to rub it off with a wet paper towel as best as I could.

After I was as presentable as I could be, we walked back to my office, and I collected my things before the agent escorted me out to the parking garage.

"Hey, don't sweat today," the agent said as she stopped at the entrance. She was smiling apologetically and didn't seem like a total dick. "You wouldn't be the first person that man has made sick. Doubt you'll be the last either."

I grinned at her. "Glad to be part of that club."

Although, I was fully aware that I might very well be part of the unemployed felons club after today as well.

Chapter Fifteen

"I mean, I wouldn't have even believed it if I hadn't been there myself," I said as I strutted across the stage of the Comedy Loft. "The cicada was literally just sitting on the senator's lapel, doing whatever the hell it is cicadas do, and he's completely unaware the giant bug is there. C-SPAN, meanwhile, has captioned the entire thing as the *Cicada Calamity* since we're in the middle of a public session. It took another hour before someone finally passed him a note to tell him what was going on."

The audience was laughing, and my mother was sitting hand in hand with Steve in the front row, smiling up at me.

"At that moment, I was expecting panic. I was expecting him to jump up and knock the cicada off or shake off his jacket or something hilarious. I was primed and ready for the pure entertainment of the moment." I imitated the motions, shaking my arms and legs like I was trying to get a bug off. The crowd laughed harder. "But that didn't happen. In fact, I have never in my life seen someone so calmly pick up a cicada with two fingers and gently place it down on the desk in front of him, and then..."

I paused for dramatic effect and the audience leaned in.

"He picked up his coffee mug and wham! Slammed it down onto the bug, making the worst crunching noise I've ever heard on C-SPAN, and I once heard Dick Cheney eating pork rinds on there. The lobbyist with the EPA just fainted right then and there."

The audience gasped then there were mixed reactions of uncomfortable laughter, disgust, and genuine amusement. If there was one thing you could trust about DC, it was that they liked their comedy on the darker side.

"Anyway, that basically sums up what it's like to work on the Hill. You folks have been great tonight," I continued into the microphone. "You can find me online and my future shows at @torimilescomedy. I'm thrilled to announce your headliner is coming up next! Please welcome...Randy Feltface!"

I clapped as I walked off the stage, trading places with the puppet and his owner. The moment I was off, I let out a deep breath and sat down in the closest chair. My first live comedy performance in front of my mother meant that I'd been limited to basically just talking about work since my golden material was either her...or the sperm app. Neither of which I could talk about on stage with my mother and her minister boyfriend in the front row.

Isa walked through the entrance to the backstage area with my mother and Reverend Steve right behind her. "Some fans wanted to say hi," she joked, gesturing toward my mother.

I squeezed Isa's hand, appreciating her escorting them here and sitting through the entire thing. "Thanks for coming, guys. I'm sorry it wasn't better."

"*Ay, no.* Don't let me ever hear you say things like that about yourself," my mother immediately countered, her arms open wide as she gathered me in for a giant hug. "You were incredible. Dark. A little scary. But the crowd loved it. You're going to be a star."

"Thanks, Mom." I glanced at Steve. "How'd you enjoy it, Steve?"

He looked thoroughly uncomfortable and like he did not want to answer that question. "Well, I did not know that puppets could be comedians, so I'm experiencing many new things today."

Steve might have a future in politics with the way he dodged that one.

My mom pulled at my hands, looking down at my fingernails and clucking her tongue. "You need to come back to the salon. You've got chips already."

"I just got them done a week ago," I reminded her, pulling my hands back.

She waved me off like it made no difference. "That was last week. This is this week. Come and let me fix your nails before your next show."

"Why don't you two grab a drink at the bar and we'll come join you in a second?" Isa cut in, motioning my mother and Steve back toward the door. "Mila just needs to get freshened up. We'll be right there."

"Okay, but will they give me free drinks since I made you?" My mother narrowed her eyes. "It feels fair, right?"

"Mom..." I warned, and she shrugged as if that was a normal question.

"Fine, fine. But employee discount?" She tried one more time. "I'll get you your favorite—margarita on the rocks, no salt."

"Oh, and get me a gin and tonic," Isa added, this time physically pushing them both toward the door. "Thank you!"

They finally left and Isa and I were alone. She grimaced at me. "How are you going to get out of drinking that margarita?"

I heaved a sigh. "You're going to have to drink both."

"Well, only because I'm a good friend," Isa agreed, a teasing lilt to her voice. "For you, I will."

I grinned and shook my head. "God, I really could use a drink right now."

She sat down next to me. "How are things at work?"

I'd already caught her up on everything that I could tell her about the investigation happening at my office or why I'd been suddenly asked to stay home for days on end. "I think I'm going to get fired."

"Really?" Isa's brow furrowed hard. "For puking? I mean, who wouldn't have tossed their biscuits in that situation?"

"I...well, there's more than that." I didn't say anything further, and she didn't ask. I released a long exhale and shook my head. "The timing of all of this—of the baby, the job—it's not ideal."

"Well, listen, you know I've got you." Isa put her hand on mine. "If you need money, I can help. If you need health insurance, I'll marry you. That baby is my little niece or nephew, and I am not going anywhere, okay? We've got this."

A lump formed in my throat, and I squeezed her hand back. "Thanks, Isa."

"You know, my neighbor works at a law firm over on Connecticut—Bushel & Hope. If you want, I can send her your LinkedIn," Isa added. "I mean, not to pressure you or anything, but you've always been too good for Abbot. Maybe this is your sign that it's time to find a new path."

I nodded, letting out a slow breath. She was probably right, except for the small possibility that if my real involvement in all of this came to light, I might not be able to work in law ever again. Let alone walk the streets free.

Sarah Robinson

"You're right. I need to find a new job." That was certainly becoming more and more obvious to me. "Literally, nothing about me matches their values anymore. Maybe they never did...but it's hard to ignore how much they helped me get through law school, paying for everything. I could have been on a partner track in a few years if I had kept my head down."

"I think it's safe to say that once you vomit on a member of Congress, you aren't keeping your head down," Isa pointed out.

I chuckled. "Okay, maybe float her my LinkedIn and if she's interested, I'm happy to talk."

"Cool." Isa nodded. "Come on, let's go appease your mom and I'll pound all your drinks."

"The hardship," I teased her as we both stood and headed toward the bar.

When we got there, my mother had already lined up drinks for all of us, and Reverend Steve was drinking a Jäger bomb—we don't use the term Irish car bomb anymore, look it up. Honestly, I was just impressed that he was drinking and seemed so at ease sitting at a bar.

"Here, baby. Drink up." My mother handed me my margarita and I took it, holding it in my hand instead of immediately taking a drink.

She didn't seem to notice yet and was already half a Corona in. "You were great, sweetheart," she continued. "Steve, wasn't she great?"

"Very funny," he agreed, seeming more at ease with a little liquor in him than when I'd last seen him at Sunday dinner. "I wish we'd stayed longer to watch the puppet guy. His opening was pretty great."

"We're not here for a puppet, Steve." My mom smacked his chest lightly—or not so lightly. "Don't listen to him, sweetheart."

I surreptitiously put my drink down on the bar, and Isa

waited a minute before sneakily grabbing it and taking a few sips behind my back.

"So, Mom, I was thinking...how would you feel if I were to consider starting a family?" I changed the conversation so suddenly, even I was surprised. I heard Isa cough as she swallowed hard behind me.

My mother blinked quickly. "What?"

Steve took a long gulp of his drink and looked away, back to being uncomfortable. He was going to have to start getting used to that if he was going to become a permanent fixture in this family.

"I'm thirty-four years old," I reminded her. "If I want to have kids, then now is the time to get serious about it. And I don't need a man to do that."

"Unless procreation has changed since I had you, you need a man." My mother frowned. "Or at least a piece of him."

I grimaced. "Okay, obviously. But, like, I can just buy that."

Or download it off an app. But I didn't say that part out loud.

"Wait...are you being serious right now?" My mother put her drink down on the bar and hadn't even noticed that Isa slid my glass back to me—now empty. "You're thinking about having a baby?"

"This seems like a private conversation," Steve finally said. "Maybe I should give you guys a few minutes."

Chicky pushed him back down into his bar seat without even looking at him.

"I mean, I'm considering it." *More than considering it*, but I also kept that part in my head.

She was silent for a moment, and I could see her brain working overtime. "Well, I'm happy you at least told me about this before doing anything, not like this comedy situation. It feels really good to know you want my feedback still. And my feedback is absolutely not."

"What?" I hadn't expected that answer. "Absolutely not?"

My mother shook her head. "Babies need a family, *mija*. You should know that better than anyone."

I didn't respond because, honestly, that really fucking hurt. It felt like she'd just dismissed my entire life—who I was and where I'd come from. And I was already pregnant. Not that she knew that, but...I could be this child's family.

"Well, she has me," Isa stepped in, draping an arm around my shoulders. "We're family. And you'd be an amazing grandma. That's family."

Isa was a master at defusing my mother, and complimenting her was usually the simplest route.

Chicky smiled. "Well, of course. That is obvious. But...is it enough? It's not the same thing as two parents. I always wanted you to have that."

I swallowed the lump in my throat and tried to remind myself that this wasn't about me. This was about Chicky and her own fears of what she felt like she hadn't been able to give me.

"Mom," I said, this time taking her hand in mine. "I never needed more than just you. You were always enough."

She didn't respond to that, and tears brimmed her eyelids. She turned back to the bar and picked up her drink, swallowing the rest in a few quick gulps. "Okay. Okay. I'll think about being on board, okay? Let's talk more about this another time. It's not like you're getting pregnant tonight unless that puppet does more than comedy."

I smiled, and despite the heaviness in my chest at her reluctance and original thought process, it meant a lot to me that she was open to discussing it more.

Mostly because...it was already happening.

Chapter Sixteen

"Lean back, heels in the stirrups," Dr. Allen said as he scooted his little stool on wheels closer to me.

A female nurse was standing by a large machine with a black screen and prepping some instruments on a tray nearby.

I did as instructed and tried to keep the paper sheet covering my bare legs as much as possible. Thankfully, I was still wearing my regular shirt and top, but the underwear and pants were tucked into a not-so-discrete pile on a chair in the corner of the exam room.

"Scoot farther down on the table," he instructed, and I did. "Great. Now knees apart and you're going to feel some pressure from the transvaginal wand. Don't get nervous if I can't find it right away. Sometimes it takes a minute."

"Find my vagina?" Wasn't that literally his entire job?

Dr. Allen laughed and shook his head, and the nurse smirked at me. "Uh, no...I was talking about the gestational sac."

Of course he was. *Please God, let me disappear into this exam table, never to be seen again.*

"I'm surprised you're here again so soon." Dr. Allen was now on to the chitchatting phase of the visit, despite the fact that he had a wand at least six inches inside me. "We were just talking a few months ago about the prospect of parenthood."

"Well, you did say I should consider starting soon because of my age." There was absolutely bitterness in my tone, but it apparently went completely over the doctor's head. Not the nurse's though, because I got another smirk.

"Smart." Dr. Allen nodded his head as he moved the wand around to the side, staring carefully at the screen beside me. "I always tell my female patients of a certain age—you just can't wait too long. Those eggs don't last forever."

I really needed to find a new obstetrician because I wasn't sure I could handle the cluelessness of the patriarchy for an entire pregnancy. Then again, it was damn hard to find a good one that took my insurance.

"Ah, there it is." Dr. Allen pointed at the screen with his free hand, but all I could see was what looked like a circle with a little white dot inside. "There's the pregnancy. The yolk sac looks great, too."

I stared at the screen and tried to feel something. This was the moment I was supposed to break down and cry—tears of joy, right? But I wasn't crying. I wasn't upset or disappointed, though. I didn't know what the hell I was aside from grateful that it was actually there and not all in my head.

"There's a baby in there?" I asked, my voice more timid than I'd expected it to be.

"Well, what will one day be a baby," he confirmed. "And look, it came from your left ovary. There's a cyst on that one."

"I have a cyst?" Timid was gone, and shrill had taken its place with a vengeance.

Dr. Allen looked up at my face, his brows furrowed. "Oh, that's not a bad thing. That cyst just tells us which ovary produced this one, and it provides things the pregnancy needs until the placenta is fully formed and can do its job."

What in the absolute science experiment is a woman's body?

"Oh. So, it's safe?" I asked again.

He nodded, moving the wand around a bit more. "You're measuring a bit smaller than I'd expected—maybe only by a few days. You probably ovulated late. Very normal in women your age."

I deserved a medal for hearing about my age mid-vagina wand and not Kegeling him the hell out of my pelvic region.

"Everything looks great, though. I'll print a few pictures for you and the nurse will take your blood, then you're good to go. I'll see you back here in four weeks." Dr. Allen removed the wand and handed it to the nurse, who de-condomed it. I mean, that's what the thing they put over it looked like, but I don't know the actual name of the condom apparatus.

"Okay. Is there anything I should be doing?" I needed a full step-by-step instruction guide and he was acting like women did this every day.

I mean, I guess they did.

Dr. Allen shook his head as he finished jotting notes on his laptop. "Nope. Just take your prenatal vitamins. Stay away from alcohol and any raw foods, minimize caffeine intake—you know, the usual. Get someone else to change the cat's litter box going forward. The receptionist will give you a packet about the first trimester when you check out, so you can peruse that if you're curious. Here's your little souvenir."

He handed me a string of printed ultrasound photographs. With that, he patted my shoulder and walked out of the exam room with the nurse close behind him.

"I'll wait out here for you to get cleaned up," she said to me before closing the door. "Take your time."

I appreciated that, but there was zero chance I wasn't about to move at lightning speed. The idea of someone being inconvenienced out there waiting for me was basically intolerable, thanks to my mostly self-diagnosed anxiety issues. The paper sheet over my legs was a great wipe for the copious amounts of lube between my legs as I squatted and tried to clean it all out before tucking the paper sheet as far into the biohazard trash can as I could.

Undies and pants on, I grabbed my purse and opened the door. The nurse looked surprised to see me—which only validated my inner critic that I hadn't made her wait too long—but then she walked me over to the lab, where I sat in a metal chair and got a blood draw. And by blood draw, I mean like five or six full vials. I don't know what the heck they're testing for, but I haven't given that much blood since that one time in high school when our captain hit me in the face with a softball during practice.

Isa was reading a copy of *US Weekly* in the waiting room when I returned to her. She looked up at me and grinned, dropping the magazine down on the table and getting to her feet. "Well? Tell me everything! Was it like that show we saw?"

"Jesus, Isa. No." I held up the pictures from the ultrasound. "All appears well with the baby. Look!"

She grabbed the photos and squealed. "Oh my gosh, look at my little niece or nephew or nibling—be whoever you want to be, peanut. Aunt Isa is going to love all over you!"

I smiled at her, glad to see her so happy but immediately envious of her excitement. That was exactly how I should be acting right now, wasn't it? Jumping up and down and all giddy? That's what pregnant women were supposed to do. Isa wasn't even pregnant, and she was doing it better than I was.

Doubt swarmed in my chest, and I tried to push it away. I could do this. *I can do this.* Everyone's journey was different—at least, that was what the blog I'd been reading about trying to conceive had said. It was normal and okay that I was experiencing this in whatever way I was experiencing it. It didn't mean I was going to be a complete failure at motherhood.

So why did it feel like I was trying really hard to convince myself of that?

"Can I take a picture of this and post it on Instagram?" Isa asked, holding up the ultrasound.

"What?" I grabbed the photos away from her. "Absolutely not. These are mine. Don't post anything online before I do."

"Oh, right." Isa nodded. "I forgot that there are rules to this whole thing for the father. I'm already getting sympathy cravings, though, so we should hit up Chipotle for lunch."

I laughed as we waited in line to check out. "Slow down there, baby daddy. Don't be getting ahead of yourself."

"What do you think about the name Maestro?" Isa asked. "If it's a boy. It means teacher—and that's what babies do, right? They teach you about life. It's really fitting in a philosophical sense."

I handed my debit card over to the receptionist as she told me the co-pay amount due, then she handed me back a few pamphlets and a card with my next appointment date written on it.

I slid the card into my wallet. "Isa, I'm not naming a child Maestro."

She tried to change my mind the entire walk back to the car, so I gave in and told her we could do Chipotle for lunch. That completely shut her up, and I'm now suspecting that might be what she had been angling for all along.

Since Isa was driving, I snapped a photo on my phone of the ultrasound photos and saved them. I quickly texted a copy to Aston with just the caption, "Success!" Then I hit share again and typed in Ari's name and sent it off to her as well.

The moment I hit send and watched my phone announce "delivered," I felt like I'd made a mistake. "Shit."

Isa glanced sideways at me. "What? What's wrong?"

"Uh...nothing. I just...it's nothing." I shook my head, but Isa grabbed my phone and looked at the screen. "Isa, watch the road!"

"You texted the ultrasound photo to Ari? As in Ari Elliot—sperm donor's superhot older sister?"

I snatched my phone back from her. "It's not that big of a deal."

"You mean the woman who published that story three weeks ago about your client? Who also had a mysterious source who gave her everything?" Isa had both hands back on the wheel, but she was bulldozing right over me with her line of questioning.

"Uh..." I wasn't sure how to respond to that. No one knew about that except Ari and me, but I should have known my closest friends wouldn't be blind. Not to mention Ari's career in crisis management and public relations made her an eagle-eyed cynic.

Isa just shook her head. "Mila, you're playing with fire. That woman is your baby's aunt. What are you going to do? Play house with her? This is taking U-Haul Lesbian to a whole new level."

"I'm not moving in with her!" I assured Isa. "She's just a friend. I can have friends, Isa."

She shrugged. "I mean, I'm your *best* friend, to be clear. But I guess you can have some second and third tiers to fill the time when I'm busy."

"How kind of you," I replied, my tone dry and sarcastic. "Really, so generous."

"Well, so then why did you seem upset about it? What's wrong with sending her the picture?" Isa turned onto my street and we both started scanning the side of the road for an open parking spot.

"There's nothing wrong." I sounded way too defensive, and Isa didn't miss it.

"Thou doth protesteth too much," she teased. "Listen, I'm not hating on the match. Ari's cool as hell. But you're on a pretty unique path. Do you know if she wants that? A high-powered journalist doesn't seem the type to settle down and build a family that quickly."

That was really the million-dollar question, and I already knew the answer.

But sometimes, I wondered what would happen if I asked again. I mean, we'd experienced things together since the first time she told me she couldn't be involved, which definitely implied she was okay with *some* involvement. At least, that's what my hopeful self wanted to believe. But how did I even ask something like that?

Hey, Ari, would you like to raise your brother's child with me? I mean, it didn't exactly roll off the tongue.

"It's a nonissue. I promise," I assured Isa, pushing the idea away as she pulled into an open spot about half a block away from my house. "Thanks for going with me to the appointment. I have to get back to work. Abbot is still pretty mad at me about the whole puking-on-a-senator thing."

"Yeah, I was going to ask how work was going." She climbed out of the car, and we reconvened on the sidewalk.

"Probation is almost over, I think," I replied. "But I'm not sure they'll be putting me back on the senator's case anytime soon."

Not that I was unhappy about that possibility. It did mean a huge loss of commission for me to lose that account and a potential step back on the future partner track, but I'd also lost a lot less sleep over the last few weeks. So, maybe it all evened out?

"I really appreciate you coming with me today, Isa." When we got to my front door, I gestured inside to Isa. "Do you want to come in and hang out for a bit?"

Isa waved me off. "Hey, anytime. I'll go to all the appointments with you. But I actually have a date tonight, so I need to go get ready. I'll see you on Sunday at your mom's?"

Isa was a regular attendee at my mother's Sunday Dinners.

I nodded and gave her a quick squeeze of a hug. "See you then. Good luck tonight."

She headed back in the direction of her car as I let myself in, carefully pushing Macavity back with my feet as he was already primed and ready to bolt out the front door the moment he'd heard my key in the lock. My cell phone buzzed in my pocket, and I pulled it out to see a text message from Ari on the screen.

Wow, it's so real now. Congratulations!

I wasn't sure what I had expected her to say in response to the ultrasound photos, but that didn't feel entirely right. It felt forced and stiff—which, to be fair, I also felt. I hadn't seen Ari since the night we'd spent at her place, and we'd only exchanged a few messages here or there in between—nothing monumental. But the ache in my chest just felt stronger and stronger with every passing day.

Are you busy tonight? I sent the text back before my rational inner voice could intervene.

I'm home. Door is open.

That was it. That was her whole response. She didn't even bother to inquire why I'd asked. She just invited me over like it was nothing. I should say no. Absolutely turn it down and head up to my desk in my bedroom and catch up on the work I'd missed taking off this afternoon. That's definitely what I should do.

Are you hungry? I can bring dinner with me later.

That was the opposite of what I should have responded, but I'd already hit send. I headed straight for my bedroom, throwing my cell phone on my bed and trying to take a few deep breaths as Macavity hopped up on the bed and batted at it with his orange-and-black-striped paw.

The phone buzzed and I ran back to it, shooing him away.

I'd eat anything.

Knowing Ari's food habits, that should have been taken literally, but I couldn't help immediately going to a sexual place in my mind. I headed straight for the shower because I swore I could still smell the doctor's lube from earlier. Not at all because I wanted to be clean and smell good when I saw Ari. That was definitely not the reason.

She was a friend. A supportive friend who just wanted to be there on a significant day for me. That's all it was.

God, I hope not.

Chapter Seventeen

T here was no reason that I checked my emails as I climbed the back stairs up to Ari's apartment floor, but this was Washington, DC, and if you weren't busy and multitasking at all times...well, you probably didn't live here.

When I spotted the email from evite.com in my unread messages, I clicked on it out of curiosity as I opened the door on the landing to Ari's floor.

Aston Li cordially invites you to the third annual Baby Mama Mingle family reunion.

He did not.

I slung the bag of take-out food over one arm as I reached up and knocked on Ari's door, and she opened it moments later.

"Your brother hosts reunions?" I asked before even saying hello.

Ari grinned and stepped aside to let me walk past her. "The Baby Mama Mingle? Yeah, I think he's due for the third or fourth one pretty soon."

I stepped past her and went straight for the kitchen, placing the bag of food down on the countertop. "You'd tell me if my child is potentially genetically linked to a crazy person, right?"

She laughed and leaned against the counter, watching me unpack the brown bag of food from Five Guys Burgers—one of my favorite go-tos when I needed a feel-good meal. "I think it goes without saying that this child is genetically linked to at least one crazy person."

I eyed her, smirking. "Now I'm not sure if you're talking about me or your brother."

She shrugged. "One of life's great mysteries, I suppose. That smells heavenly. What is it?"

"Double cheeseburger with bacon for you," I said, handing her a large aluminum-wrapped burger that was bigger than my fist. "And a chili cheese dog for me. Have you had Five Guys before? I do a whole bit on them in my set."

"I've definitely never had five guys before," Ari said with a smirk and clear innuendo. "Although most of my meals come from the freezer. But good call on the bacon burger."

I shrugged. "I figured a salad wouldn't be your cup of tea."

Ari grinned and offered me a wink. "You already know me so well. Want to sit in the living room? Sorry, I don't really have a dining room. I usually just eat on the couch at the coffee table while watching television."

"My roommates and I do that sometimes," I replied, picking up my food and following her over to the living room that was exactly as it had been last time—large, soft sectional and at least eighteen different plants and greenery.

She chose to sit on the couch all the way to the right—I'm assuming to give me space to sit beside her, but something about that felt like too much. Instead, I opted to sit on the end of the chaise that stuck out from the far side of the sectional and was perpendicular to her. It still put me close but with boundaries. We both began eating and there were a few minutes of quiet as we focused on the food.

"So, how's that going to work when the baby comes?" Ari asked, breaking the silence.

I was drawing a blank to whatever she was referencing and just stared at her.

"The roommate thing," she clarified. "Like they're going to keep living there? Or are you moving out?"

"That's all still in the works," I replied. "Basically means I have no idea. I mean, I own the place and they rent from me. But I don't know if it would even be suitable to have a child there—with or without roommates? I'm not sure."

"Hmm," Ari hummed, then swallowed the bite she was working on. "Well, I don't think I can help you much there. I've spent my life actively avoiding pregnancy and babies at all costs. It's admirable that you're doing this whole thing on your own."

"Thanks." Though I wasn't sure if that really felt like a compliment. "Motherhood is something that's always been important to me. My mom is a huge part of my life, and she did it all on her own. She is always telling me that I'm a blessing and I hope this kiddo feels that way, too."

"Chicky is a force, that's for sure," Ari confirmed.

"Yeah, I would be lost without her." I looked down at the hot dog in my lap and then shook my head. "I'm going to tell her this weekend about the pregnancy. About everything."

"Really?" Ari's gaze lifted to me, her eyes wide. "You feel ready?"

I nodded. "Yeah, I mean...it's a little early still, but since I had my first ultrasound today, I want to show her the pictures. I want to tell her she's going to be a grandmother."

"She would kill it as a grandmother," Ari agreed. "You should meet Nomi sometime soon—she'll probably be at the reunion. You'd love her. Being a grandmother to a ton of children that aren't technically her grandkids is basically half her identity."

"I spoke to your mom on the phone," I replied. "Before going through with this whole thing. She seems like quite the personality."

Ari grinned. "She's a trip. Very supportive, super loving. You remind me a bit of her."

I didn't know what to do with that comment at all, so I just pretended it hadn't happened. "I'm sure she'd get along with Chicky then. But, yeah, I'm looking forward to this little nugget being here one day. It feels kind of strange still—a bit disconnected. I don't *feel* pregnant yet, you know? I mean, nausea is a thing, and my boobs are sore, but like...it still doesn't feel completely real yet."

"I'm sure that's normal." Ari took another bite of her sandwich. "But again, I'm not the person to ask."

She'd broached the topic of motherhood, so that meant I could pry further, right? "Well, babies aren't for everyone. Pregnancy has certainly been interesting so far. You don't ever see that for yourself? A family one day?"

I shoved the hot dog into my mouth quickly to stop myself from piling on more questions. This was just a casual conversation between two friends. Absolutely not a scoping mission for intel gathering.

"There are a lot of ways to be a family without biology or shoving a watermelon through my vagina," Ari replied. "Hell, that's the whole reason I got married—to *not* have a child."

Intel gathering hotspot. I needed to know more. "I was curious about that," I asked super nonchalantly, not a big deal at all. "I wouldn't have pictured you as the type to be married to a man. But then...you've got a stepson."

"I've been vibrantly out of the closet since I was fifteen,"

Ari replied. "There's no one who meets me who doesn't imme-diately think—*oh, she's definitely gay.*"

"That was certainly my line of thinking when we met," I joked. "But you married a cishet man...with a son? Make it make sense."

"Lukas's dad—John Elliott—was my college professor and I did some teaching assistant work for him as well. I knew back then that birthing babies was not in my future, but I couldn't find a single doctor who was willing to snippety-snip my tubes." Ari took another bite of her burger and chewed much slower than I would have preferred because she could not just leave me hanging like that. "Anyway, one finally agreed to sterilize me if *my future husband agreed.*"

I frowned. "But you weren't married back then?"

"Nope. Single, queer college student." Ari shook her head. "I was venting to John about the plight, and he said he'd marry me just so I could get sterilized if I wanted."

Excuse me. "That is wild."

Ari shrugged. "It was, but it worked. My uterus is just deco-ration at this point."

I filed that away in my brain so I didn't have a visibly emotional reaction in front of her. It wasn't lost on me that I was currently pregnant and sitting in front of a woman I was very attracted to who was blatantly telling me she'd done every-thing medically possible to avoid children. "So then, how long were you two married?"

"A year," she answered. "The paperwork took some time. I even lived with them during recovery and that's when Lukas and I became closer. They really are like a second family to me. We joke that I'm Lukas's stepmom, but he feels more like a dumb little brother to me—not all that different from Aston, honestly. Plus, John and my mom are like best friends now. Which is a little weird, but sometimes I think they'd actually be a really good match if either was ever ready to let go of their deceased first spouses."

It made sense why she felt family could be displayed in many ways, and I was acutely aware of the small feeling of relief in my gut at hearing that her marriage had been for a practical, nonromantic purpose. Not that I'd hoped for her not to fall in love. Or not to fall in love again. I needed to stop this entire train of thinking. "Is that why you kept the last name? Elliot? To stay part of the family? I mean, if your mom marries him, then he'd be your dad and ex-husband and you would have been the most proactive name change in history."

Ari laughed at that but shook her head. "Maybe at first." She swallowed the last bite of her burger that she'd basically inhaled. Once she'd cleared her throat, she continued. "But I realized pretty quickly that having his last name really furthered my career. Ari Elliot is ambiguous in both gender and ethnicity—enough to potentially pass as a white man in a newspaper byline. Something written by Ari Elliot is a lot more likely to be read and shared than if written by Arielle Li. It was hard to even get a recruiter to return my call when I used my original last name, and I didn't score a job at the *Washington Times* until I went by Elliot. That's certainly not a coincidence."

"I hadn't thought about it like that," I admitted, but I knew she had a point. "That's why I go by a stage name, too. Tori Miles is more popular than a Torres."

Ari nodded. "It's crazy how pervasive it is, right? This need to fit in with a world that overlooks us when we are our most authentic selves?"

She definitely wasn't wrong. "People are uncomfortable with being real if it doesn't fit their perfect and narrow definition of right, wrong, or normal versus not."

"My motto is that everyone needs to get comfortable being

uncomfortable. It's the only way to grow. Or maybe that's just something my therapist told me." Ari laughed as she stood and headed for the trash can, throwing away her aluminum foil. "Do you want anything to drink?"

"Water would be good," I replied. "I didn't know you went to therapy."

"Don't you?" Ari furrowed her brows at me. "I thought everyone our age did."

I laughed at that as I stood and followed her, tossing my own trash away after her. "If they did, the world would be a much better place. But, yeah, I have a therapist over in Rosslyn I see. She's a very no-holds-barred, gives-it-to-me-straight type."

"In Rosslyn?" Ari curled her upper lip and furrowed her brows as she poured water from a Brita pitcher into a clean glass from the cabinet. "You cross the bridge every week to see her?"

"Sometimes we do telehealth," I admitted, taking the glass from her when she was done. "But she prefers to drag me there in person whenever she can. Something about working on my avoidance issues and not always hiding behind a screen."

I drank a long sip of water—avoiding explaining further about my personal issues and insecurities. Maybe I should book a second appointment this week...

"So, what's going on?" Ari leaned one hip against the kitchen counter and watched me finish off the water she'd just poured. "Is there something you wanted to talk about?"

The way she said the last sentence hinted that she already knew the answer to that and she was just waiting for me to tell her, but talking was the last thing I wanted to do. I placed the now-empty glass of water down on the counter and cleared my throat.

"No, uh...nothing specific." *Lying again.* "I just wanted to see you."

She tilted her head to the side just enough to make her hair fall away from her shoulder. "You did?"

I looked down at my feet because the way her gaze was currently piercing me was making the hot dog churn in my stomach. "I mean...is that okay?"

My voice sounded so timid I barely recognized myself. This effect she had on me...I hated it and loved it all at the same time. I was *not* a timid person. I was a boss bitch at work and in my friendships. I was the very opposite of a wilting flower, but the moment I got around Ari, all the words became jumbled in my mouth and I just wanted to curl up in her arms and let her love me.

Jeez, I sounded like a bad R&B song.

"I told you when you left last time that you're always welcome back here." Ari stepped closer to me and ran her fingers up the length of my arm until she reached my shoulder. She pushed my hair behind my back and lifted my chin to lock eyes with her. "I say what I mean, Mila."

Part of me wished that wasn't true, given our conversation earlier, but the sincerity in her voice was undeniable and I loved that side of her. There was never any doubt when I was with her that she was telling me the truth—the full truth—and that I could trust her. Which probably only made this entire thing even stranger between us.

"Right," I whispered as she stepped even closer, now pinning my body between hers and the kitchen counter.

She dipped her head down, her lips mere centimeters from mine. "I'm glad you came back."

My heart leaped in my chest, and I silently cursed at the fantasy that was already playing out in my head of the two of us together. That was not going to happen. She'd just been very, very clear—she didn't want what I wanted.

Except right now, all I wanted was for her to kiss me.

I pushed forward and kissed her. My hesitation was only momentary as she leaned into my kiss and deepened it. I had no idea what to do with my hands in that moment, so I just placed them on her hips to hold her tighter to me. I just needed to feel closer to her, and it wasn't something I'd ever felt before. It wasn't for lack of experience—believe me. I'd been with men, women, trans, and nonbinary folks in the past, but nothing felt like this. Nothing felt like there was a fire inside of me that only she could put out.

"Take these off." Ari was pushing at the top of my jeans now—and why was I always wearing jeans?

"Okay." I didn't hesitate to unbutton my pants and drop them to the kitchen floor, stepping out of them as fast as I could.

"These, too," she said, pulling down on the sides of my underwear. This time I'd purposely chosen a cute pair of dark-pink cheeky undies in an attempt to make up for whatever granny panties she'd seen me in last time.

The moment I stepped out of them, she grabbed me by the waist and lifted me with only minimal effort onto the kitchen counter. I was not a large person, but I wasn't tiny either. I had a density to me that mostly sat in a pouch on the front of my stomach, which I'd lovingly named my ice cream holder, but I wasn't even thinking about that as she pushed my knees apart and stood between them.

Her lips were still on mine, but the cold granite beneath my ass cheeks was sending thrills of anticipation through me. I could feel the skin across my spine prickling into a million little goose bumps and I shivered, despite how hot I felt.

She pushed me back just enough that I leaned onto my elbows, looking down my body at her as her lips moved to my chest—grazing over my breasts with gentleness (thank God, because those ladies were still very achy)—and placing several pointed kisses across my stomach. Her hand slipped beneath the hem of my shirt and pushed it up enough to kiss my skin directly this time, and then she kept moving lower.

I could feel the tension growing in my body as she placed soft, slow kisses on my skin. Sometimes, just a kiss. Sometimes, her tongue trailed across me. Sometimes, a soft nip of her teeth. She pressed my legs apart, propping my knees up on her shoulders as she began giving the same attention to the inside of my thighs, switching back and forth from one side to the other until I felt like I couldn't even keep my eyes open anymore to watch her. My head fell backward as my chest heaved with every breath I tried to pull in, but breathing had never been so hard before.

When her tongue made contact with the most sensitive part of me, I groaned and my eyes fluttered to a close. *Thank fucking God I'd showered before coming over tonight.* But that was the last coherent thought I could put together before she continued and my mind wasn't words anymore. Instead, it was colors, sounds, sensations, and when her lips closed around my clit and applied the perfect amount of suction, all I could see was fireworks exploding behind my eyelids with the same intensity as the waves pulsing through my body.

"Ari," I gasped as I felt it getting so close I could no longer stop myself. Minutes passed, but it felt like torturous, wonderful hours as she found a rhythm that threatened to rupture through my defenses. "Oh, God...Ari..."

My voice sounded choked, and I pushed my hips up against her face, wanting more, wanting deeper, wanting harder. And sweet Bebe Bennet, did she oblige. Her finger slid inside me with a come-hither curl to it at the same time her tongue ran across my clit in quick flicks. My entire body responded like I was being hit by a Mack truck, but she only held me down tighter and doubled her efforts as I unraveled around her.

When she did finally slow down, I was careening toward overstimulation as my body twitched and shuddered with every touch. Somehow, she seemed to know that, lightening her touch and moving to kiss the inside of my thighs again and then back up to my stomach and then my neck and then she just watched me for a minute—her eyes locked onto mine.

"There's literally nothing sexier than hearing you say my name when I'm between your legs." Her voice had a huskiness to it that reverberated like desire against my skin.

I wanted to make her feel everything she'd given me—twice now—but when I reached for her, she pulled away. Instead, she reached down and picked up my underwear and jeans and slid them one by one back up my legs until I was fully dressed again. She was gentle and nurturing, and there was a sweetness to the way she took care of me that made my heart pound.

I slid down off the counter once dressed and my hands went to the front of her pants—she was sporting sweatpants instead of jeans like I was. "I want you to feel this, too."

But she grabbed my hands and lifted my wrist to her mouth, kissing gently on the inside of my lower arm. "Maybe next time."

I frowned, feeling a sting of...rejection? I wasn't even sure what. I stared at her in confusion, struggling to understand. She cupped my cheek.

"Don't overthink it, Mila." She placed a kiss on both of my cheeks. "I just...I need some boundaries here. Not because of you—they're for me. For my heart."

Oh. I swallowed hard, realizing for the first time that she was having as hard a time with all of this as I was. It hadn't dawned on me that I could potentially be hurting her coming over here like this—honestly, I hadn't thought this was much more than physical for her. But the way she said that last sentence was strained and deeply emotional and I felt her ache in my own chest.

"I'm sorry, Ari." I shook my head and turned away from her, now looking for my phone and wallet. The pressure to just run was pounding at the door of my heart, and my entire body felt jittery. "I shouldn't have come here. I'm really sorry."

"Mila, stop. That's not what I said." Ari's hand wrapped around my wrist, but I shook her loose as I grabbed my stuff.

"I'll see you later, okay?" I wasn't even looking at her anymore but rather actively avoiding any sort of eye contact.

"Mila..." She called after me one more time, but she didn't follow me to the front door, and she didn't stop me from closing it behind me. She didn't open it again, and she didn't ask me to come back inside, and I walked to the stairwell alone, feeling like I'd just lost something I'd never even had.

Chapter Eighteen

I knew the day would eventually come, but it still felt too soon.

My hand grazed over the bumpy, paint-peeled hood of my Ford Taurus one last time before I finally stepped aside and allowed the tow truck driver to do his thing.

"Are you going to be okay?" Isa put one arm around me. "That car was...a legend."

"Yeah, she was," I agreed, but then my hand rested on my lower belly where somewhere a fetus was forming. "It's not like I could keep her, though, once I have this baby. That car is a death trap already, so I definitely wouldn't have put an infant in it."

"Fair." Isa saluted the car as the tow truck driver finished loading it onto the flatbed and pulled away from the curb. "But you know what that means?"

I raised one brow and looked at her.

"Your birthday present to yourself is clearly going to be a mom mobile." Isa grinned and waggled her eyebrows at me. "Does Subaru make a minivan? You need a minivan."

"Absolutely not." I shook my head with fervor. "I will never be caught driving a minivan."

Isa frowned. "But you have to. That's what moms do."

"My mom drives a Volvo," I remind her. "Works just fine."

"Okay, okay." Isa shrugged and followed me up the steps to my house and inside. "But I think it would still be a perfect birthday present. You're turning thirty-five this weekend and we can't go out and party too hard, so let's do a day trip to CarMax or something like that."

It didn't sound like a terrible idea. I hadn't been so sure I was ever going to replace the Taurus once she died for good, but with a baby now on the way, I was rethinking that decision.

"CarMax?" I asked, pulling open my laptop as we both sat on the couch and I typed in the car company's website. "I mean, they do have some nice ones on here. We'd have to go out to Potomac Mills or Dulles, though."

"They have some in Maryland." Isa pointed to the screen. "Your mom could come, and it would be a whole thing. You know she'd want to be involved in picking something with you."

"Yeah, but then I'd have to tell her about being pregnant. Remember how that last conversation went?"

Isa took the computer from me and began searching by CarMax lots closer to my mom's house. "She didn't say she was opposed to it entirely. She just needs some convincing. I mean, who wouldn't? We all did going into this."

That was fair.

I pulled out my cell phone and sent a text off to my mom asking if she wanted to go car shopping this weekend. She responded instantly that she was wholeheartedly in, but she wanted to also make me my favorite birthday dinner at the house after. I wasn't about to complain.

Rachel walked into the living room. "Are you guys looking at cars?"

171

"Yeah, I think we're going to go car shopping this weekend for my birthday. Want to come?"

Rachel leaned down across the back of the couch to look over my shoulder at the screen. "CarMax? What about like an actual dealer or something nicer?"

"But then I'm just putting an infant in it," I reminded her. "Imagine spit-up in the back seat of your Audi."

Rachel grimaced and shook her head, definitely the car fanatic out of the group. "Yeah, no. Get something practical then. Have you thought about what you're going to do living-wise yet?"

I knew I needed to give Yasmeen and Rachel a game plan at some point and soon. It was already a lot to ask them to keep doing the litter box for Macavity, and I'm sure they both felt anxiety not knowing if I was about to kick them out or not. "I promise whatever I decide, I'll give you two plenty of notice. I'm not trying to make this more difficult for anyone."

Rachel nodded before heading for the kitchen. "Yeah, I know. I get it. Just wondering."

My phone vibrated in my hand, and I glanced down at the screen to see Ari's name pop up.

The Secret Service is trying to subpoena my emails and text messages. We're fighting it, but I can't make any promises.

My stomach lurched, and I closed out of the text message and pretended like I hadn't just read that. Nope, no. Absolutely not. If they managed to actually get those records—which seemed unlikely legally, but it was also the government—then it would be clear that Ari's inside link was to me. Hell, my pregnancy would also be put on blast, and that would add a really colorful component to the whole senator-hides-a-pregnancy story.

"What's wrong?" Isa caught the change in my expression and frowned.

I shoved my phone in my jeans pocket and wiped any evidence from my face. "Nothing. Just work stuff."

"They don't know about the baby yet, right?" she asked.

I shook my head. "No. I figured I'd disclose once I'm actually starting to show. I'm only ten weeks right now, so that feels like it's still pretty far away."

"Are you worried about how it will impact you there?"

It was a fair question. "I'm trying to lean on the hope that maybe they won't act like this is the stone ages and I can't be both good at my job and pregnant at the same time."

"Yeah, sure." Isa's tone was laced with sarcasm. "This is the same firm supporting the face of ending women's reproductive rights, but I'm sure they'll be super supportive about your pregnancy."

Point made. "I need to leave this job."

"Ding ding ding!" Isa waved her hand like it was obvious. "I honestly don't know how you've stuck it out this long. I sent your LinkedIn to my friend, and I think they'd be a much better fit. I can give you her email if you want. Maybe follow up with them?"

"Yeah, maybe." The thought of job hunting while pregnant seemed just as daunting. I wasn't even sure how all of that would work out in terms of my health insurance, which I definitely needed more than ever right now. Not that I had that great of a plan, to begin with. "New car, new job, new baby, new place to live...it's all a little overwhelming."

Isa squeezed my hand. "You're not doing it alone," she reminded me.

God, I had the best friends.

A few days later, Isa was still right beside me as we walked onto the CarMax lot in Gaithersburg, Maryland with my mother. She'd driven separately and met us there, but she'd brought with her an entire binder full of printouts from their website marking the cars that she thought were the best.

"Let's start with the Nissan Rogue," Chicky said, pointing toward an entire section of her binder that was earmarked *Nissan*. "Steve has one of those, and I'm telling you, it drives like a dream. Really great, practical car."

"What about sports cars? Something flashy and fast?" Isa asked, already knowing full well we weren't going that route but clearly loving to agitate my mother whenever she could.

"*Ay*, no." Chicky shook her head. "You're thirty-five. It would just look like you're trying to relive your youth."

"I'm still young!" I replied with a bit of defensiveness.

She waved her hand like that was obvious. "Of course. You're my baby and always will be, but sports cars are for middle-aged men having some sort of low testosterone crisis."

I hadn't even yet told her about the baby, but the practical aspect of her car shopping was right on target, so I wasn't about to argue with her.

"Fine, let's just go look at the Nissans." I shot Isa a look that we'd already discussed in the car, which meant that I needed to talk to my mother alone for a few minutes.

"I'm going to check out the coupes," Isa replied, pointing toward the opposite side of the lot where a tall man was standing, looking at one of the smaller sports cars. He was definitely handsome, even from this distance, and I knew immediately that Isa planned to try to hit that. "Just for, you know, research purposes."

Chicky and I walked over to a row of crossovers, and she began peering in the window of the closest one. "Mila, come look at this one."

"Hey, Mom," I began, keeping a step back. "Can I talk to you about something?"

She turned around quickly, her eyes sharp as she examined me from top to bottom. "What's wrong? Are you okay? What's going on?"

I put both hands up to slow her down. "It's nothing like that," I assured her. "No need to panic."

Her gaze narrowed as if she wasn't buying it. "Okay..."

I walked around the car to the next row of crossovers, and she followed me, the binder now tucked under her arm.

"Remember when you came to my show and I asked you about your thoughts on me starting a family?" I posed the topic with as much gentleness as a hand grenade being lobbed at her. "And you said we'd talk about it more later."

The tension in her shoulders seemed to ease. "Oh, is that all you wanted to talk about? Jesus, you scared me for a second there. Sure, baby. Let's talk about it. You want to start a family."

I nodded my head. "Well, yes. I...I *am* starting a family."

The tension returned and her shoulders crept up. "What do you mean?"

"Mom...I'm pregnant." I didn't look at her when I said this, instead pretending to be really fascinated with one of the cars in the lot in front of me.

She didn't say anything for a second, and then she laughed. "Sweetheart, I appreciate the near heart attack, but you should warn your mother when you're doing one of your comedy bits. Is this for an upcoming show?"

I turned to face her, and her expression said she was finally reading the seriousness on mine. Her smile faltered, then fell to a straight line. "You're pregnant?"

I placed a hand on my belly. "Technically, I'm eleven weeks pregnant today."

Her eyes flickered down to my hand and then back up to me. "Eleven weeks?"

I nodded again. She looked at me harder, like we were in this staring match that neither of us knew how to break.

"You folks find a car you like?" A short-statured salesman walked over to us, pulling his belt up over his round beer belly as he did. "This one right here has been getting a lot of heat. I can bet it's going to be gone by the end of the day if you don't act fast."

My mother and I continued to look at each other, completely ignoring his introduction. He looked between the two of us, finally sensing that there was something going on he did not want to be a part of.

"You know, when you're ready, I'll be right over there." He motioned to the doors to the showroom. "Happy to answer any questions you guys might have."

And then the man literally speed walked away as fast as his tiny legs could carry him.

"You're pregnant." My mother repeated it, but this time like a statement. Like something she was slowly swallowing and coming to terms with. "You're having a baby. You—my little Mila—are having a baby."

"Mom, I am thirty-five years old," I reminded her. "And I didn't go into this rashly. I've been thinking about it for years."

She nodded and pushed a smile that only felt mostly forced onto her lips. "This is wonderful. Yes, you're thirty-five. You're not my baby anymore, *mija*. You're having your own baby. I'm going to be an *abuela*."

I couldn't tell if she was asking me for confirmation or just trying to hear herself say all of that out loud. Either way, I just nodded.

"Okay. Okay." She repeated herself a few more times before shaking her shoulders and arms out as if trying to refresh her entire life view. "This is wonderful. Tell me how this happened. Who's the father?"

I shook my head. "There is no father."

"There has to be a father," she replied, her head cocked to the side and her hands on her hips now. "Someone put that baby in you."

"I did. By myself. With a really long syringe thingy." Probably not the right technical term, but it painted the picture close enough. "I...uh, well, I used a sperm donor. A friend I met not too long ago on a, uhm, on an app."

"An app?" My mother's brows lifted, and I could tell I was losing her. "What are you talking about right now?"

I pulled out my phone and clicked on the Baby Bank app. "I used this app to meet a guy named Aston, who regularly does this for women who want to have kids. He's already helped a lot of families and there's actually a reunion next week that I'd love you to come to so you can meet everyone."

"A reunion?" The color was draining from her face, and Isa walked up in that same moment.

"I think I have a date lined up for this weekend with that cute salesman," Isa began, pointing back toward the tall man she'd been talking to. When she looked back at us, she realized she'd come back sooner than she should have. "Oh. Are you guys...are you guys done talking?"

"I need to sit down." My mother put her hand out and both Isa and I immediately grabbed an arm. We walked her over to the showroom and found her a chair to sit in as she waved the binder in front of her face as if it was a fan.

"I'm guessing that didn't go well," Isa said quietly to me.

I shook my head. "She's going to come around. It's just a lot at once."

"So, help me understand—" my mother cut in, looking up at me now. "You went on an app. You met a man you're not dating. You got pregnant with his child."

"Well, it's *my* child," I clarified.

"Right, right." She nodded. "And now you're going to raise this baby together?"

Clearly the concept was taking her a minute to swallow.

"No—just me. He's not involved."

"But she has all of us," Isa added. "Rachel, Yasmeen, me, you...we're all going to be there and help."

"Yes, of course," my mother agreed. "I'll be there every step of the way for my grandbaby. In fact, I think you should move back home."

I shook my head adamantly. "I'm *not* moving back home. Mom, I know this is a lot to digest, but I can do this. I promise. I'd love your help, which is why I asked you to come car shopping with me. Help me find a car that's baby safe."

My mother looked down at the binder in her hands and then chucked it in the closest trash can. "Well, we're going to have to start over from scratch. None of these are child focused. My grandbaby has to have the safest car on the market."

I grinned as she stood up, a look of determination on her face. "So, you'll help me?"

Chicky pulled me in for a hug and kissed my cheek. "Of course, my baby. This is wonderful. You're going to be a mama!"

"And you're going to be a grandma!" Isa tossed the word out there, but Chicky gave her a cutting look.

"This is a lot to digest in one day," Chicky told us both. "Give me a few more days before I'm ready to actually call myself an *abuelita*. No one would believe I'm old enough for a grandbaby. I mean, look at me!"

"Fair enough." I squeezed her back in a tight hug because, as awkward as this conversation had been, at least she was on board. She was going to try, and I wasn't going to be in this alone.

Isa threw her arms around both of us. "Ah, we're going to be one big, weird family!"

Something about that felt really comforting, and I tried hard not to think of Ari and wish she was part of that.

Chapter Nineteen

"Oh, good Lord, he had a banner made." My mother pointed ahead of us as we climbed the grassy hill on our way up to the covered pavilion next to the playground at Lubber Run Park in Arlington—God, why did I keep getting dragged out to Northern Virginia for events?

My gaze followed Chicky's gesture and sure enough, hanging across the side of the pavilion was a large, rainbow-colored banner that read *Aston's Baby Mamas Mingle*. There were rainbow balloons on either side and streamers decking out the inside ceiling of the wooden covering. Several picnic tables filled the space and were covered in plates of food, drinks, and a full assortment of donuts hanging on a donut wall in the back.

"This is...very festive," I tried to find the words as we closed in on the reunion, but honestly, this entire situation was indescribable. I paused in my tracks for a minute and grabbed my mother's arm to hold her with me. "Please promise me you'll be civil to everyone."

She clucked her tongue at me. "I've had a week to process

all this grandbaby, stranger-sperm news, and look, they also have beer. I'll be fine."

I eyed her suspiciously, but honestly, she had handled the news a lot better than I expected. All week long, she'd been emailing me decor ideas for a nursery or sending me applications to preschools that she insisted I needed to get on the waiting list for now.

I'd just been deleting her emails so far, but I appreciated the gesture.

"Mila!" Aston spotted us as soon as we reached the top of the hill and began crossing the playground area. He waved furtively high above his head and motioned us over.

"Hey, Aston," I said, giving him a side hug when I got to the pavilion. I stepped back and gestured toward my mother. "This is my mother—Chicky Torres."

"It's Grandma!" Aston pulled my mother in for a hug, and she looked a bit startled at first but then smiled and returned the embrace. When he stepped back, Aston pointed toward my stomach. "Are you excited for the little grandbaby brewing in there? How many weeks are you now, Mila?"

"Twelve weeks," I replied, my hand running across my lower pelvis, which still looked like I'd just enjoyed too many tacos for dinner for the last few nights—or years. "It's still pretty early. I don't want to get too ahead of myself."

Everyone had been telling me to keep the news to myself until I entered the second trimester—though when the fuck that actually was is a hotly debated topic because half the websites say twelve weeks and the other half say fourteen weeks and you can't divide forty weeks by three anyway. But that wasn't my style. If something happened to this pregnancy, I wasn't about to keep that news to myself and suffer in silence. I was going to want to lean on friends and family if, God forbid,

I had a miscarriage. It wasn't like I thought it was shameful or something I needed to hide.

"We have a newcomer this year!" A woman walked up to me with a toddler hanging around her legs and a belly that looked like she was about to give birth right here on the playground. "I'm Jana. What's your name?"

"Mila." I put out a hand to her and she shook it, her smile wide and welcoming. "You look like you're due any day now."

She rubbed a hand over her engorged belly. "Yep, I have a C-section scheduled for next week. And this little one is Alex."

I gave a small wave and smile to the little boy who'd now ducked his head between his mom's legs like he was trying to hide from me but just peeking out enough that I could see his smile. "Hi, Alex. Are you excited about being a big brother?"

"Mommy baby tummy," Alex chattered, and his little voice was so freaking cute that I felt the swirl of excitement at the thought of having my own little one of those one day soon.

"My husband is over by the beers—shocking, right?" Jana pointed to a transgender man who had a jawline that could kill. "Jay, come meet the new girl!"

Jay turned to look at us, raising his beer in the air. "Anyone want a beer?"

"Ooh, me!" Chicky's hand shot up and she walked over to him.

Jealous. This whole no-drinking thing for ten months was a real vibe killer.

Jana leaned backward a little more, seemingly trying to offset her center of gravity as she held her stomach with her free hand. "I told Jay that the moment I wake up from that C-section, there better be a margarita waiting for me."

I think I might like Jana. "That sounds like something I would do."

She grinned at me. "Come on. Let me introduce you to the other moms. How far along are you, by the way?"

I gave her the rundown of my pregnancy so far and how I'd met Aston as she led me over to the sloped climbing wall for kids, with a group of women standing at the top supervising their children scrambling up and down the hill.

"Ladies, this is Mila," Jana introduced me to the group, all of whom turned to look at us with big smiles. Jana took turns introducing everyone to me, pointing to each woman as she went around the semicircle. "That's Emily—two kids, Max and Lily. This is Marta—her second kid is on the way and her first down there is Felix, but he's not from Aston. Merrick and her wife Jules have Cody and Delia, and Hailey is pregnant with her third—her first two are Nicky and Benson. Hailey's husband is a firefighter, so he couldn't make it today, but you'll meet him eventually."

I immediately forgot everyone's name within three seconds of Jana saying them but waved hello anyway. "Hi, everyone. I'm Mila. Twelve weeks along. First-time mom doing this on my own."

"I love that for you," said one of the women, her name already a blank, but her stomach visibly pregnant, so I'm sure I could narrow her down at some point. "That's what I've done, too. Felix is already six years old, and I decided, why not do it again? I'm due in two months."

"Are you completely overwhelmed yet?" Another woman asked, leaning forward and offering me a genuinely kind smile. "When I first came to this reunion thing after having Cody two years ago, I was like...what the hell is happening right now?"

"I mean, the sign did spark some of those thoughts," I said, pointing to the banner on the pavilion.

The woman laughed—I want to say her name was Merrick.

"Aston's sense of humor is one of the reasons why I went for kiddo number two with him. I can already tell Cody is going to have some of it, but Delia's just learning to walk, so the jury's still out of her."

Delia was on her hip and had the cutest little cheeks I'd ever seen on a baby. It would be wrong to pinch them, right? I held myself back. "Wow, she's adorable. So, is this how you all met? I'm guessing from the rainbow banner that everyone here is queer, too?"

"I'm not." Hailey raised a hand in the air, and the only reason I remembered her name was because she was introduced last. "My husband is a firefighter and lost his testicles in a mishap on duty a few years back."

I grimaced. "Whoa. That sounds like a nightmare."

Hailey laughed. "Yeah, it wasn't his favorite shift at work, that's for sure. On a firefighter's salary, buying sperm was just a little out of our wheelhouse. When we found Aston, everything seemed to align. Now we have the family we always dreamed of."

I felt a little lump in my throat. "That's really wonderful. I'm glad you guys were able to do that."

"How's the process been for you? We talked on the phone, I think, at the beginning of it," one of the women said.

I recognized her voice from one of the reference calls I made before getting pregnant. "Yes, Emily! Thank you for that. It's been pretty smooth sailing so far. I'm doing okay, and I have a lot of support—my mother is over there drinking all the beer."

I pointed back toward the pavilion where Chicky was laughing and chatting with an older woman I didn't recognize. Chicky very literally had a light beer in one hand and what looked like a shot of tequila in the other, and the older woman was holding up a lime slice to her. *Jesus, Mother, this is still a*

184

public playground. I looked away when Chicky licked the back of her hand and drank the tequila in one go, then took the lime and sucked on it. *I just cannot.*

"She looks fun," Emily replied, and her voice sounded sincere despite the fact that I was thoroughly embarrassed. "Looks like she and Nomi are hitting it off."

"Nomi? That's Aston's mom?" I looked back at the older woman with my mother. She was shorter than my mother by at least half a foot, and her thick black hair was tied back in a loose braid.

"Yeah, she's incredible. You definitely have to meet her." Jana was already pulling my arm back in the direction of the pavilion. "Come, let me introduce you two. Hey, Nomi! This is Mila."

"That's my daughter," Chicky boasted with a smile that was clearly partially influenced by the booze—her cheeks a darker red than normal.

Jana pushed me toward Nomi and then abandoned me to return to the other moms. *Please take me with you.*

"This is Mila?" Nomi put out both of her hands as if asking me to come hug her. "Oh, she's beautiful. How's my grandbaby?" I awkwardly went in for the hug but was not prepared for her to pat my stomach and lean down and talk to it. But she did. So, that was happening. "Hey, little baby! This is your part-time grandma. You bake real good in there, you hear me?"

I blinked. "Uh..."

"Or whatever you want me to be, hun," Nomi quickly assured me. "You can ask any of the girls—I'm as involved as you want me to be. No pressure. At some point, if Aston keeps populating the entire city, I'm not going to be able to keep up, but for now, it's still doable."

I forced a smile, trying not to let the awkward side of me

rear its ugly head. "Yeah, I can imagine that's a unique experience for you."

Nomi laughed, and her head tipped back so far that when she did, that I could see the faint scar lines around the side of her face and ears from an old face-lift surgery. *Interesting.* I averted my eyes quickly when she looked back at me.

"Oh, honey, you won't even believe the stories I could tell you," Nomi continued. "Both of my children are unique souls—beat to their own drum, you know?"

I tried to keep my expression totally neutral at the inclusion of Ari in this conversation. "Are they?"

"Absolutely." Nomi waved a hand as she poured another shot of tequila—actually, two, one of which she handed to Chicky. "Arielle's out of town on a work assignment, but I'm sure you'll meet her at some point. Ari is a great aunt if you want her to be—she just doesn't want to have her own. Wild, right? I have one kid who is closed for business and the other who is giving it away for free. I don't know where I went wrong with them."

I tried to smile, but her words felt like a familiar sting I'd become all too acquainted with when thinking about Ari. Hell, I didn't even know she wasn't in town. The only message I'd gotten from her last week had been about the phone records potentially being subpoenaed, but so far, their lawyers had been able to squash it.

"Wait, Ari?" Chicky sniffed the second shot of tequila before shooting it back quickly. After she swallowed, she exhaled loudly and then looked at me. "Wasn't that your friend's name who you brought over for dinner? The gay one?"

¡Dios mío! I had never wanted to disappear more.

"Oh, that sounds like Ari." Nomi nodded. "You guys have met?"

I had not come into this with a preplanned story, and I was already trying to remember the new names I'd heard today, so scrambling to pull a fake meet-cute out of my ass was not in the cards for the day. "Um, yes...that was Ari, Mother. Ari and I met through Aston, of course. Totally casual. Just friends, nothing going on there. We're just friends."

My mother rolled her eyes way too goddamn loudly, so Nomi definitely caught it.

"I've been learning so many new things about my daughter lately," Chicky replied, her tone dripping in her classic passive aggressiveness. "New friends, new career, new car, new baby. How will I ever keep up?"

And I would have to be the one to drive her home. Ugh. The drive here—despite being gloriously smooth in my brand-new crossover that we'd successfully picked out last weekend—had already been enough to get under my skin as I'd had to explain everything happening at my work to her. I mean, I didn't *have* to, but it felt like the floodgates were open after all I'd revealed to her. It seemed a bit pointless to also hide that I was still on probation at work and that Senator Murphy had demanded my boss open an internal investigation on me that would be at least a few more weeks of tedious audits. And he didn't even know about the whole selling-him-out-to-the-world-thing unless this subpoena went through.

All of this was literally over some vomit. Old white men are fucking fragile.

Nomi laughed, but it sounded more nervous than amused. "We could always do a third shot?"

Chicky grinned at her. "We're going to get along well, Nomi."

"I'm going to continue mingling with the other moms," I said, pointing back toward the women who weren't pounding tequila at two o'clock on a Saturday afternoon at a children's playground. "It was nice to meet you, Nomi. Mom, I think you've had enough."

"See? She's already trying to mother me," Chicky said to Nomi as she sipped her beer. "She's going to be great at this whole baby thing. She learned from the best."

I gave my mom *the eye*, holding up one finger to reiterate my point that she'd had enough. She waved me off and returned to chatting with Nomi as I walked back to the other mothers.

Other mothers. That felt weird to even think of myself in that context—as a mother. But being here around everyone who my future child was quite literally biologically related to was making it all feel a lot more real than it had before. And I was feeling excited. Not that I wasn't before, but something in the air today just felt like it solidified the entire thing.

I was really doing this. I was bringing another life into this world—a life that would have half siblings and part-time grandmothers and a full-time Chicky and that just all sounded so full of people and love.

It sounded like family.

I swallowed the lump in my throat as I reached the other women, not wanting to get emotional the first time they met me despite the fact that I one-hundred-percent was. I didn't need Ari to fall in love with me and raise this baby with me—even if that was what the fantasy in the back of my mind had been playing out.

I already had the most unique but clearly involved support group I could imagine. I *could* really do this on my own. I'd gone into this with the confidence that I could, and while that had wavered a bit in recent weeks, I was feeling the surge inside of me again, finally.

I was going to be a mother. And one hell of a mother at that.

I checked my phone before reaching the other mothers and paused at the new email from my boss that had just appeared on the screen. I clicked it quickly and my stomach sank.

The jig was up. The subpoena had gone through.

Chapter Twenty

"Gender-reveal parties literally kill people," Yasmeen informed me as she finished taping up the pink and blue streamers against the wall of the living room. "And they are an archaic symbol of a binary gender system that doesn't actually exist. What if the baby grows up and decides they are trans? Or enby? Or fluid? What if they're born intersex? Statistically, that's as common as having twins."

"Gender-reveal parties do *not* kill people." I huffed, spreading the cookies I'd picked up from a local bakery out on a tray on the dessert table. I swear to God, my friends could be so dramatic...

"Oh, no?" Yasmeen stopped what she was doing and pulled out her phone, typing something in quickly. She held up a *Newsweek* article for me. "Look, this one says their gender-reveal cannon exploded and killed grandma with blue shrapnel."

"A cannon? Who the hell uses a cannon at a baby party?" I frowned. "Yas, I literally just have a cake and we're going to cut into it to see what color it is inside. Unless the baker buried anthrax in there as the secret ingredient, I think we're going to be fine."

"Ooh, you can't make a joke like that in DC," Yas commented, clicking her tongue as she put her phone back in her pocket.

I grinned. "Sorry. I forgot the Pentagon is probably listening."

"I don't know her!" Yasmeen called out into the air as if someone was listening in. "Who is coming to this thing anyway, Mila?"

"Some of the other moms from Aston's group, Chicky, Isa, Rachel, Kari, Lukas...the usual." I shrugged because I definitely hadn't gone all out or anything like that. I wasn't trying to be one of *those* moms. I just wanted to have all the experiences and not miss out on anything my first time around. After all, I wasn't sure I'd ever do this again.

Not to mention I desperately needed the distraction from work as my job—and probably my license—was tenuously hanging on by a thread.

"I'm interested in meeting the other Stepford wives," Yasmeen commented, carrying the cake in from the kitchen and placing it next to the cookies I'd arranged. "God, this thing smells good."

"I ordered it from a queer bakery in Dupont—they never fail to deliver the yummiest cakes." I placed a serving cake knife next to it on the table. "But you better not call anyone a Stepford wife when they get here."

Yasmeen laughed. "I'm teasing, of course. But, like...it's all a little strange. You have to admit that."

The front door to our apartment opened without warning— I mean, to be fair, we had left it unlocked for guests.

"What would you call your stepmother's brother's sperm baby?" Lukas was walking into our apartment backward, holding his phone in front of him and clearly making a live video on TikTok. "That's the question of the day, folks. Let's ask the mom-to-be."

Lukas glanced over at me, lowering his voice. "Tori?"

Despite his complete lack of boundaries, at least he knew to use my stage name on any live video.

I nod my head. "Are you doing a live video?"

"Tori Miles, we have eighteen hundred people tuned in right now and everyone wants to know—" Lukas flipped around and turned his phone to face me now. "Is that my brother? Or my nephew? Or my cousin?"

"Uh..." I hadn't really thought out the extent of the connection. "It's your...nothing. I'm pregnant with *my* baby. No one else's."

Lukas turned the camera back to get his face on the screen. "You heard it here first, folks. Tori Miles, up-and-coming comedienne and lesbo, is pregnant with her very own baby."

"I'm not a lesbian," I reminded him, this time grabbing the phone from him and hitting the end button. Thank God I'd already announced it on social media a week ago because I'd be pissed if this was how the world found out I was pregnant. "And who the hell outs someone on live?"

"Oh, my bad." Lukas rubbed a hand across the back of his neck. "Is that bad? Are you not out? I thought you were gay. You look gay to me now."

"Why did you invite him?" Yasmeen stepped up next to me, her arms crossed over her chest. "His cis-hetero whiteness is pungent."

Lukas grinned and pretended to bow. "Thank you, ma'am."

"That was *not* a compliment." Yasmeen's nostrils flared and she turned away to head back to the kitchen. "Tell me when someone palatable gets here, Mila."

"You don't have to make it so difficult, you know," I told Lukas, this time shoving his phone back into his hand.

Lukas pulled the most innocent puppy-dog face he could, then snatched a cookie up off the table and inhaled it in two bites. "What am I making difficult?"

I rolled my eyes at him and handed him a stack of napkins. "Liking you. Here, be useful. Put these out on the end table over there."

He grinned sheepishly and did as I asked. "Hey, I brought a present, at least. Two, technically."

"Wow, that doesn't seem like you." My tone was dry. I finished setting up the rest of the dessert table and glanced around to see if there was anything else I needed to do before people arrived.

"Well, one is from me. The other one is from Ari. She asked me to bring it since she's overseas right now."

"She's overseas?" I wasn't curious. Not at all.

"Some assignment in Jordan. She'll be back in two weeks, I think. But, yeah, she sent it with me." Lukas dug in the pockets of his canvas pants but couldn't find it on the first try. He started digging around the second pocket, then the third, and he kept coming up empty until the fifth pocket. "Ah, here it is."

I put out my hand and he placed a long brown object in it. "What is this?"

Lukas looked way too proud. "A Cuban cigar. For after the baby gets here."

"Ari gave me this?" That felt...weird.

Lukas looked offended. "Hell, no. That's my gift to you. It's illegal, you know. I had to break some serious knees to get that. Ari just got you a stupid trinket."

He fished out another package from what was probably his seventh pocket and handed me a small box that was wrapped with a pink-and-blue bow. "Here. This one's from Ari."

I handed the Cuban cigar back to Lukas and took the box instead. "Here, why don't you keep the cigar safe for me."

"Sweet. I'm on it." He held it under his nose and rubbed it against his nostrils, taking a deep whiff, then shoving it in one of his many cargo pants pockets.

Gross.

Ari's gift was flat and small enough to fit in my hand, and I didn't wait to open it until everyone arrived. I pulled at the ribbons and slid the top off the box. Inside was a sheet of tissue paper, and when I lifted that off, there was a small silver picture frame beneath it.

On the frame, there was an inscription etched into the metal—*family is who you choose.* Inside the frame was a blank white background with a yellow Post-it stuck to it that said in Ari's handwriting—*ultrasound goes here.*

Shit. Of course she'd get me something super fucking meaningful like this. I traced a finger over her handwriting and then put the tissue paper back over it and closed the box, trying to blink away any potential tears that I could already feel beginning to build.

"A picture frame?" Lukas scoffed before turning around and plopping down on the sofa in a dramatic fashion. "The cigar trumps that by miles."

I was about to tear him a new one, but the knock on the front door pulled my attention. I shot Lukas a look instead. "Hey, look at that. Some people knock."

When I got to the door and opened it, Emily was standing there with Merrick and Hailey.

Emily lifted a bottle of wine in the air and smiled. "We have babysitters for the rest of the afternoon!"

I laughed, getting a little glimpse into my own future. I didn't hate it. "Come in. Come in. Drinks and glasses are in the kitchen—help yourself!"

Hailey didn't join them as they headed for the drinks, instead stopping to talk to me. She rubbed a hand over her own burgeoning belly. "You look amazing. How far along now?"

"Fourteen weeks." I touched my still mostly tacos belly. "I mean, it's still so early and all that, but since the blood test confirmed the gender, I figured...why not?"

"Pfft. You should totally celebrate because the second trimester is the best," Hailey replied. "I'm about to enter the third trimester here and feeling every bit of it."

"I can only imagine." I offered her a sympathetic look, though, in reality, I had zero understanding at all about whatever she was experiencing because I barely knew what was happening to my own body. "Has anyone heard from Jana? How was her C-section?"

"Girl." Hailey's eyes went wide. "You didn't hear?"

Oh god. "No, what?"

"I mean, that probably sounded more dramatic than it needed to be." Hailey waved her hand. "But, yeah, the baby is in the NICU for at least a few more days. Swallowed meconium in the amniotic sac right before they got it out, so some respiratory issues the poor little nugget has to outgrow under monitoring."

I frowned. "What's meconium?"

"Poop," Emily filled in for her as she walked back into the room with a very full glass of wine. "The baby pooped in the amniotic sac."

"They can do that?" My eyes widened. "Like poop inside of you?"

"Between that and you shitting on the table during delivery, there can be a lot of poop in childbirth." Emily looked so laissez-faire about the news she'd just dropped on me and how had no one told me I was going to shit on the table when giving birth?

"Oh, she looks pale," Merrick said, joining us now with an equally full glass of wine. "You're going to scare her, ladies."

"Please, keep going because this is gold," Lukas called out from the couch, and I glanced over to see him holding his phone up, filming us.

I gritted my teeth. "Lukas, I will shove that phone so far up your ass that you'll be shitting yourself."

"Christ, those hormones are really getting to you." Lukas put the phone back in his pocket and rolled his eyes.

I looked back at Emily. "But like...what do you mean shit *on the table*? Like in one of those little bedpans when no one is watching behind a draped curtain?"

Merrick laughed a lot harder than I was comfortable with.

"Uh...no." Emily grimaced and patted me on the shoulder. "I mean, it's a lot of pushing, you know? Sometimes the body just doesn't know what it's pushing out...so everything goes."

Logically this made sense. Emotionally, I was close to passing out. *Someone, please stop the thought spiral I was quickly scrolling down.* "Okay, okay, but hear me out...does that mean I could potentially expel my child from my vagina into a pile of my own shit after my child already swallowed its own shit?"

Emily looked over at Merrick, then at Hailey. "I mean...I guess? I'm not sure what the stats are on that specific combination—seems like a perfect storm."

"A perfect shitstorm," Merrick clarified without even a smirk.

That was helpful. *Not.*

"Maybe you should sit down, Mila." Hailey placed a hand on my back and guided me toward one of the chairs by the dessert table. Was it that obvious I was on the edge of a nervous breakdown? "We can change topics! Let's cut the cake! That'll definitely distract you!"

I sat down because the odds were I was going down, whether voluntarily or not. Someone put a glass of ice water in my hand, and I sipped it slowly while Yasmeen reentered the room with Rachel and took over, answering the door as everyone else arrived.

"Am I at least allowed to get the cake cutting on camera?" Lukas asked me as I finally stood up a few moments later and headed toward the cake, where Yasmeen was already setting up for the big reveal. "Ari asked me to send her the video since she can't be here."

Well, I obviously wasn't going to say no to that. Because Ari and I were purely platonic friends, and what friend would deny something like that? Completely normal, absolutely casual. What was a video between friends slash sperm donor's sister slash baby's aunt?

"Yeah, that's fine," I told him. "But no posting it on social media. Send it to me and Ari—that's it."

"Fiiine." He rolled his eyes like every bit of the frat boy he had refused to grow out of. I didn't know why he was getting on my nerves more than normal today, but I felt like I had no patience for his antics, whereas a few weeks ago, I seemed to tolerate him just fine.

He was not a bad kid at all—in fact, I'd seen some really sweet sides of him over this strange new friendship, but things had shifted the more pregnant I felt. Or maybe it was the more pregnant he perceived me to be? Like he had to be the center of attention and sharing the spotlight with a baby was not comfortable for him.

Good Lord, was my baby's sperm aunt's-stepson jealous? That was a topic to explore with my therapist on Monday.

"Do we sing a song or something?" Rachel asked as everyone started gathering around the cake table that I was now standing behind. "Is it like a happy birthday song, but like the happy assigned sex at birth day?"

Emily laughed and elbowed Rachel with one arm as she held her third glass of wine in the opposite hand. "We would be friends."

Great, my pre-mom friends were mingling with my mom friends. Definitely nothing that could go wrong there.

"There's no song," I assured her as I picked up the cake knife. "We just cut it and see!"

"Wait. First, you have to tell everyone what you hope it is," Yasmeen called out.

I absolutely wasn't falling for that. "I just want it to be a happy, healthy baby—boy or girl or somewhere in between."

"Cut the cake!" Lukas shouted out from the other side of the room and started to make a pretend drumroll sound.

I slid the knife into the pristine white icing on the surface of the small round cake. It was decorated with pink and blue sprinkles on the top, all mixed together. After one full cut, I pulled the knife out and began slicing the other side before sticking the knife under the piece and sliding it out so everyone could see.

"It's a..." Rachel had now joined in on the drumroll and was banging two spoons against the table in quick succession.

The piece slid out of the cake easily and I looked at the side. It was...purple.

"It's a girl!" Rachel shouted out.

Yasmeen immediately cut her off. "No, it's a boy! Purple means there must have been blue dye in there."

"What the hell?" I was thoroughly confused.

Emily and Hailey both came over and inspected, but neither of them could tell which it was either.

"Did it come with a letter or something to clarify?" Rachel asked, taking the knife from me and beginning to cut up the rest of the cake to see if there were better answers hidden somewhere inside.

Nope, the entire inside of the cake was a pinkish-blueish-purple color. "Maybe check the bottom? The baker could have written the answer there?"

Yasmeen started divvying up pieces of cake onto plates and passing them out to everyone in the room until the cake stand was empty, then Rachel flipped it over. Sure enough, there was an envelope taped to the bottom.

I grabbed at it and quickly ripped it open. There were two pieces of cardstock inside and the first one simply read, *Your child will choose their own gender one day.* I flipped to the second one and that one read, *But if you have to follow an antiquated tradition, the blood test indicates you're pregnant with a girl.*

That was the last time I would use a queer bakery.

"It's a girl!" I held up the card and shouted a lot louder than I intended. Everyone in the room cheered back.

Yasmeen took both cards from me and read them. "Plus, a lesson on gender identity and assumptions. Who's the baker? I'm going to give her five stars on Yelp right now."

I ignored Yasmeen's probe, but truthfully, I wasn't upset about any of it.

"This is going to be the most boring video ever," Lukas said, looking down at his phone. "You sure you want me to send it to you?"

"Send it," I confirmed. While it certainly hadn't gone according to plan, it also kind of felt like it had...exactly the way it was supposed to.

I didn't know who my child was, but I didn't love them for the type of genitals (internal or external) they brought with them into the world. I ran a hand over my belly and felt a rush of warmth in my chest. I loved this child because they were mine, and I was climbing mountains to bring them into this world. And I'd keep climbing mountains to fight for them every day once they got here.

No matter what that meant for my future employment options.

Chapter Twenty-One

"**S**hout-out to all the uterus owners in here tonight," I said as I walked across the stage of the DC Comedy Loft, the microphone in one hand and a glass of water in the other. "I'm seventeen weeks pregnant right now—I know, shocking. This isn't just tacos."

I gestured toward my only slightly more swollen stomach at that last remark and the audience laughed lightly.

"But you know what that also means?" I continued, this time turning to look back at the audience. "I haven't had a period in seventeen weeks. I went over twenty years bleeding profusely without dying every single month, and suddenly, I've been on a four-month vacation, absolutely free."

The audience was laughing a bit louder now, a chatter going around the crowd. There was movement by the door near the bar and I glanced toward it to see Ari walking in.

Ari? Last I'd heard, she had been out of the country on an assignment, and so, I had not expected to see her here...or anytime soon. She walked over to the bar and took a seat on one of the stools.

I cleared my throat, trying to find my spot again in my set. *Shit.* I was distracted. "Uh, so...yeah, four months. Totally free. Except for the co-pays I've spent on OB appointments. Or the ginger drops I buy by the pound for nausea. Or the prenatal vitamins that are an insane cost for what—folic acid? So, technically, it's actually been a pretty expensive four months, and from what I hear, it only gets more expensive after the baby gets here."

Someone hooted from the side, and I pointed toward them. "Are you a parent, ma'am?"

Don't look over at Ari. Focus on your set. Involve the audience. Make them laugh. "If you had to estimate how much money you've spent on your child since they were born, what would you say?"

She hummed for a moment, then shouted out her response. "He's nineteen now, so if you count college, at least a quarter million dollars."

"A quarter million dollars," I repeated her answer louder for the entire audience, my brows raised and my tone purposely sounding incredulous. "And, ma'am, what did you get in return for that investment?"

"Nothing yet!" She laughed, and it almost sounded like a cackle. "But that's my retirement plan."

I pointed at her and smiled. "Smart. I like that. Forget a 401(k). Just have a human and let them impose on you for eighteen years in exchange for you imposing on them for the last few years of your life. It really does sound like a solid deal."

The audience was calling out different suggestions and costs now, and I went around checking in with a few people about what their child investment had gotten them, making witty remarks from their answers. I wasn't looking at the bar. I wasn't focusing on Ari watching me at all. Nope, not even a little bit.

"I signed with a comedy agent not too long ago," I told the crowd in a bit of a segue. "I'm having this baby, you know, and now I'm like...shit, I have to pay for this thing. And as you all have just informed me—children are expensive as hell. And guess what happened? My agent pitched me for a group comedy special that Netflix was going to stream, and I was like, holy crap, this is it. This is the big leagues."

The crowd clapped for me, but as in most comedy, my jokes often came from a place of pain and my roller-coaster journey in Hollywood so far—if you can even call it that—had been nearly as tumultuous as my legal career.

"So, I got the call—I was in, I was going second. They had to have a man go first, right? Patriarchy. But then two days later, I'm opening for a puppet here on this very stage, and I get a different call—I'm out. They gave my spot to Ali Wong because they said they needed more diversity. I am a Hispanic pansexual female, but that's not diverse enough."

That earned a big laugh from the crowd, and a few people shouted out how much they loved Ali Wong.

"I love her, too," I agreed. "That's why I asked for tickets to be in the audience. Hell, if I can't be on stage, at least let me watch the greats!"

I grinned at the audience and tried my best not to look at Ari.

"You guys have been amazing," I finally told the crowd as I began wrapping up my opening bit. "I'm excited to welcome the main artist to the stage next, a good friend of mine and a hilarious comedian and former wild child—Shayne Smith!"

With that, I walked off the stage while clapping as Shayne sauntered past and gave me a hug. His hair was long and down, and his body was covered in tattoos—like face, neck, arms—everywhere. I'd opened for him three times so far, and each time the crowd was amazing, and he was gracious and kind.

As I stepped off the stage into the audience to go walk out the side door backstage, I glanced over at the bar area. *Don't do it.* Too late. Ari was still sitting there, but she wasn't alone anymore. She was talking to a woman sitting on the stool next to her who had long platinum-blonde hair that nearly reached her butt. I couldn't see her face from this angle, but the way her bright-red dress clung to her from the back, I couldn't help but feel a stir of jealousy.

Stop torturing yourself. I walked through the side door to the backstage area and paused to take a deep breath, but then I felt my phone vibrating in my pocket. Fishing it out, I glanced down at the screen and felt my entire body tense as Ari's name appeared on the display.

I'm at the bar. Come chat if you have time before your next set.

Well, I certainly couldn't pretend I didn't know she was here now. She'd basically just called me out on slinking away and acting like a coward. Okay, no. My therapist would ask me why I was going straight for catastrophic thinking. Maybe Ari just wanted to say hello. Maybe she just wanted to check in on her future sperm-niece. That was probably all it was. Just a friendly hello. Completely platonic.

Does it count as lying if you say it to yourself?

I quickly typed up a response, telling her I'd be over in a few and then headed for the bathroom to check my face. After confirming in the bathroom mirror that I looked as good as I was going to get for now, I walked around the entry hallway of the venue and came back in through the door by the bar to the back of the crowd. From this angle, I could see the woman Ari was talking to clearly, and she was basically the real-life version of Jessica Rabbit.

Good God. Even I forgot about Ari for a second just looking at this woman.

Ari noticed me in her peripheral, however, and waved me over. "Hey, Mila."

"Tori," I reminded her, since we were still on-site at the venue where everyone knew me as Tori Miles. "I didn't expect to see you here. I thought you were on an assignment overseas."

Jessica Rabbit's brows lifted, and she looked even more interested in Ari. "You were traveling overseas?"

Ari nodded. "I was, but I got back last weekend. Just working on wrapping up the article now, but I should be done by next week."

"That's so cool." Jessica Rabbit leaned in closer to Ari, batting her lashes. "I've always wanted a job that let me travel like that."

"What do you do?" I asked Jessica Rabbit, forcing myself into the conversation as if I could verbally step between them.

"Eyelashes." Jessica Rabbit batted her very-long lashes at me this time, then turned back to Ari. "Don't you just love them? Eyelash extensions are such a hot trend right now. I'm completely booked. But, you know, if you ever wanted to come see me, I bet I could find some time in my schedule."

Vomit. "Oh, cool. Do you have a card? I might make an appointment." I stuck my hand out toward her, even though she was very clearly talking to Ari, not me.

She glanced back at me, looking a bit confused. "Card for what?"

"Your business?" I asked, not trying to talk down to her but also having a really hard time not doing exactly that. "Like a business card?"

Jessica Rabbit chuckled and then placed a hand on my arm as if to comfort me. "Oh, sweetie. No. My generation really prioritizes being environmentally conscious, so I have a QR code on my phone and that will take you to my Instagram. You can book through my DMs."

I know she did not just age me out of her generation right to my damn face.

"Oh, I don't use QR codes. The only phone I have is still attached by a cord to my kitchen wall," I responded, the sarcasm clearly audible. "I hear they make these handheld ones now that you can take with you. Wild, right?"

Ari's mouth was set in a tight line like she was actively trying not to smile. But I could tell by her wide eyes that she was thoroughly enjoying the exchange.

Jessica Rabbit chuckled sympathetically. "You are just so cute. Do you want to sit down? You can have my stool. I can absolutely stand."

"Thanks," I said, taking her offer and sitting my old ass down on her stool. "It's hard on my hips to stand for too long, you know?"

"No, I don't," Jessica Rabbit responded. "I'm going to run to the bathroom, but I'll be right back."

That last part was flirty and definitely aimed at Ari, not me. But whatever, at least she was gone.

"Should we be here when she gets back?" Ari asked me, now grinning. "I was a bit worried I might have to referee a smackdown there."

"Yes, please. Let's run." I laughed but grabbed her hand and pulled her toward the entrance.

Ari tossed some cash on the bar top and then followed me—hand in hand—out into the main entry. We walked past the bouncers, and I told them I'd be right back before we exited into the night on the street.

She let go of my hand when we reached the bottom of the steps and our feet landed on the sidewalk. I pretended I didn't notice.

"So, how have you been?" Ari asked, now leaning back

against a metal parking sign and looking at me. "How's the baby?"

I placed a hand over my stomach. "All good and healthy so far. It's a girl—I'm not sure if Lukas told you that or not."

Ari grinned. "He sent me the video from the gender reveal. Congratulations."

"Yeah." I laughed, a bit nervous. "That whole ordeal was a clusterfuck, but I'm seventeen weeks now. I don't think I can feel her moving yet, but sometimes I think I do. I'm not sure if it's her or just gas though."

Did I just tell Ari about my gas issues? Lord, help me.

"I think my mom said that around twenty weeks is when she felt Aston and me moving around." Ari was grinning even wider now, and I knew she was just letting me save face. "I bet that's going to be really exciting when you do feel her."

"I think so." I was smiling now, and it wasn't out of nervousness but rather excitement at the prospect of feeling this little girl bouncing around in my belly soon. It felt like this big unknown and the excitement was slowly trickling in. Not to mention, there was a warmth in my chest at the fact that Ari was asking me about my pregnancy. She didn't say things she didn't mean, and this didn't feel like lip service. It seemed like she genuinely cared. "I have the big anatomy scan in a few weeks, and that will basically tell us everything about the baby. So, I'm looking forward to that."

"Your mom going to go with you?" Ari asked.

I nodded as I sat on a stone ledge to rest my feet a few feet apart from where Ari was standing still. "Yeah, she is one hundred percent on board now. Well, more like a solid ninety percent. There's still some mild disbelief over how I went about the whole process."

"Nomi said she loved meeting her at the reunion." Ari was looking down at her shoes, and I couldn't see her eyes, but I could see her thick lashes brushing against the tops of her cheeks. "They've been texting every day since apparently."

"Really?" That was new—and mostly unwelcome—information to me. "She said that? Chicky hasn't mentioned it at all."

"For a mother and daughter who are super close, there's a lot you two don't tell each other," Ari commented.

If anyone else had said that, I'd respond defensively or probably smack the shit out of them. But there was only gentleness in Ari's tone, and for some reason, my defenses stayed firmly secured in safety.

"It does kind of seem that way, doesn't it?" I admitted, now picking at a loose piece of stone on the ledge next to me. "I'm starting to wonder if there are a lot of things in my life that aren't everything I'd once given them a pedestal for."

"Work?" Ari's brow lifted as she looked up at me. "I had been meaning to check in when I got back to town. I know the subpoena went through, but I haven't heard what they've done with the records yet. Or if they've even gone through them. Has anything smoothed over there yet?"

I shook my head and the loose stone fell off and tumbled onto the sidewalk. Oops. "No, I'm still on probation. I've started reaching out to other firms, looking for a different job. My firm requested a copy of your phone records from the Secret Service, so it's just a matter of time until they tie me to it."

"Shit." Ari sighed. "I'm sorry, Mila. I feel like I'm to blame for all of this."

"Technically, none of the current probation is related to you. Plus, I knew what I was doing and made my own choices. It was the right thing to do—the article you wrote was amazing."

"Did you see his bill was shot down in the house?" Ari's

frown lifted into a small smile. I had forgotten how much I loved her smile until this very moment. "I can't say it's directly linked to the article...but it did help."

Of course I'd seen that. "Yeah, that was the best news I'd gotten all week last week. If I wasn't pregnant, I would have had a margarita to toast the occasion."

"Makes it all worth it," Ari replied. "Still, I'm sorry for the difficulty you've experienced because of it. I really hope you don't lose your job or your license."

"Me, too," I agreed, my mind mostly centering on the thought of health insurance. I had some savings, and I owned my own house, so I didn't feel too frightened financially. But... still, giving birth in America is fucking expensive, and I wasn't sure I'd have enough to pay for that out of pocket as well as support a baby after. Not to mention the money I needed to set aside for maternity leave if I wasn't going to be getting paid maternity leave.

God, this was all so damn complicated.

"You okay?" Ari looked concerned, and I'm sure she was referencing the pukey look on my face as I was tabulating the never-ending list of dollar signs around the next few months.

"I'll have to be. Either way, I'm going to have to figure out my career options pretty soon, or the decision might be made for me. Maybe it's because of how I was raised, but doctors, lawyers, engineers—were considered careers to be proud of when I was younger. It's all I aspired to be, something that would bring pride to the Torres name." I found another loose piece of stone, and, this time, picked it up, turning it over in my hand. "But, when I'm on stage, I feel like my soul is alive in a way that it doesn't even come close to behind a desk. Maybe it's just because of what desk I'm sitting at though. Maybe it's not law entirely."

"Maybe you don't have to choose," Ari suggested. "When I

told my mother I wanted to be a writer, the first thing Nomi said was that I wasn't allowed to live at home in my thirties."

I laughed because I could definitely picture Nomi saying something like that.

"My work has gotten great acclaim and reach, but I'll probably never be rich from it," Ari continued. "But my life *feels* rich. At least, the professional part of it."

Her last sentence was quieter, and I swallowed hard at the thought of what she might be saying. *What was she saying?*

"All I mean by that is," Ari quickly continued, looking down the sidewalk now and watching a couple cross the street holding hands. They were sweet, but I wasn't looking at them. "You can have comedy, you can have art, you can have writing, you can have anything you want and still do law. Maybe even law that you're passionate about, though I'm not sure you'll find that at your current firm."

"I suspect you're right about that," I agreed, now squeezing the piece of stone tightly in my palm. So tightly that the sharper edges of it almost felt like they would break the surface of my skin, but I didn't let up the pressure. "Isa is trying to hook me up with a boutique, all-female law firm that specializes in refugee work. With the dozens of busloads of people being transported to the US Capitol steps from Texas over the last year, they've had their hands full and been expanding pretty rapidly."

"Sounds like you're already beginning to find your way off the pedestal." Ari's expression looked proud in that moment and something about it fanned my soul. "That's a lot of potential changes in a short period of time."

"It is, right? But it doesn't feel like it," I admitted. "Instead, it feels like I'm settling into a place I've been looking for. I'm not there yet, but things feel like the puzzle pieces are beginning to come together slowly. Well, most of them, that is."

Ari's gaze focused on me, and it was sharp. "What puzzle piece is still missing?"

I looked at her with as much sharpness as I could muster back, but I didn't respond. Not verbally, at least. She knew exactly what I meant. I knew what she'd meant earlier. We both knew we were talking about one another and yet neither of us said a thing.

Why couldn't I open my mouth and just tell her I missed her? I wanted her in my life. I wanted her to be the person I rolled over in bed to cuddle up next to. The realization was like a dull knife twisting in my chest, but with how much I did care about her...I couldn't ask that of her. I remembered the hurt in her eyes the last time I'd been at her apartment. I remembered how anguished she'd been when she'd told me she couldn't be involved with my pregnancy. She didn't want the life I had or was about to have. And she'd asked me—in not so many words —to not play around with her heart, and so...I wouldn't.

She deserved better than that. I did, too.

"What time do you go back on?" Ari said after a moment of quiet passed between us.

"The second show starts at nine thirty. Are you going to stay?" I tried not to sound eager or hopeful, but I wasn't ready for her to leave yet.

Ari shook her head, and her gaze avoided me this time. "I think it's better if I go."

I could learn a lesson from her in how to set boundaries because she had that shit locked down. Just another thing to admire about her. "Yeah, that makes sense. Jessica Rabbit might still be in there looking for you."

"Who?" Ari looked confused, her brows furrowed.

"The big boobs in the red dress who was fawning all over you," I reminded her. "I named her Jessica Rabbit in my head."

Ari just smiled, but she didn't respond, and she didn't feed into my fear or insecurity that she might be interested in those big boobs in the red dress, but she didn't say she wasn't either. "I'm going to go, okay? But if you ever need anything, reach out. Otherwise, I'll see you around."

I stood up from where I was sitting on the ledge, dropping the stone in my hand onto the sidewalk. It had left an impression in my palm print, but I rubbed it against the outside of my pant leg. "Okay. Well, get home safe."

Ari stepped closer to me and reached out her hand to me. I placed my hand in hers and she just squeezed it softly while we kept eye contact. "Good luck with the second show, Mila. You're really great on stage."

"Thank you." With that, she took her hand back and shoved both of her hands deep into her pockets as she turned away from me and walked down the sidewalk.

I just stood there watching her walk away, and I wanted to ask her to turn around, come back, change her mind, want what I want...want me.

"Tori, are you out here?" One of the bouncers stuck his head out of the door at the top of the stairs.

I looked up at him and waved. Once upon a time, I might have been concerned that he—or anyone in the bar——had seen me with Ari, but now that everything was out, or on the verge of being out, the secrecy seemed pointless. "Hey."

"You're up for the closing in two minutes," he informed me. "Ready?"

I climbed the stairs to head back inside. "Yeah. I'm ready."

It's showtime.

Chapter Twenty-Two

"What do you mean Reverend Steve broke his penis?" I couldn't even believe those words were coming out of my mouth, but to be fair, everything about this phone call with my mother sounded sinful. "Mother, what did I tell you about playing with the minister?"

"It could happen to anyone," Chicky's voice rang through the other end of the phone at a slightly shriller than normal pitch. "You just sit on it wrong, and, boom, it snaps like a twig. Penises are very delicate."

My twenty-week anatomy scan was in less than thirty minutes uptown, and I wasn't about to be late because my mother had a sex mishap. I grabbed my keys and swung open my front door, still on the phone with Chicky. "Can you please not tell me what you did to Steve's penis? I don't need that kind of imagery in my mind."

I stepped out into the hallway and nearly ran into Ari, who looked as stunned as I felt. In a black top and blue jeans, Ari was dressed casually and had one arm raised as if she was about to knock on the door that I'd just opened.

"Oh, uh, sorry...I didn't mean to interrupt," Ari said, her voice a whisper as she pointed to the phone.

I waved at her that it was fine. "Mom, I have to go. You can fill me in on the rest of the details later. Tell Steve I hope his dick feels better."

"I absolutely will not say that to Steve," my mother responded. "Bye, honey! Send me some ultrasound pictures!"

"Will do. Bye." I hung up the phone and gave Ari an apologetic smile. "Hey, sorry about that. I wasn't expecting you to be here."

"I wasn't expecting you to be talking about dicks," Ari replied, grinning with her brows raised.

I shrugged my shoulders because, at this point, I couldn't even be embarrassed. "Yet here we are. So, what's up? Sorry, I'm in kind of a rush. I'm headed to my anatomy scan, which my mother was supposed to go to with me. But she just canceled on me because she's at the hospital with her boyfriend —the minister—Steve, who apparently broke—or bent? I don't know how it works—his penis during sexual intercourse with her."

Ari's brows rose somehow even higher, and she pulled her lips in between her teeth, trying not to smile. She failed. "That is...a lot of information."

"Story of my life," I replied, my tone drier than the Sahara.

"Well, uh, do you want me to go with you to the scan? You shouldn't go alone. Unless you want to. No pressure or anything. I'm not trying to invite myself." Ari was suddenly rambling and almost a bit twitchy in how she wasn't looking at me directly. Her usual calm, cool, collected vibe seemed very off today.

I debated saying no for all of zero seconds. "Actually, that would be really great. I really don't want to go to this alone."

"Okay." Ari nodded and then stepped to the side to let me out. "Let's go."

I closed the front door to my house behind me and double-checked that it was locked. It was going to be weird next month when I moved, but I'd finally made a decision about the entire living situation. I was going to continue to rent out this place to Rachel and Yasmeen—or whoever wanted it if they didn't—so that their lives weren't disrupted and I was still able to cover the mortgage with their rent. For myself, however, things were going to be very different.

I was moving, and possibly to Northern Virginia.

I know, I know. Look how far the mighty have fallen. But the reality was I needed to think about my financial future carefully now that my job prospects were grim. My boss had already scheduled a meeting for him, myself, and the head of human resources on Monday, so I knew what was coming. They were going to fire me. They'd seen the records, they'd made the connections, and they knew what I'd done.

There was literally zero chance I wasn't going to be fired and then reported to the bar association. At this point, it was just a matter of time.

The one-year rental I'd found in the heart of Ballston was definitely a bit more kid-friendly than my current DC neighborhood, and the rent was more feasible when compared to district prices. I'd briefly considered buying something cheap and small just to feel a bit more secure, but it felt like there were too many unknowns to do that yet. It seemed crazy to me that so many people bought homes before becoming parents because that just feels like a lot of unknowns about what my future child is going to need or where they'll be best suited that I just can't know until they're out of the womb. But it also seemed crazy to me that people got married before having kids too, so I know I'm slightly off-center from societal norms to begin with.

Ari didn't say anything as we drove to the obstetrician's office—though she did remark on how much she loved the new car. Seconds after that compliment, I clipped a curb trying to parallel park. Normally, I would have gotten at least a snide remark or two about my driving abilities, but she seemed subdued today compared to normal. A few minutes later, as we got inside, the receptionist asked us which one of us was the patient—uh, I'm clearly the only one with the belly, but okay—Ari still barely had a reaction. If I wasn't pregnant and someone had asked me if I was pregnant, I would probably have had to book an emergency therapy session, but Ari acted like the comment barely registered.

What the hell is going on? She was beginning to make me nervous now. Had I done something? It occurred to me that I still didn't know why she'd been at my front door, but I didn't have time to ask as the ultrasound technician asked me to lie on the exam table and tuck a towel into the top of my pants and underwear.

"The gel is warm, don't worry," she said as I lifted my shirt to expose my belly. She globbed on a ton of blue lube-looking gel, and she was right—it was warm. Like, shockingly warm. Not that it burned me or anything, but I was still startled.

Ari was seated in the folding chair next to me and we were both facing the same direction, looking at a large television screen on the wall. The ultrasound technician was on the other side of me and had her own screen, but it was easier to see the projection of what she was looking at on the television rather than twist my neck to look at her screen.

"We're going to take a lot of pictures today," the technician began as she rubbed the wand against my belly. "So prepare to be here for a while. I might also ask you to turn to one side or the other as we try to obtain different images of the baby."

I mean, I wasn't going anywhere. "Okay."

The technician frowned at the screen and then looked over at my stomach. "Oh, could you hold up your stomach for me? Just right here."

She guided my hands to the bottom of my tummy-pouch-pooch-flap thingy and had me lift it up so she could swipe the wand underneath. *That wasn't embarrassing at all.* Not even a little. Definitely not, because Ari was sitting right there next to me and not only heard the entire exchange but was now staring at me while I was lifting my belly flap as high as I could stretch it. No, this was totally chill and normal. Just a regular day.

"Perfect. There she is." The technician smiled at the screen, and I looked over at the television. "Wait, did you guys already know the gender?"

I mean, if I hadn't, I would now. "Yes, we knew."

"Okay, whew. That was a close one." The technician laughed. I don't know what she thought was funny. "So, there's the head—oh, she's looking directly at us."

"Yikes," Ari commented in a stark tone. Her first reaction of the day and it was that. "She looks like a character from *Aliens vs. Predators.*"

I cast her a long look. "Gee, thanks, Ari."

"I mean it in the most affectionate way. Like a really cute alien creature," Ari kidded, squeezing my arm gently. When she pulled her hand away, I immediately wished she'd put it back. Even if she did think I was pregnant with an alien.

"They all look like that at this stage," the technician told us, and honestly, Ari wasn't lying.

When the baby looked at the camera, her eyes were just big black sockets and her skull looked enormous. Her body was smaller, but I could definitely make out the legs and arms and what looked like a snake coming out of her stomach. Wait, that's the umbilical cord. Health class really did not prepare me for this whole living-in-a-female-body thing, but it certainly did teach me how to put a condom on a banana.

"Okay, turn onto your right side and continue to hold your stomach up if you can," the technician instructed.

One of the first things I worked on when starting therapy in my early twenties was my struggle with body image, and I was proud to say that I felt like I had a pretty good handle on feeling good about myself. All that being said, this appointment and all the talk about my stomach flap were definitely going to challenge that.

I turned to face Ari, though nothing about my movement was graceful. It was reminiscent of an upside-down turtle flailing those little legs to try to get back up.

"Do you want me to hold your stomach for you?" Ari asked, the grin on her face huge.

I squinted my eyes at her in a dramatic fashion. "Does your family have a familial burial plot? Because I might need you to save me a spot after this."

"I'll see what I can do," Ari joked. "You can be next to Lukas."

"God, no."

Ari laughed as the technician kept taking pictures and rolling her wand around my side. She then had me turn to face her, my ass to Ari now, and did the same thing. Finally, I was on my back once more as the technician finished up all the rest of the photos and videos that she needed, including letting us hear the heartbeat, which absolutely got me in my feels. I noticed Ari was quiet during that, too, and her hand was on her own chest. I could see the heart beating in the video imagery, and it all felt so real like I wanted to hold my future daughter right now.

"Chicky is going to be so upset that she missed this," I said, my voice slightly thick with emotion as I watched the screen.

"I'll send a link to your phone with all the videos and photos so you can share them with friends and family," the technician said as she handed me an additional towel. "Go ahead and clean up, and the doctor will review the images and come in and talk to you shortly."

"Great." I rubbed the towel against my belly and under my tummy flap in an attempt to wipe up as much goo as I could. "You guys don't print the photos anymore?"

"You can print from the link I'll text you, but this way, you'll also have videos." With that, the technician left the room.

"I never considered how high-tech obstetrics has gotten," Ari commented.

Sure enough, my cell phone dinged a moment later and an automated message with a link came through from the doctor's practice. "Right? This feels very fancy for something women have been doing for centuries."

Ari was quiet as I buttoned up my pants and sat up, finally goo-free, or at least as good as it was going to get. I crossed my legs underneath me on the exam table and angled my body toward her. "Thanks for coming with me to this. I can't imagine this is how you planned to spend your day."

She shook her head. "I'm actually really glad I got to be here. I've never seen something like that before—it was really beautiful. Your daughter is going to be special, Mila."

Crap, there was that lump in my throat again. I nodded but didn't say anything because if I spoke, I was going to cry, and she'd already seen me hold my stomach flap today, which was enough.

"I, um, actually, on that note, I do have something I want to talk to you about," Ari said, her tone shakier than before. Was she nervous? I hadn't seen a nervous Ari yet, but I got the distinct impression she was right now.

I waved at the room around me. "I should have asked sooner what you had come to talk to me about this afternoon. But I was so focused on all of this happening."

Ari shrugged it off. "No, it's...honestly, I don't know if this is the right time. But I don't think there will be a right time."

Butterflies swirled in my stomach—oh, wait, that was the baby. "Is everything okay?"

"I just feel like I haven't been honest with you, or not honest...but more transparent." Ari looked away from me now, and the bottom lash line of her eyes welled with tears.

I reached my hand out to her, squeezing her arm. "Okay, well...you can. You can tell me anything."

This felt big, like a moment I'd been waiting for all the answers to unravel. Everything about Ari was shaded in discretion, and this felt like a huge step for her to come here and want to bare her soul to me. At least, assuming that's what she was doing.

She looked down at my hand on her arm, then up at me. "It's been hard keeping my distance these past few weeks," she finally admitted. "I...Mila, I really like having you in my life."

I swallowed hard, my heart racing faster. "I like having you in my life, too."

"But..." Ari looked away now, and my heart deflated. "I think we have to just be friends. I don't want to lose you, and I don't want to not know you. But anything more? I...I've been down this road before, and I just can't do it again."

What road? I wasn't entirely sure if she was referring to relationships, my pregnancy, or what the hell she meant by all of that, but I could see how twisted up she felt over it all. The tension and stress in her expression made me want to pull her into my arms and hug it all away, but I held back. My heart ached that I'd put her in any sort of position to feel so overwhelmed like this, and clearly, something was being triggered in her.

What the hell that was, I had no clue.

"Ari, I don't want to push you into something you don't want. I would never do that," I clarified. "If you want to just be friends, then okay. We'll just be friends."

Her shoulders sagged slightly, almost as if she was relieved to hear that. "Mila, I'm really sorry. I know you were hoping for more than that."

I could feel my cheeks heating. Had I been that obvious? Okay, yes. Yes, I had.

"I'm just glad you're part of my life, Ari." I shrugged my shoulders as if my heart wasn't tearing into pieces. "If this is what you need, if this is what you want, then it's what I want."

Liar.

Chapter Twenty-Three

*Y*our license is currently under review with the District *of Columbia Bar Association. All current legal counsel must cease until the conclusion of this investigation when a finding is determined.*

Well, fuck.

The next email that came after that doozy was from Bushel and Hope Law Firm—the all-female firm that Isa's neighbor had hooked me up with an interview. An interview, might I add, that had gone really wonderful two weeks ago, right after I'd found out I was being given a severance package at my current job and shown the door. I mean, honestly, that was a lot more than I'd expected to get, but apparently, they wanted to make sure I kept my mouth shut about what I'd done since it reflected badly on the firm. In exchange for a signature on a nondisclosure agreement, I was walking away from a job I hated with six months of pay in one lump sum. But no health insurance. Thankfully, I could use the package to extend my previous plan until I found a new job, even though that meant paying a ridiculously high premium without any help from the firm.

With the interview at Bushel and Hope so shortly after, I felt like I'd fallen onto a bit of a safety net. Things could have been much worse—after all, I was moving to Virginia—and my silence had also guaranteed me immunity on any charges for the information I leaked. The firm was so embarrassed that they had had a mole they were willing to jump through hoops to keep my name —and, more specifically, their name—out of any legal filings.

I clicked on the email from Bushel & Hope, not completely shocked to find that it was an offer letter. *Bushel and Hope Law Firm would like to extend the offer of the position of associate attorney to Mila Torres, Esq.*

Of course it was an offer letter.

Clearly, they hadn't gotten the news from the bar yet that there was an investigation happening, so I was going to have to be the one to tell them—which was completely awkward and would most likely mean that they would pull this offer.

I scrolled down to look at the next page of the offer letter, which had the start date—*flexible, we'd love to work around your maternity leave schedule as we prioritize motherhood and the work/life balance*—and the salary—*starting at one hundred and eighty thousand dollars a year but with room for bonuses.* Well, fuck me. Abbot paid me barely above six figures, which I already thought was generous, but this salary offer was the most I'd ever seen in my life. And they loved working with mothers.

God, why did they have to be so perfect?

"What's wrong?" Ari glanced up at me as she placed the large cardboard box down on the floor of my new kitchen. "You look like you're about to puke. Is this morning sickness again?"

I exited out of the email on my phone and shoved it in my back pocket, trying my best to wipe any sign of existential dread off my face as quickly as possible. There simply was not enough time to deal with this emotional and professional crap on top of everything else today.

"I'm fine," I clarified. "Nausea comes and goes."

Sorry, future kid, for already blaming things on you, but you should get used to that.

"Well, sit down." Ari gestured toward the kitchen table and chairs that we'd already brought in. "I think this was the last box, so you should just put your feet up. I can start unpacking."

"Thanks," I agreed, though she wasn't exactly twisting my arm. I grabbed a water bottle off the counter and sat down at the kitchen table, leaning back to accommodate my expanding abdomen. At twenty-four weeks pregnant now, I was definitely showing, but not like falling over large. Just semi-uncomfortable, "freshman-fifteen" kind of large.

"Where does this go?" Ari asked a few minutes later, holding up a yellow plastic gadget she pulled out of a cardboard box. "Actually, what the hell is it?"

"That's my banana filler." I had zero plans on telling Ari about the emails I'd just gotten. We'd spent the last month trying to find some version of friendship, and things had been... touchy. Or, more factually, no touching at all. I wasn't going to upset the balance we'd finally reached between us by sharing the latest disastrous development in my legal career. We were friends now. Or friendlier friends? I don't know what the hell we were, but whatever it was, it was a lot better than the back-and-forth roller coaster we'd previously been on.

"Your banana filler?" Ari held it up in front of her face and turned it over in her hands. "Are you actually completely straight and have just been lying to me for months?"

I laughed and motioned for her to hand it to me. When she did, I began demonstrating how it worked. "No, look. The banana goes here and then you can put any filling here—I prefer Nutella—and it stuffs it inside the banana for you. It was on Shark Tank."

"Oh, well, if it was on Shark Tank." Ari put her hands up defensively, but she was chuckling as she continued unloading the packed box of kitchen supplies. She held up a sponge with a smiley face on the front. "You have a Scrub Daddy, too?"

I grinned and wiggled my brows. "You're really beginning to question my sexuality now, aren't you?"

She laughed, then shook her head. "I would, except I know how you respond to a woman's tongue."

Bebe Bennet, please set me on fire. I was not prepared for that response or the way my body reacted immediately to it.

"Sorry," Ari immediately followed up, shaking her head. "That was...too far."

I wish it wasn't though. The baby immediately started kicking.

"The baby is kicking," I said, trying to divert attention from what both of us were thinking.

Ari looked up, her brows raised. "Really? You can feel it?"

"I think you can, too?" I offered, lifting the hem of my T-shirt to expose my bare belly. "Do you want to try?"

"Sure." Ari sounded reluctant, but she came over anyway and placed her palm flat against my stomach.

I waited for the baby to move, but nothing was happening. "Hold on, she'll move soon."

"Okay." Ari just continued to stand there, her hand on my stomach and the baby suddenly stone still.

Definitely not awkward at all.

Finally, a kick. "Ooh, did you feel that?"

Ari shook her head. "No. Am I in the right spot?"

I moved her hand slightly to the right, where I'd felt the kick. "There's another one. Did you feel that?"

She shook her head again. "Nothing. Maybe it's still too early for an outsider to feel something?"

"Maybe." I was a little disappointed, but I'm sure that's normal. "Sorry. Maybe soon?"

Ari removed her hand and straightened up. "What's it feel like for you?"

I thought for a moment, focusing on her movements inside me to try to figure out how to describe it. "Like a wiggle? Or fluttering, flip-flop kind of sensation, little pangs here and there? It's not consistent, but it definitely is different from, like, gas pains or digestion or anything like that. It's a feeling all on its own."

"I don't know how you do it." Ari shook her head, her lips pulled in a flat line. "I couldn't imagine having something inside my body like that. It's all so...science fiction."

I laughed, but mostly because I was a little uncomfortable by her comment. I mean, what was I supposed to say to that? It's too late now. The thing is in me and will come out one way or the other. "Well, yeah. Pregnancy is weird. It's not, like, terrible though."

"Definitely not for me." Ari crossed her hands over her chest. "More power to you and other uterus owners though. You guys are doing the hard work."

I think that was a compliment, but all it did was remind me of how different Ari's vision for her future was from mine. But that was okay because we'd agreed. Just friends. We were just friends.

"Is this a dinosaur ladle?" Ari had changed the topic to the next item she was pulling out of the kitchen box.

"That's Nessie," I clarified, trying to swallow the lump that had been forming in my throat. I didn't have time for emotions today—not about Ari and not about my potential job cluster-fuck of a situation. "She's a brachiosaurus."

"What?" Ari's brows furrowed and she stared at me, blinking slowly. "You're also secretly into dinosaurs? Okay, maybe you are queer."

I grinned. "See what you learn about someone when you become friends who help each other move?"

"Oh, you're going to help me move?" Ari asked.

"I will help you find movers," I clarified. "Like a good friend."

She laughed and shook her head. "Are you hungry? We should take a break. There's a cute breakfast place on the corner."

I *was* kind of hungry. "It's almost dinnertime."

"Breakfast time is anytime," Ari added. "Come on. Let's get you some home fries."

"Ooh, and an omelet." I pushed myself up from the chair, definitely excited now. My stomach growled in anticipation. "Extra cheese. And peppers. Can they put bacon on it?"

"Baby, I'll let you get as many toppings as you want," Ari teased, using her fake-theatrical-sensual voice, pretending to pull out her wallet and make it rain dollar bills all over. "It's on me tonight."

"Ooh la la," I joked back, but it took effort not to look at the way her body moved with the little wiggle-dance thing she was doing. Ari clearly worked out regularly, and her masculine side was one of the things I loved most about her, but there was a delicateness to the way her muscles rounded her body that made her somehow even more desirable and when she danced, it was all the more on display.

Wait, did I just say love? *I meant like.* One of the things I *liked* most about her. Because we're friends. Friendly friends. Friends who are friendly and occasionally flirty. But shouldn't be flirty. Because...friends.

Ari did a little theatrical twirl and then opened the front

door. "Come on. I'm already picturing a stack of pancakes slathered in butter and syrup."

"Shocking," I teased but followed her out. I grabbed a set of my new keys, cell phone, and my wallet and then locked the front door to the townhouse behind us as we exited onto the sidewalk.

We got to the end of the street and there was a small hole-in-the-wall restaurant or café that didn't seem to have a name to it. There was just a light-up neon sign in the window saying, "All-Day Breakfast" and a faded paper sign that said, "World's Best Coffee." Doubtful. The front door stuck as Ari pulled on it and she had to yank it hard to get it fully open, a bell chiming once she finally did.

When we stepped into the dimly lit room, there were only four small round tables with mismatched chairs around them and then a hole in the back wall that looked into the kitchen with a sign over it that said, "Order Here."

"Either this will be the best food we've ever had, or we're both getting food poisoning," Ari whispered to me as we approached the wall-hole-counter thing.

"I can't get food poisoning when I'm pregnant," I reminded her, already feeling a little nervous. "You try it first."

Ari whirled her head to face me, giving me a smiling but indignant look. "Now I'm your taste-test dummy?"

"Also, my mover and unpacker," I added, grinning.

"Fine." She rolled her eyes but was clearly laughing. "I'll do it, but only because I'm as invested in your alien baby as I am in you."

What the hell does that mean?

Ari began ordering from the old guy wearing a net around his bushy beard behind the wall and I didn't have time to ask or consider the implication of her words. But she had said that, right? She'd said she was invested in me...*and* the baby?

Not just me. *The baby.* That did not feel like "friendly-only" friends, and the hope blossoming in my chest felt dangerous and completely impractical.

It must be the pregnancy hormones. That's all. Definitely just the hormones talking.

Chapter Twenty-Four

"Try to become friends with your vagina as it stretches," the instructor standing at the front of the room was saying as I did my best not to make any eye contact with Ari who was sitting behind me.

Or with my neighbor, Naked Becky, who was seated next to me with her partner. Although, thankfully, she was fully clothed now. Really wasn't expecting her to be part of my pregnancy journey. Rachel was definitely going to be disappointed.

To the other side of Ari and me was a straight couple who very clearly hated each other, though they seemed to be under the impression that their whispered fighting wasn't audible to the rest of us. It was. She was mad that he was late to the class. He was mad that she signed them up for the class in the first place. She was mad that he never supported her. He was mad that he was missing the game on television tonight.

I'm mad that I'm listening to this in the first place.

"What am I supposed to be doing?" Ari whispered to me now, and that was enough to at least pull my attention from the angry heteros next to us.

"Uh..." I glanced back at the instructor, who was currently squatting and showing us a breathing exercise. "I guess breathe?"

Ari seemed confused. "We have to take a class to learn how to breathe?"

"Like Lamaze breathing for labor," I tried to clarify. "It's different."

She didn't let up. "How?"

I tried to show her what the teacher had done earlier, but then I quickly got dizzy.

"Mila, Ari—pay attention," the instructor called out to us, her bony finger pointing in our direction. "Don't skip ahead. Right now, we're focusing on feeling our vaginas. Imagine the stretch as the baby crowns. Feel at one with the primal energy of bringing a human onto this planet."

"Can I keep my pants on?" I asked.

The instructor cut her eyes at me. "Metaphorically, Mila. Metaphorically."

"Metaphorically feel your vagina or metaphorically keep your pants on?" Ari whispered to me, and I tried very hard not to giggle but immediately failed.

She rubbed a hand against my back from where she was sitting cross-legged behind me, and I leaned into her touch a bit more. It felt really soothing from a sore and pregnant stand-point—all the back massages, please. But it also felt affectionate and meaningful, and I was trying so hard to remember that we were just friends, but things were beginning to feel muddy, at best.

Nothing had happened between us, not physically, at least. She'd been very clear that she couldn't be more than friends with me. Loud and clear. But now we were "just friends," and we still spent an intense amount of time together. She came to at least half of my doctor appointments—my mother insisting on coming to the rest now that Steve was on the mend—and she'd, for some reason, agreed to chaperone me through this birthing class that Isa swore her coworker loved.

Twenty-eight weeks into pregnancy and this strange friendship, and I was trying my best to figure out both of them.

This birthing class, however, was a wash—why had I taken pregnancy advice from someone who'd never been pregnant?—and we'd been warned that we'd be ending the class by watching a birthing video, which I was now beginning to think was a very, very bad idea. The instructor wasn't at the video stage yet, though, and she led us through a few more positions for birthing, breathing exercises, and general knowledge about labor.

But then she announced it was time for the video.

What she didn't announce though, and what we only realized as the video began and panned out from the woman's hairy naked and bloody vagina to the woman in labor's face, was that it was the instructor's personal birthing video. *It was her giving birth.* I was now watching her son—who she informed us was now eighteen years old—bludgeon his way through the blood-streaked forest between her much-younger legs, and that was honestly an image I would never be able to erase from my mental trauma bank.

"Holy shit," Ari whispered, and her entire body stiffened behind me. "Is that...?"

I just nodded, swallowing hard. "I can't look away."

"I have to close my eyes," Ari said. I glanced at her for a brief second before returning to the scene of the crime and Ari had her eyes shut as hard as she could. "Tell me when it's over."

I didn't think it would ever be over in my mind's eye, but I couldn't form words out loud just then. The instructor was describing how she was unmedicated in this video while she was standing to the side and describing what was happening in each part and I was pretty sure Naked Becky fainted for a second next to us, but her partner smacked her cheek a little and she seemed to revive.

I was going to absolutely verbally murder Isa the moment we got out of this classroom.

"Any questions?" the instructor asked as the video came to an end. "If not, you're all welcome to head out when you're ready and send any thoughts or feedback via email. You'll also get a survey in your email about this class to review it."

Oh, I had a lot to say in that review.

Not so surprisingly, no one had any thoughts to share or questions to ask, and the entire crowd of us looked half-paralyzed, half frantically restless. Just your basic traumatized bunch of future parents.

"I need a drink," Ari said as we stepped out onto the sidewalk a few minutes later.

My knees were still feeling a little weak. "Me, too. But I guess I'll settle for a mocktail."

She grinned at me with a sympathetic tilt of her head as we walked down the sidewalk in the direction of a patio bar on the corner. "Damn. I don't know how you're going nine months without booze when what we just saw is the final result you get to look forward to."

I grimaced and the baby kicked at one of my ribs. "I just keep telling myself that I have no choice. She's got to come out one way or the other—but you can bet your ass I'm asking for every drug possible. I want to feel absolutely nothing from the waist down."

"I've never had a woman say that to me before," Ari joked.

I laughed and shook my head at her. "How do you always find a way to make a sexual joke out of everything?"

"It's a lesbian right." Ari shrugged as she held open the gate for me onto the patio bar area. "Men get dad jokes, and we get vagina jokes."

We sat down at a small, round table and a hostess dropped off two menus with QR codes and instructed us how to order from our phones. Of course, the option to order a Shirley Temple was not on there, so I had to settle for a Sprite and wrote "add grenadine" in the comments. Ari ordered a whiskey neat.

"It's like two o'clock in the afternoon," I reminded her, mostly just teasing.

"It could be nine o'clock in the morning, and I'd need a whiskey after watching that woman give birth." Ari shook her head, and thankfully a waiter arrived moments later with both drinks.

My phone lay flat on the tabletop when I saw a notification come through on my Instagram that said Ari had been tagged in a photo. I quickly put my hand over the screen in hopes she hadn't seen the notification. Was having my notifications turned on for her profile a sign of being clingy? Or just friends? I had no idea, but I wasn't about to give her the impression that I was desperado.

"What are you doing?" Ari frowned at me.

I guess the way I was awkwardly leaning across the table to hide my phone didn't seem super natural. "Uh, nothing. Just enjoying my mocktail." I took a sip. "Mmm, Shirley Temple."

"Thank God I'm fully snipped and not equipped," Ari commented. "That video will haunt me for the rest of my life."

"It was...informative," I added. "Never thought you'd be turned off by a vagina, huh?"

"Gold star lesbian over here," Ari replied, grinning and wiggling her brows. "Not that *that* matters. When I was in college, anyone who said they were a lesbian was usually a huge asshole about it. Like you were either a gold star or you didn't count. If you had so much as crushed on Justin Timberlake one time, you're out of the lesbian club. Such fucking bullshit."

I understood that sentiment all too well. "I used to literally avoid lesbians because of that. That whole wave of trans and multisexual exclusionary feminism is toxic as hell."

"Right?" Ari took another sip of her drink, nodding in agreement. "I used to worry I wasn't gay enough to be considered a lesbian. Like, what does that even mean? There was literally a group of women in college that told me that and it messed me up for years."

"The Comparison Olympics." I took a big gulp of my drink and then leaned back and took a deep breath. "I definitely didn't feel like I belonged in queer spaces for the longest time. I'm not a lesbian, though when people call me that, I don't mind. I'm just not *one* thing—whether it be sexuality or gender identity or whatever. I'm just...me. Still not really sure what that means, but I don't want a single label to define me."

"We get the chance to do things differently going forward." Ari motioned to my stomach. "You get to raise the next generation to not feel like they have to fit into any strict definitions at all. That kid there is going to know that they can be anything—or with anyone—they want to. You're going to be a really great mom at that, that's for sure."

A lump immediately lodged itself in my throat. "Thanks. I hope you're right."

"Oh, I one-hundred-percent am," Ari continued. "There's not a doubt in my mind. I'm just impressed you're still going through with all this after watching that video."

I laughed. "I mean, I'm twenty-eight weeks. This child could literally survive on her own outside of me at this point—hypothetically. She's going to have to exit my body somehow."

Ari grimaced and then pulled out her phone to scan the

menu QR code again. "On that note, I'm going to order another drink. Want another?"

I shook my head no, but then picked up my phone, too. Scrolling through it just to pass the time, I opened Instagram. Truthfully, I hadn't stopped thinking about the notification from before, and with Ari distracted ordering, it felt like a convenient time.

But that was a mistake. A Jessica-Rabbit-sized mistake.

Ari had been tagged in a photograph and the caption only read "future bae." The photo itself was even worse—it was Ari and Jessica Rabbit both holding shot glasses up in the air at some bar and looking like they were in the middle of a cheers. They were both smiling and looking happy, and it was definitely not the same night we'd all been at the comedy show because they were in very different outfits. This time Jessica Rabbit was in a silver cocktail dress that still barely reached the bottom of her ass cheeks, and Ari was in her usual muted blacks and browns.

"Mila? Did you hear me?" Ari's voice tugged me from the existential void I'd tumbled into. "I'm asking if you want mozzarella sticks. They have happy hour pricing on appetizers right now."

I looked up at her and her face immediately changed from curious to concerned.

"What's wrong?" She frowned and put down her phone. "You look like you've just seen a ghost."

I shook my head. "Nothing. Nothing's wrong."

She clearly wasn't buying that because she reached out and snagged my cell phone from my hands, looking at the screen for herself. "You're looking at my Instagram? Or I guess Cindy's Instagram."

"Cindy? Jessica Rabbit has a name now?" My tone came out a lot more snide than I intended, but I didn't take it back.

Ari handed me my phone back and let out an exhale. "Yes, I ran into Jessica Rabbit again. Her name is Cindy. She's very nice. Why does any of this matter?"

I looked away, my jaw set and my nostrils flared. "You didn't mention this to me."

"I didn't know I was supposed to?" Ari shrugged her shoulders, and I could see the conflict on her face. "I thought we talked about this. Am I supposed to be checking in with you everywhere I go?"

"That's not what I mean," I cut back. *My God, someone, please stop me.* The words were coming out of my mouth like arrows, and I could see the self-sabotage happening, but it was like I wasn't in my body. I was just watching myself speed toward a huge friendship-ending crash. "You know what I mean. You didn't tell me you ran into Cindy. What, are you guys dating now?"

Ari gritted her jaw and didn't say anything for a moment.

The waiter chose that second to arrive and drop off her next drink and a basket of mozzarella sticks, glancing between us and clearly feeling the stony silence at our table. He scurried away as quickly as possible.

"Mila, you're speaking to me as if you and I are dating. We're not." Ari's words were firm and clear, not angry, but also not gentle. "We are friends. We decided that two months ago, after what felt like months of back and forth that neither of us was enjoying."

"I know we did," I tried, but my voice sounded more like a whine.

"So, then, you cannot be angry at me for meeting or going out with other people when I'm completely single and available to do so. You are, too." Ari took a sip of her drink. "I'd support you if you found someone. That's what friends do."

"Friends." I huffed out the word like a toddler. *Oh my God, what the hell is wrong with me right now?* "Yeah, friends. Whatever, *friend.*"

Ari took a long swig of her second drink and then grabbed a single mozzarella stick and stood up from the table. "I'm going to head home. I don't deserve to be spoken to this way, and honestly, this has all been a lot harder on me than I expected. You're welcome to call me when you're ready for us to talk like adults. The tab is paid."

She took a few steps away, then turned around and walked back. My heart leapt at the chance to make things right, but Ari didn't wait. Instead, she reached for two more mozzarella sticks and then was back on her way out of my life.

I didn't say anything but purposefully looked away. My forehead was literally beginning to hurt from how hard I was frowning and getting myself in a twist, but my mad-mugging expression felt like it was there to stay.

Goddamn her and her stupid, healthy boundaries advocating for herself. Clearly, we couldn't just be friends. And clearly, I needed to book an emergency session with my therapist this week. I groaned and dropped my chin to my chest, but all that did was have me staring at my stomach.

How the hell was I supposed to raise a child when I still reverted to acting like one over the smallest emotional trigger?

Chapter Twenty-Five

"So, you have to do the gender reveal, then the baby shower, then after the baby is here, you have a sip-and-see party?" Lukas's face was scrunched up in confusion as he stood in front of the giant diaper cake—which is not a cake at all, but rather a giant tower of rolled-up decorated diapers—and spoke with Nomi, who currently had two blown-up balloons under her shirt like some sort of double pregnant alien belly.

"Kid, you just don't get it." Nomi shook her head, her hand patting one of her clothed balloons. "Babies are celebrations!"

"But, like *three* parties? What has the baby even done yet to earn the celebration? I hit three million followers on TikTok last week. I should be the one getting a party." Lukas clearly was already very comfortable with Nomi, which was nice to watch. The way they all intermingled as this strangely dynamic family felt special and like I was seeing behind a curtain that maybe my child would one day enjoy.

But Ari wasn't at my baby shower today, and I hadn't seen her since we'd had our little spat. Argument? *Fight* seemed too strong of a word. But still, it had been two weeks and no contact except an RSVP notification on evite.com that she wasn't able to attend today. She also hadn't posted on Instagram since or been tagged in anything new. Not that I was checking daily. Except for the whole checking daily thing.

"Do you want to open the presents during the party or after?" Chicky asked, bustling up beside me with rosy cheeks and an excited lift to her brows. "I want you to open my gift in front of everyone, *mija*."

That was a bad sign. "Uh, I hadn't really thought about it."

We had decided to go a little fancier than the gender reveal, and this time we were hosting it in the lounge area of a local restaurant in the early afternoon on a Saturday before they opened for big crowds later this evening. Chicky had taken care of all the decorations, and it looked like pink streamers had thrown up everywhere. She even had asked the manager to put Taylor Swift—sorry, I mean Gaylor Swift, if you know, you know—over the sound system and it was gorgeous. There were literal baby bottle confetti on all the tabletops, which the restaurant manager had been very clear I was responsible for cleaning up before the dinner shift began, and there was a table full of open diapers smeared with different brown smushy stuff that we were supposed to guess what it was. They all looked like shit—literally. That was the point. Except the one that had a few nuts mixed in there—that was either a melted Snickers or someone with serious gastroin-testinal issues.

"Well, are you hungry? Let me fix you a plate," Chicky doted on me, leading me over to a bench seat by the table and encouraging me to sit down. "Sit. Sit."

That wasn't a hard request because at thirty-one weeks, my belly was very clearly protruding and I was still figuring out how to readjust my center of balance without tipping forward.

I let out a sigh as I melted onto the bench, leaning back and letting my stomach take up all the space it wanted to.

Isa plopped down on the bench next to me with a huge sigh. "Can you believe you're like two months away from being a mom?"

I lifted my brows and glanced over at her. "Sometimes it already feels like I am, though I'm sure it's going to be an entirely different ballgame once she gets here."

"Have you decided on a name yet?" Isa grinned and nudged me with her shoulder. "I know you said you were keeping it quiet, but like...I don't count, right? I know everything. And if you're going to name her after me, I should be the first to know, don't you think?"

"I'm not naming her Isa." I chuckled and shook my head. "I haven't made a firm decision yet, but there are a few ideas that I'm contemplating."

Isa pouted. "I mean, I guess, but like, you can tell me and then always change it later."

"Or not," I commented as Chicky returned and placed an overflowing plate of food on the table next to me. "Thanks, Mom."

"Eat." She picked up a tamale and handed it directly to me. "The baby is starving."

"The baby is fine," I assured her, but I swear to God, if she kept up with all this baby-slash-pregnancy advice for the next nine weeks, I might lose my mind. She visited my new place at least once a day, which I didn't totally mind because she brought food or cleaned something, and I was getting pretty exhausted at this stage. But still, it was an insane drive from her house and made me feel super guilty. Plus, I needed some space, and the constant recommendations and mother-knows-best vibes were getting exhausting. "But I'll eat because your daughter is hungry."

Chicky grinned. "Okay, I'm going to go make sure everyone got a chance to put their guesses in on the game before we figure out who won."

Aside from the diaper game, there was also a giant bottle full of M&M's candies that people were supposed to guess how many were in there. There was also a trivia game about...well, me, to see who knew me the best. And then there was my cell phone sitting on the table next to my plate, lighting up with Ari's name on the notifications.

I swallowed the bite of food I was eating and felt it sink like a stone in my gut. I picked up my phone so carefully it probably seemed like I thought it might electrocute me or something, but it had been two whole weeks. Two weeks in which I had not once reached out to apologize. Honestly, I wasn't entirely sure if I was sorry yet for how I'd spoken to her. I wanted to be. From a logical standpoint, I knew I'd been super petty, but the rejected, bitter part of my soul wasn't ready to rejoin the high road just yet.

Hope you have a great baby shower today! Sorry I couldn't make it. Traveling for work. I sent a gift with my mom.

Simple, unemotional, factual. Pretty much exactly what I should have expected in a text from Ari. Somehow, I still felt let down. As if she was supposed to have texted me how much she missed me and loved me and how much she wanted to make things work and be a whole damn family together. A family she didn't actually want, and I really, really did. I rubbed a hand across my belly, and nothing felt truer in that moment than the fact that I wanted this baby girl and I wanted to be her family. However that looked.

"You look so in love with her already," Nomi commented with a sweet smile as she came and sat in a chair next to Isa and me. "I remember that feeling with my first. Ari was a kicker. I swear to God, she came out of the womb punching and kicking everything she could."

"That tracks," Isa agreed.

I grinned because I could absolutely see that. "Motherhood is going to be wild, huh?"

Nomi nodded. "But when she was in my belly, I'd sing softly and rub my stomach when I wanted her to calm down. Worked like a charm. She'd settle immediately. Same when she was a baby. When I'd be trying to get her to fall asleep, she'd roll over onto her back and say, *'Mama, rub my belly.'*"

She paused for a moment, like the memory was playing out before her right then and there. My heart lurched at the thought of that one day—my daughter asking me for love and comfort. Emotions during pregnancy felt like they were under a magnifying glass and ready to burst from my chest whenever I thought about life with my daughter.

"I miss those days," Nomi continued, her voice softer, with a slight catch to it now. "Ari, especially. Aston's always been a mama's boy. Still lets me cuddle him and rub his head when he's sick. Ari, though...she doesn't let anyone touch her. Not unless her guard is one-hundred-percent down, and that's something I don't get to see in her often. You try your best with your kids, you know? But they all grow up to be their own people and you get to just love them as they are."

"She seems intense," Isa added. "But she's definitely brought a smile to my best friend's face more than once. That goes a long way with me."

Nomi tilted her head to the side and her gaze pierced through me as if daring me to not say more. "Chicky told me about Ari coming to her house a while back for Sunday dinner with Lukas. Sounds like you guys have become pretty quick friends."

"Friends?" Isa let out a very unceremonious snort. "That's the most complicated friendship I've ever seen then."

"We are friends," I clarified, though the tremble in my voice threatened to out me. "We were. Are. I mean, she's...she's really wonderful. I'm sure she's going to be a great aunt."

"There's no doubt there," Nomi agreed, leaning back in her chair and smiling wider. Her investigative stare seemed to relax. "She's always wanted a big family."

"I mean, not really though." The words cut out of me a bit harsher than I intended. "Not given everything she's done to prevent that from happening."

Nomi's brow furrowed like she didn't understand.

Shit, was Ari's sterilization not public information? I immediately started to backpedal. "I mean, like, it doesn't seem like she wants to become a mother. She's been open about that."

"She doesn't want to be pregnant," Nomi clarified, then waved her hand around the room. "But Ari's pretty intent on the fact that family comes in all forms. Heck, this room is a good example of that."

Isa stood up and glanced at me, her brows raised. "I'm going to go grab a drink and let you two talk in private."

The moment she walked away, I turned back to Nomi. "Are you saying that Ari doesn't want to be pregnant, but she does want to be a mother?"

Nomi shrugged. "I haven't asked her recently, but that's the last information I had. With everything that happened with her first girlfriend during the summer between high school and college, Ari keeps her heart pretty guarded, you know? That kind of trauma can take a toll on someone, and it certainly did on her. She takes time to warm up, but I've never met anyone more perfect for motherhood one day, however it may come to her."

My throat felt like it was swelling closed, but I managed to gasp out one more question. "What happened with her first girlfriend?"

Nomi's expression faltered. "Uh, well, I'd encourage you to ask Ari for the details. It's her story to tell, you know? But the basics that most people know are when she was a teenager, her girlfriend was assaulted and a pregnancy resulted from that—a pregnancy that her girlfriend didn't survive after an attempted termination led to an infection that wasn't found quickly enough."

I tried to inhale, but I couldn't. The breath was stuck in my chest with the aching throb of a completely broken, devastated heart. Why hadn't she ever told me this story? Why hadn't I ever asked? The realization hit me like a cinder block—it had always been about me. Every interaction with Ari had been based on something I needed or wanted. And she gave—over and over again, she gave to me in every sense of the word. But I didn't give back. I didn't ask her what she needed. I didn't ask her who she was or what made her into that person.

"Nomi, I'm..." I tried to find the words, but, fuck, what words are there? "I'm so sorry."

She waved me off. "Maybe you should talk to Ari. She gets back into town tomorrow morning. I know she'd be open to telling you the full story. She talks about you a lot, you know."

I didn't respond to that either because everything in my chest was a mixture of guilt, love, heartbreak, sorrow, and God knew what else. A sob lifted in my chest, and I swallowed hard to try to contain it.

Nomi stood and squeezed my hand. "You're going to have a wonderful family, Mila."

"It's time for gifts!" Chicky was clapping her hands loudly from the gift table and motioning me to come join her. "Mila, come. Let's open the gifts!"

I pushed myself to my feet on autopilot because I couldn't

even hear the rest of what Chicky was saying. My entire body felt numb, and all I wanted to do was run—okay, waddle—out of my own baby shower and find Ari right now. *I need to apologize.* I needed to beg her to forgive me for being so fucking selfish because, at this point, I definitely didn't deserve to be with her in any romantic sense since I hadn't even earned her friendship. In fact, I might be the worst fucking friend out there.

"Mila, open mine first." Chicky pushed a large, wrapped gift into my hands once I was seated on a chair in the center of the pile of gifts. I fumbled with the wrapping paper as people gathered around to watch, and I didn't even blink when I pulled out a Beebo.

"What the hell is that?" Yasmeen shouted out from where she was standing to the side on her third or fourth baby-themed cocktail. "It looks like an adjustable boob."

Chicky grabbed the Beebo from me and held it up for the crowd to see. "It's an over-the-shoulder hands-free baby bottle holder! Meet the Beebo!"

When she put it on my shoulder, I didn't even move and I barely registered that it was happening. Suddenly, I stood up and the Beebo fell off my shoulder onto the ground.

Chicky frowned at me, her hand on my arm. "Are you okay? You look so pale."

"I need some water," I found myself saying, but the words sounded like they were coming from someone else.

"Okay, people, move aside." Chicky began parting a path in the crowd of people toward the drinks station. "Pregnant lady needs water. Move! Move! Move!"

Someone shoved a cup of cold water into my hand, and I drank it faster than I used to chug beer in college. I couldn't stay here any longer. I needed some air. "Mom, I'll open the gifts later. It's too stuffy here. I need to take a moment."

"Let me walk you outside," Chicky offered. "Fresh air is so good for you and the baby."

I shook my head. "No, I've got it."

For once, she didn't push back but just nodded and let me go. I didn't have enough brainpower to think about what a big step that was for the two of us. I just walked to the exit.

Isa met me at the exit and said nothing. She just walked alongside me and held the door open for me until I got to the sidewalk and took a seat on the curb—which, by the way, is actually very hard to do with a pregnant belly. But Isa sat next to me, and we both just stared out in front of us.

"Am I a bad friend, Isa?" I asked after a few quiet moments.

Isa put her hand on my knee and squeezed. "The fucking worst."

Uncontrollable laughter bubbled up from my chest and I shoved her with a push of my elbow. She grinned and laughed with me, and we didn't say anything else at all because that was more than enough. When I felt ready to go back inside, Isa held my hand, and we walked in together and I made a vow to myself and my future daughter right then and there that I was going to make all the changes I needed to make in order to be the mother she deserves. The self-focused, lying-prone version of me was in the past, and it wasn't going to come into my daughter's future.

Or Ari's.

Chapter Twenty-Six

The law offices of Bushel & Hope were on the top two floors of a three-story building downtown—the retail stores on the bottom being a Starbucks, a queer-aligned bookstore, and a bakery that only sold CBD-oil-infused products. So, you know—typical DC.

When the elevator doors opened on their floor, I was immediately impressed at how the inner decor had transformed the space. Everything about the office was minimalist and plant-focused—seriously, what is it with everyone and plants? The wallpaper was a pattern of green leaves, the floor was a rich, dark wood, and every corner of the room had a ficus tree that seemed like it might outgrow the space pretty soon.

The receptionist gave me a cheeky smile and motioned me over to the front desk, immediately handing me a bottle of cold water from the mini-fridge behind her. "Good afternoon, ma'am. Who are you here to see?"

I took the water, a little surprised at the immediate courtesy. Points for them already. "Uh, Patty Bushel and Genevieve Hope."

"Oh, are you Mila Torres?" The receptionist's eyes widened like this was the most exciting thing that had happened to her all day. "Come on back. I've got everything ready for you all in the conference room."

I followed her down a hallway lined with glass window offices until she motioned for me to enter a glass-walled conference room with one long table in the center surrounded by soft-looking fabric chairs.

"Take a seat wherever you're most comfortable," the receptionist said. "I'll let the partners know that you're here. They'll be here in two shakes."

I had no idea what that meant, but I did as instructed and picked a chair on the longer side of the table that was close to one end. I was seated a bit farther back than I normally would be to accommodate room for my belly, and the pencil skirt I was wearing threatened to rip at the seams if I tried any other position. Not that it wasn't already burgeoning with the pants extender I had holding the buttons closed in the back or the blazer I had worn, despite the heat, to cover up evidence that the skirt wasn't able to fully zip up anymore.

"Mila, thank you so much for coming in," a woman in tall heels said as she walked into the room and reached for my hand. I went to rise, but she shook her head. "Please, don't get up. I'll come to you. I'm Patty, and this is Genevieve."

Another woman was behind her, a bit stockier and shorter but with bright-blonde hair and a large, extravagant hair clip on the side of her head. We all shook hands, and Patty took the seat perpendicular to me and laid a folder out in front of her, while Genevieve sat across from me.

"So, let's cut straight to the chase," Patty began, her hands flat on the table in front of her as she looked at me. "The DC Bar sent us the same notice that I'm sure they sent you. Your current investigation is in the final stages, and they plan to have a decision on record by the end of next week."

I had gotten that email notice earlier this week, and I had no idea what way they were leaning. "Correct. I understand if this means that you're going to pull your offer."

Patty nodded her head, her lips in a straight line. "Frankly, we've spoken to our contacts down there, and it doesn't look like the investigation is going to go in your favor."

Fan-fucking-tastic. I swallowed hard.

"We are, however, willing to wait out the decision before moving forward. If, by some small chance, they do return your license, we'd be willing to continue with the offer as originally intended."

"And if they pull my license?"

Genevieve leaned forward, her elbows on the conference room table. "That would clearly be the worst-case scenario, but it would mean we wouldn't have a choice other than to pull our offer. We love your résumé, and we love what you've done in your career, but this is something we can't overlook."

Do not get choked up in front of two female powerhouses. I cleared my throat and nodded my head to give me a few seconds to consider my response. "That is, uh, well, that's completely understandable. I know I've put you all in a difficult situation, given the way I had to leave my last firm."

"Here at Bushel & Hope, we consider confidentiality to be of the utmost importance to our ethics and standards that we provide clients," Genevieve began. Patty nodded beside her. "But we also are very selective in the clients that we choose to work with. We champion women's rights, queer issues, and anything related to female empowerment."

"One of the things I love the most about this place." I hoped a little flattery might help smooth things over.

"Definitely," Genevieve agreed. "So, we have to make clear

—if we were to move forward and your license was reinstated, there can be no leaks here. Period. And while we certainly are not saying you were the leak at your last firm—that is for the bar to decide—we do want to know what your thoughts are on the reason for the leak in the first place."

I could hear what they were asking without actually asking it. "While I can't speak for the source of this leak, I would imagine that given the content leaked, it was for social justice purposes. That bill Senator Murphy was championing would have pushed women back decades, and I can't imagine whoever leaked it felt like they could sit back and watch that happen. Not when they could do something to help."

Patty and Genevieve looked at me a moment longer, then looked at each other. They seemed to share a private conversation in just their expressions, but then they both nodded and looked back at me.

"That's what we want at Bushel & Hope—someone who's willing to go above and beyond to protect women. But, in order for us to do that, to truly champion women's issues, we have to play within the lines of the law. It can be frustrating and limiting at many times, but it also has made us very successful in pushing legislation and helping women in need. Do you feel that that is something you'd be able to do one hundred percent of the time, including strict confidentiality?"

"Absolutely. I can definitely do that, and even more so because this is a cause that means a lot to me. It aligns with everything I'm passionate about, and I wouldn't want to do anything to jeopardize that."

They both seemed satisfied with that answer. "So, for now, we wait," Genevieve said. "Hopefully the bar will give us good news soon and this can all be a distant memory."

"I appreciate that," I replied.

"One more question," Patty added, this time a small smile

appearing on the corners of her lips. "Can we bug you for some tickets to your upcoming comedy show this weekend?"

I blinked quickly because it had not occurred to me that they knew about Tori Miles. "Uh, wow. I'm sorry, I wasn't expecting you to be familiar with my work outside of...work."

"Huge fans," Genevieve replied. "We were at your show at the Arlington Drafthouse a few months ago for a corporate outing—most of the staff were there. We just loved it. You're very funny."

"And we're big proponents of having interests, hobbies, whatever, outside of law," Patty reminded me. "So, we're absolutely on board with the whole stage-self versus courtroom-self dichotomy thing you've got going on."

Holy shit, I didn't realize such a perfect workplace could possibly exist. "That's incredible. I'd be happy to get you guys tickets, absolutely."

"Yay!" Patty clapped her hands, then stood from her seat. "So, we're all set, and we'll be in touch as soon as the bar makes a decision."

I shook their hands and told them how much I appreciated their time. I walked out of Bushel & Hope, feeling the first sliver of hope I'd felt about my career in a long time. That hope, however, seemed to run out the moment I hit the sidewalk and knocked shoulders with Ari as she was walking out of the queer bookstore next door.

"Oh, sorry!" Ari said before realizing that it was me. "Mila. I didn't expect to see you here. I'm sorry I ran into you like that. Are you okay?"

She was gesturing to my stomach, and I nodded my head to assure her that, physically, I was fine. "Yeah, barely a bump. Everything is fine."

"Okay, good." Ari stared at me for a moment, like neither of us knew what to say.

"I'm actually glad I ran into you," I blurted. "I was hoping we could talk."

I certainly could have said that via text or phone call at any point since the baby shower, but I had struggled with finding the words. Or even emotionally figuring out what to do.

Ari glanced around and then pointed to the Starbucks on the corner. "Want to grab a coffee for a bit?"

"Sure." I followed her the short walk over, and we placed our orders with the barista—decaf for me, extra shots for Ari— then we staked our claim to two armchairs in the corner that were diagonally facing one another and forward at the same time.

"What brought you back to the district now that you're a Virginia resident?" Ari asked, fiddling with the receipt for her coffee in her hand.

"Job interview. Or, I guess, an almost job offer until the bar makes a decision about my ability to continue practicing law or not." I spied our drinks being placed out on the counter, and Ari got up to go fetch them. I resumed my explanation when she returned, drinks in hand. "It seems like a really lovely place to work, so I'm excited about all of that if it pans out."

"That would be amazing," Ari agreed, sipping her caffeine cocktail. "I know I've said it before, but I'm sorry about every-thing with the bar. My editor told me about the investigation. I wanted to reach out, but it seemed like you wanted space. Or maybe I needed space. I don't know where we left things, to be honest."

Her candor was jarring and refreshing all at the same time. "I think I did need the space, but I needed it to take a good hard look at myself."

Ari's brow furrowed as she looked at me.

"Everything between us has been really one-sided," I continued, avoiding her gaze now. A lump was beginning to form in my throat and my skin felt hot and clammy. "I've been really focused on my own journey—my pregnancy, my career, my comedy, my love life, my everything. There hasn't been room to focus on anyone else. There wasn't room to focus on you. And there should have been."

Ari took another sip of her drink and cleared her throat. "Hey, you took a big risk for me with the senator's file."

"Even doing that was for me—it was me pushing my own agenda." I waved a hand, dismissing her nicety. "I've become very comfortable over the last decade only thinking about myself, saying whatever I need to say—true or not—to get what I want or need. I've been realizing lately that that *has* to change —not for me or you, but for this baby."

I rubbed a hand over my stomach, my smile wry and grim. I took a deep breath because my chest felt restricted. "She deserves a mom who puts her first and who does the same for the people in her life that she loves. It can't keep being about me."

"You sound like you're going to be a great mom," Ari replied softly. She leaned forward and placed a hand on my knee. "Look, there's no bad blood between us. I appreciate the apology, but I've known who you were since we met, and I've really liked that person. I still really like that person."

"She's not going anywhere," I assured her, this time with a light chuckle. "But she's going to make some changes. Starting with being there for a friend. Like, as a real friend this time."

Ari squeezed my knee, and I reached for her hand, taking it between both of mine. My hands were shaking, and I worried she might feel that, but I couldn't seem to control them.

"Nomi told me about your girlfriend after high school," I admitted, my voice lower and more solemn now. "Not every-thing, but the gist. I'm so sorry I never asked more about you and your life. I'm so sorry I put myself over your needs and wants again and again. That was shitty friendship on my part."

Ari's eyes lifted to mine, and I was pretty sure there was a hint of tears on her lower lashes but they didn't feel sad. I wanted to wipe them away, but they mesmerized me at the same time. She was normally so stoic and seeing this side of her felt like a gift—one I'd chosen not to unwrap for way too long.

"I would like to tell you more about myself, about my past," Ari finally said, clearing her throat. "What Nomi told you... that's not the full story. I want to be more transparent and tell you everything. I've done a lot of work on healing from it, but it's always hard to tell the whole story over again. Mila, I..."

She paused like she was struggling to find the right words. The expression on her face was vulnerable, timid, and I wanted to pull her into my arms and kiss her until she could feel how deeply true my words were. I wanted to ask her to give us a chance to be together, to try again, despite the fact that that would go against the promise of friendship I had just offered.

But as I opened my mouth, my breath hitched, and the room seemed to dim at the edges.

"Mila? Are you okay?" Ari's voice sounded farther away than it had a moment ago. She was still sitting in her chair, but she seemed to be tilting to the side in a way that didn't seem like it would work with the laws of physics.

I frowned at her and tried to respond, but the dim edges rushed into total darkness, and Ari disappeared with it.

Chapter Twenty-Seven

All I could hear upon rousing back to consciousness was loud wailing and crying, like the kind you might hear at a funeral. I opened my eyes slowly, trying to adjust to the harsh fluorescent lighting above me. *Am I dead?* My gaze finally landed on the back of Chicky's head where she had placed it in my lap, most of her body seated on a chair next to the hospital bed I was apparently in.

Not dead. Just around a very dramatic mother.

"Mom," I said, my voice cracking like plaster as I realized how dry my mouth was. "Why are you crying?"

"Oh!" Chicky's head shot up and she jumped to her feet, clapping her hands. "Mila! You're alive! Ari, call the doctor! She's alive!"

I hadn't noticed Ari was there at all, but now I saw movement from the other side of the bed and looked over to see her grinning at me from a plastic chair.

"You're awake," she said, just a bit breathless and I wondered if she'd been holding it for me. She was pressing the call button on a giant remote pad attached to the wall. "Good to see you back in the land of the living."

"I am awake," I confirmed, quickly glancing down at my stomach. Everything appeared normal—still pregnant. I didn't feel any pain, but just an overall sense of fatigue, which I'd pretty much gotten used to over the last seven months. "But also very confused. What happened?"

"Oh, sweetheart, it was horrible," Chicky volunteered. "You were just sitting with Ari, and then the next minute, you were slumped over like an overstuffed rag doll."

Gee, thanks for that image. "I fainted? Were you there? I don't remember."

Ari shook her head and stood beside the bed, holding the railing with both hands. "No, you and I were at Starbucks, remember? I called your mom when we were in the ambulance."

"And good thing she did," Chicky added, her tone stark and dramatic. "Oh, my baby girl, anything could have happened. I was so worried."

Okay, her tone was starting to freak me the hell out. I looked to Ari for something coherent and sane. "Is the baby okay? Am I okay? What did the doctor say?"

"You're fine and so is the baby," Ari assured me, her hand on my arm now. "That was the first thing I asked them to do—check on the baby. The doctor said it was most likely due to low blood pressure. They're just monitoring you and the baby now to make sure that doesn't happen again, but they said it can be normal in pregnancy—especially when someone isn't getting enough rest."

"When I was pregnant with you, I called them my sparkly moments," Chicky added. "But I never fully fainted. Have you been eating enough? What about sleep? How's your rest?"

I hadn't *not* been taking care of myself, but the recent stress of the bar investigation and the argument with Ari had been weighing on me. I'd tossed and turned for the last few nights, and I'd wanted to blame that only on pregnancy insomnia and trying to get comfortable in this new body, but the truth was that my mind was racing, and I'd felt this heavy sense of numbness over the last two weeks. It wasn't the first time I'd had that experience—depressive episodes had always been something I'd struggled with—but this was my first time living alone during one. Normally, I'd turn to my roommates for extra social time or comfort, but now, being on my own, I'd just been focused on finding a job or isolating myself from the world.

"I guess I could be better at both of those things," I said hesitantly. "It's been a hard few weeks. I feel okay right now, though."

"I'm going to go check on the doctor and see why he isn't in here yet," Chicky said as she walked for the door to the hallway. "Shout out if you need me and I'll come running back."

I definitely was not going to do that.

"I'm glad you're feeling better," Ari said, sitting back down in the chair and propping her elbows up on both knees. "You really scared me there for a minute."

I could see in her eyes how true that was. "I appreciate all you did to get me here and calling Chicky. That was really nice of you to care like that, especially after everything that happened between us."

"Nothing happened between us." Ari shook her head. "We're good, Mila. I promise we're good. You just need to focus on you and that baby. Also, Chicky said she's going to move in with you until the baby is born, so if you need an escape plan, I'm here to brainstorm."

"Good God," I grunted, though that idea sounded exactly like my mother. "I can't decide if that would be more helpful or detrimental to my mental health."

"Yeah..." Ari shrugged. "Aston and Nomi checked in as well, plus Isa, Yasmeen, and Rachel, of course. Everyone is eager to hear from you when you're back up on your feet to see how you're feeling."

That felt really good. My own little cheering section waiting in the wings. Despite the concerns I had about people I may have pushed away or the type of friend that I hadn't been, there were so many wonderful, good people who'd stuck by me for years. I was going to make sure that they knew how grateful I was to them. Not for me or to make myself feel better for being a bit more self-focused than I had realized, but to prioritize this baby's future village.

She deserved them a hell of a lot more than I did.

"Ari, can I ask you a question?" My mother wasn't back yet, and I just needed to know.

Her brows perked up. "What's up?"

"You were saying...you were saying I didn't have the full story." There were still pieces of our conversation that I remembered, and even though we were in the hospital for me, I wanted to give her a moment just about her. "Would you tell it to me?"

Her expression faltered for a moment, like she was deciding how much she really wanted to share with me or how honest she could be after I'd passed out on her the last time. Finally, she cleared her throat.

"When my girlfriend found out she was pregnant, she was...she was really desperate to end it. It was like this permanent reminder inside of her that that man had attacked her, taken a piece of her..." Ari shuddered at the memory, and I reached out a hand to her. She let me hold her hand and didn't try to pull away. "Her parents wouldn't sign for her to get an abortion like she wanted—they were the type who believed everything happened for a reason—and she was younger than me and not able to legally consent to the procedure without them. So, she...she could only think of one solution and that solution meant I'd lose her, too."

I swallowed hard. "Ari..."

She continued. "I couldn't let her hurt herself. I couldn't imagine living without her, you know? She was my first love. My first everything. I had to help her. Teen hormones were running the show and I couldn't think logically—I just felt like I had to be her white knight. I had to help her get rid of the pregnancy, or I'd lose her entirely."

Her voice strained and caught in her throat. I squeezed her hand tighter, dreading where this story was going.

"I didn't know what I was doing," Ari was whispering now, but her voice was strong and tense. "We had asked a few friends, looked up random things online, and finally bought some off-script medications from this pharmacist who lost his license a few months later. I gave her the pills."

I pushed my legs to the side of the bed and tried my best to sit up, putting my arms around Ari's shoulders and pulling her into my chest. "It isn't your fault, Ari. None of that was your fault."

"I know," she whispered back. "Believe me, I know. I've been in therapy ever since then, and I've done all the steps. The grieving, the self-forgiveness, all of it. But, healing isn't linear and meeting you, going through this pregnancy with you...I had to set boundaries and work on healing those old wounds again."

It dawned on me how often she had set boundaries with me over the last few months, whether it had been physical touch, or the way I spoke to her, or the way she wanted to be treated. In fact, her consistent modeling of healthy boundaries was probably what pushed me toward realizing I didn't have many of my own.

"Sorry," Ari finally said, looking away from me. "I know

that's a lot of information. And it's not on you. It's not your fault that this whole thing has been a trigger for me and my own past."

"I wish I'd asked earlier," I said. "I'm sorry, Ari. I'm sorry I didn't. You've talked a lot about how family can be whatever you make it. I should have asked what that meant for you."

"For the longest time, I thought that was completely off the table for me," she admitted. "But, now sometimes I dream about what it would be like to be married to a woman who loves me just as I am, raising children together who feel supported and cherished. Having all the things I had said were so off-limits to myself at one point."

I swallowed hard because her admission made me feel hope, and that was scary. "Ari..."

"Baby, guess what!" Chicky burst into the room with so much gusto that the curtain literally flew open. "The doctor's coming right behind me, and he goes to Steve's church. What a small world, right?"

"Just miniature," I responded to my mother, though my eyes didn't move off Ari. We continued to stare at each other a moment longer, and I wanted to say so much more, but not in front of my mother. And not in a hospital gown.

"It looks like your mom has a handle on things," Ari finally broke the silence. "I'm going to head out if that's okay. I have a deadline I have to hit by midnight."

"Of course," I replied. "I'm just grateful you came at all."

She reached for my hand and squeezed it. "Feel better. Call me if you need anything."

I nodded that I would and then she left the room, her jean jacket hooked on her finger over one shoulder.

"Did you guys hook up while I was out in the hall?" Chicky asked, wiggling her brows at me. "Is that the term the kids use? Hook up?"

"What?" I let out a huff. "Mom, God, no. What are you talking about?"

She shrugged her shoulders and took a seat at the bottom of the bed. "The sexual tension in here...I'm going to be the next one to faint if you guys don't cut it out, *Dios mio.*"

"Mom..." I groaned and rolled my eyes like I was fifteen again. "I don't know what to do."

"About what? The baby? The job? The woman? Sweetheart, you're juggling a lot of balls for someone who prefers *coño.*"

I cringed. "Okay, you're definitely not moving in with me."

"Sweetheart, you're delirious. You don't know what you're saying. *Ay,* where is that doctor? Someone should check you." She got up to look out the door into the hallway then looked back at me. "I swear, I have to do everything myself around here."

I lay back on the pillow and stared at my vitals on the monitor next to me. All I wanted was to be out of this room, out of this building, and begging Ari to give me a second chance. Or maybe it was a first chance. Either way, I couldn't just be her friend anymore.

And I thought she might feel the same way.

Chapter Twenty-Eight

"Wait, it still needs something." Emily squinted her eyes as she surveyed my outfit from top to bottom, where we were standing next to the concrete platform on the edge of the playground that was covered with a wooden pavilion.

Isa nodded in agreement next to her, her arms over her chest.

Emily snapped her fingers like she suddenly got an idea. "Ooh, here. Hold on." She reached into the diaper bag on the bench next to her and pulled out a tube of travel-sized toothpaste, unfastened the top, and then squirted it at my top, just like...plop.

"What the hell!" I jumped back, but it was too late. White-and-green toothpaste was dripping down my right breast and onto the top of my now-quite-large baby bump.

Emily reached forward and rubbed it into the fabric further, turning it from a gross mess into a lifestyle choice. "There. It looks like a baby spit-up. More realistic, you know?"

"I do not understand mothers," Isa said, grimacing as she looked down at my shirt. "Y'all are your own special brand."

"Since when is baby spit-up green?" I asked, looking down at the mint green streak in the toothpaste.

"Children are disgusting," Emily assured me, waving her hand like it was no big deal. "Anything goes. Your hair is too tidy, as well."

"I got that one," Isa stepped in, wiggling her fingers in front of my face, then running them through my hair and creating half a bird's nest in front of the messy bun that was trying to contain the rest at the back of my head. "Perfect, now you look like you just rolled out of bed like that."

"In, like, a sexy way?" I asked, hopefully.

Emily grimaced. "Uh...sure. If that's what you need to tell yourself."

"Guys, I'm already nervous enough!" I groaned and stepped back, pulling out a mirror to examine my makeup-free face and the tired bags under my eyes. "I look seriously tragic."

"You look like a mom," Emily countered. "Not tragic—just tired."

Isa laughed as she looked down at her phone. "Okay, they are almost here. Yasmeen said less than five minutes. Rachel is finding them a spot to park now."

Nerves raced up and down the skin on my arms. "And the family?"

"Nomi says that Chicky is mad that she has to stay in the car until it's over," Isa informed me. "But they are here. Aston is on bodyguard duty and Yasmeen installed the child locks on the back seat doors."

Only a really good friend would kidnap your mother and your sperm donor's mother for you.

"Okay, okay. Good." Holy shit, I was beginning to get sweaty. "Does anyone have a towel? I'm getting hot."

"All the better for the whole look," Emily assured me. "When you're chasing a newborn, you're either naked or you're sweating, and since we're at a public playground, you can't really go the naked option."

I cut my eyes at her. "You're really not selling this whole motherhood life to me, you know."

Emily waved her hand nonchalantly. "Don't worry. Eventually your brain will completely erase the newborn years from your memory. It's like a trauma response, you know? Then just when you've forgotten how horrible it is, you'll be ready to do it again."

The baby kicked me hard in the bottom of my lungs and I let out a forced exhale. "The human body is shiesty."

I walked over to the picnic table that they'd helped me set up and carefully examined it. A red gingham tablecloth laid the foundation for the weekend midday picnic setup, and on top was a short bunch of Gerber daisies, two sets of plastic cutleries still in the wrapper, and then two white foam to-go boxes sat in front of both seats.

It was takeout chic at its finest.

"Mila, it looks good," Isa assured me. "They're pulling up, so we're going to go hide behind that playhouse so that I can record the two of you."

"What if she says no?" My eyes widen with sudden fear as I grip my best friend's forearms.

She shrugged. "Then we delete the video and bury her in the Potomac, obviously. No evidence left behind."

God, I loved Isa. The way she always knew how to ease my mind in every situation was an art form only she possessed. "You're seriously the best friend I ever could have asked for."

"I know," she agreed. "You don't deserve me. Now, hurry up! They'll be here any minute."

She and Emily rushed away from the pavilion and found a

spot to hide where they could still stick their iPhones up and zoom in on me. No pressure though. I glanced around the picnic area one more time, making sure everything was set up the way I'd pictured it. I mean, I hadn't really pictured anything other than chaos, and the scene certainly depicted that and then some.

I glanced down at my own body—a zip-up sweatshirt over a tank top and a pair of pajama bottoms with Adidas sandals rounding out the whole look. Plus, the toothpaste, baby spit-up and messy hair. I tried to settle my nerves with some deep breathing and then sat down at the end of the picnic table bench, my eyes trained on the entrance to the playground. There were little kids roaming around and acting like someone had just piped sugar into their veins all around, but all their screams sounded muted and drowned out to me. I could hear the blood pulsing in my ears, the breath in my lungs, and I swear I could even hear the baby moving inside of me—like she was shouting at me to "Get it the fuck together, Mom."

Love you, too, kid.

I was doing this for me, but I was doing it for her, too. I wanted to so badly for her—for both of us. Now I just needed to find out if Ari wanted that as well.

Ari walked onto the playground through the entrance with a confused look on her face, glancing behind her. I could see Yasmeen literally pushing her forward and pointing to where I was. Ari followed her gesture until her gaze found me. She smiled first, then immediately frowned, and I could see her lips moving as she said something to Yasmeen, but I couldn't hear what she was saying at this distance.

Oh, God, I think I'm going to be sick.

Whatever Yasmeen said to her, she finally began walking toward me and Ari's expression turned from confused to concerned and then determined and then cautious and then the cycle just kept repeating. I knew she had no idea why I'd had Yasmeen and Rachel bring her to a playground in Virginia —the same playground her brother hosted baby mama reunions at—on a late Saturday morning out of nowhere, mostly against her will, though they had promised her a free six-pack if she went along with it.

"Mila?" Ari called out to me as she got closer. "Are you okay?"

I stood up from the picnic bench, wobbling only slightly as I tried to find my balance. "Hi."

She came to a stop in front of me, and the concern was back on her face, but then her eyes scanned the picnic area behind me, and her expression slipped to amused. "What's going on?"

The words felt lodged in my throat, and I shook my head. "Hold on, I wrote it down."

I pulled my cell phone out of my pocket and clicked on my notes, opening the tab where I'd jotted down what I wanted to say. My eyes stayed glued to the screen as I began to read. "Ari, I asked you to come here today because..."

Ari's hand covered the phone screen, and she took it from me gently, then placed it on the picnic table behind me. She then returned her hand to mine and intertwined her fingers with mine, her voice gentle and soft. "Just talk to me, Mila."

I let out a shaky breath and lifted my eyes from our hands to her face. "I was wondering if you'd like to have a picnic with me."

"Sure." She smiled at me and gestured toward the table, and led me to one side, where I sat down as she walked around to the other side of the picnic table. "What did you bring for us?"

"Breakfast tacos, or brunch tacos, I guess at this time of day." I opened the take-out container and showed her the insides of mine. "Extra bacon and cheese on yours."

She grinned. "Appreciate it."

When she opened her own take-out container, she paused, and I saw the moment her eyes caught the words I'd written on the inside of her container's lid. Her eyes lifted above the edge of the container to find me. "Mila..."

I was definitely sweating harder now. "Ari, I don't know what you see for yourself in the future, and I don't know if I fit into it or if this baby fits into it. I also know it's a lot to ask and a bit past insane, but I know without a doubt in my mind that I'm head over heels in love with you and I know that I have nothing to offer. I'm dressed this way for a reason because if you say yes, then this is what you're signing up for. A mom on the playground with baby spit-up—actually, it's toothpaste—and messy buns and three-day-old pajamas I haven't washed all week. A woman who's made a lot of mistakes with you. Prioritized everyone but you and has been completely selfish and dickish again and again. A lawyer who just found out the bar took her license, and I am completely unemployed with zero prospects. A flailing comedian who was asked to travel to Los Angeles to audition for a pilot with no idea how I'll manage doing that with a family. And I know it's not the romantic or glamorous package you'd probably pictured for yourself, and I know that I can't give you any guarantees on if we'll be happy or if I'll be insufferable or if I'll spend the first year postpartum crying and leaking milk, but I'm all I have to give right now and I just want it to be enough. I know that I can't promise you anything other than this moment right here and now. All that to say..." I took a deep breath and tried to slow my ramble. "I love you, Ari. Gracie and I want to be your family if you'll have us."

"Gracie?" Ari's smile was wider now. "You're naming the baby Grace?"

I nodded my head, but the lump in my throat was preventing me from saying anything in response.

Ari stood up from her side of the picnic table and circled around to where I was sitting, placing one leg on either side of the bench as she sat down next to me.

That damn Tiffany song was playing again somewhere in the recesses of my mind. *I think we're alone now...the beating of our hearts is the only sound.* My eyes searched hers, daring not to breathe until she said something. *Please say yes.*

Instead, Ari's hand came to the side of my face, and she trailed a finger down the length of my jaw, then hooked it under my chin and lifted gently. "Mila, you and Gracie have always been enough for me—*as-is* condition and all. I'm sorry it took me so long to get out of my own way to see that."

Her lips pressed down on mine, and I could no longer hear the fan club cheering in the background because all I felt was her softness. My lips parted just enough to allow her closer as my hands came to either side of her face and anchored myself to her. Her hands dropped to my lap and held my knees, pulling me as close to her as possible until we were right up against one another on the bench, just kissing like our lives depended on it.

"Ari, I love you," I whispered in between kisses. "I promise the only roller coaster I'll put you on from now on is parenthood."

She grinned against my mouth and squeezed my leg. "I'm looking forward to it."

"Okay, this is still a playground," Nomi's voice broke us apart after a moment. "You guys have to keep it at least PG."

"Mom?" Ari looked surprised and I grinned, feeling like I'd accomplished the surprise I'd been going for. "What are you doing here?"

"You asked me to hold on to something for you until the right moment." Nomi wiggled her brows and held out a small key-sized envelope to Ari.

Ari's jaw dropped and she let out a slow breath, then glanced at me before she took the envelope from her mother. "You brought it?"

Okay, this wasn't part of the surprise. *What the hell is going on?*

"What's that?" I asked, but Chicky waved me silent from where she was standing next to Nomi.

"Isa, come closer for this shot!" Chicky called out to Isa, who was already walking over from her hiding spot. "Did you get all that?"

"I did. Great video so far. Emily took some photos for stills," Isa agreed, then pushed my mother and Nomi to the side so that they weren't in the shot.

"Wait, this is *my* surprise, and now I feel like I have no idea what the hell is happening," I called out to my friends and family, all gathering around as I stood up from the picnic table. "What are you guys doing?"

Yasmeen pointed behind me, and I turned to follow her gesture, only to see Ari kneeling down on one knee.

I gasped, my hand flying to my chest. "Ari, what are you doing?"

"Mila, I gave my mother this ring months ago, and I told her I was going to marry you. I was just waiting for you to be ready and for me to be ready, but there hasn't been a doubt in my mind since we met that you're the person I want to spend the rest of my life with." Ari lifted a thin gold band between her fingers, one sparkling stone set in a golden embrace.

"You what?" My jaw dropped open. "You remember that I'm pregnant with your brother's child, right?"

"I'm cool with it!" Aston's voice called out from the sidelines, and I turned to find him standing beside Rachel, her elbow on his shoulder as she towered over him. "Kiss my sister!"

I grinned, a laugh bubbling up in my chest.

"He's cool with it," Ari repeated, and tears sprang to my eyes as I looked at her. "I want you and Gracie to be my family, Mila. I love you both and I'm not scared anymore. Be my wife. Let's start our family."

"I want to kiss you, but I can't bend down," I said, laughing and pointing at my large belly.

Ari jumped to her feet. "Is that a yes?"

I nodded, tears falling onto my cheeks. "Of course, yes. Absolutely."

She slid the ring onto my finger and took me back into her arms, her lips finding mine for the first of hopefully many, many more times.

"Are you sure you're ready for this?" I whispered to her when our lips parted. "I'm...a lot."

Ari pulled away just enough to wipe some toothpaste from my shirt. "I would never want less."

We kissed again, and I felt the baby moving. "Grace is kicking," I said out loud, too loud, because Chicky heard it.

"Ari, move. Let me feel the belly," my mother said as she literally pushed my future wife out of the way to place two hands on my stomach. "*Mi nieta*, say hi to your *abuelita!*"

I shook my head, my gaze not leaving Ari's over the top of my mother's head. I mouthed the words *I love you* to her and she did the same in response, and I couldn't believe I was standing here with my future child and my future wife and my current mother in pure bliss all because of a man's sperm donation.

Goddamn patriarchy.

Epilogue

"What do you think about an edible panties subscription box—a new flavor every month?" Yasmeen asked me. "I feel like that would sell, right?"

My brows lifted close to my hairline as I finished placing a tall pink candle in the center of the smash cake. "I think we're at a child's first birthday party, is what I think."

"Brainstorming can happen anywhere," Yasmeen countered. "That's what makes an entrepreneur great—always open to the next big thing."

"Is it? What happened to the nonbinary romper clothing line you were working on?" While I loved Yasmeen, she always had wild ideas she was working on that she was sure would take off. So far, that had never come to fruition and her family had a lot of thoughts about her lack of direction.

"Customer feedback was not positive," Yasmeen admitted, this time letting out a long sigh. "Apparently people don't like having to get totally naked just to pee—and rompers and jumpsuits with a zipper in the crotch are suspect."

I tried not to laugh, but a small chuckle slipped out. "I mean, I love a good jumpsuit, though."

She sighed. "Well, jumpsuits are out. Edible panties are in. What do you think of the company name *Chewing on Love?*"

I grimaced and shook my head emphatically. "Absolutely the fuck not. Don't you dare."

"Mila?" Ari popped her head into the kitchen from the entrance to the hallway. "Can I see you for a second? We have an issue with the laundry."

"Oh, God," I groaned, quickly getting up and following her into the hallway. "Did Chicky put the nonorganic stuff in Gracie's load of clothes?"

We got to the laundry room at the end of the hall, across from the entrance to my bedroom and the farthest away from the living room, where party decorations were currently being set up for Gracie's first birthday celebration in an hour. Ari grabbed me by the wrist and pulled me into the laundry room, then locked the door behind us.

I looked around the room, and nothing seemed out of place. Then I glanced back at Ari, noting the devilish grin on her face. "Oh, *this* is a booty call."

Ari stepped closer to me and wrapped her arms around me, pulling me flush to her as her lips met mine. "I couldn't resist. It's so rare we have someone watching Gracie."

"Bless Chicky for this moment alone." I lifted my arms around her neck, turning my head enough to kiss her fully. God, she still tasted as amazing as she had the first time I'd kissed her over a year and a half ago, but now everything about her felt familiar. Not in a bad or boring way, but in a comfortable way like this was my person and every inch of her body just confirmed that over and over again.

She pressed me back and my heels hit the bottom of the washing machine. Her hands were flat on the machine top, casing me in on either side, but I had very different plans for that moment. I pushed Ari back a step, this time putting my hands on her hips and tugging at the sides of her pants. Her brows lifted and she quickly helped me with pulling them, as well as the boy shorts she had on, the rest of the way down and stepping out.

I tapped the top of the washing machine. "Sit."

She didn't waste any time and with a small hop, she was on top. I reached behind her and turned it on—spin cycle—then pushed her knees apart as I stood between them. Her mouth was on mine again, leaning down to find me as my hands tangled through her hair and pulled her closer to me.

"I've missed this," she groaned the words against my lips. "We need to plan more date nights. Just-us time."

"God, yes," I panted back.

The first year of motherhood had been a whirlwind, and it had certainly bonded Ari and me in ways that I couldn't even imagine—we were like a formidable team; hell, we were a family. But one of the areas that had taken a bit of a back seat was the romance and physical intimacy, which was hard to fit in around diaper changes, feedings, and co-sleeping. I wasn't worried, though, because we'd lost nothing even in the change of pace. In fact, I'd argue we gained so much more. The physical connection between us wasn't going anywhere, and the way my body felt right now proved it.

"Lean back," I directed, my lips slipping down to her jawline and then her neck, lingering a moment on her collarbone—God, I loved her collarbone—until I pressed her knees farther apart with both hands.

She did as instructed, and her gaze was heavy as she looked down at me as I started with a soft kiss on her inner thigh, not too far above her knee. I let my tongue trail against her skin, inching closer to her center, and I could feel her tremble beneath me, even with the shaking of the washing machine. I loved touching this woman, and I loved the way she opened up to that touch. It was something that she'd held back on for so long, but now that we were in this—we were a team—she had given me every bit of herself and more.

My short fingernails lightly scraped up the skin on the inner thigh of one leg as my tongue did the same on the other leg. Her breathing was erratic, and I reveled in the feeling of her response to me. I reached behind her and scooted her hips closer to the edge and pressed her torso just enough to instruct her to lean back farther. She moved down until she was propped up on her elbows, still watching me, and I made sure our eyes were completely locked onto one another as my tongue found her center.

She groaned and lifted her hips against my mouth, her eyelids getting heavier as I played small circles across her clit. I moved lower and sucked her into my mouth, flicking my tongue against her as I did so, and she shook against me.

"Mila..." Her head fell backward, and I knew if we weren't just a hallway and door away from half of a party, she'd be screaming my name right now. "Oh, just like that."

My mouth moved lower as I released her and slid my tongue inside of her as far as I could reach. She was warm and wet, and every sweet bit I remembered as she pulsed around me. Her hips were bouncing off the machine now, moving up to meet me every time I slid my tongue inside of her. She was getting closer, and I could feel her desperation now.

"Please..." She was panting and I pushed her knees wider apart as my finger replaced my tongue.

I used a come-hither motion as I slid a second digit inside of her and coaxed her G-spot. My tongue lapped at her clit in a frenzied motion, pressing harder for a moment then moving to a soft touch, then back to fervent. Ari's head had completely fallen back at this point, and all I could see was her long neck and chin as her chest heaved up and down. I felt her begin to tense around my fingers, and I applied just a bit more pressure, knowing that would take her over the edge and it absolutely did. She shook around me, her body moving of its own will as I begged each and every tremor out of her until she was loose and limp in my arms.

When she finally stilled, I pulled her toward me in an embrace as she slid off the top of the washing machine and into my arms. She wrapped her body around mine like a cocoon, and we just held each other for a moment. Her breathing was soft against my ear, and I reveled in the warmth of her hug.

After a few long moments, she finally pulled away and slid her pants back on from the pile they'd been in on the floor. Once dressed, she placed one arm around me and pulled me against her, her other hand resting on my jaw and gently caressing my cheek with her thumb. "What do you say we ask Chicky to babysit overnight tonight and we get a hotel downtown?"

"She'd be thrilled for the chance to spoil Gracie rotten without our commentary." My arms squeezed around her waist, and we kissed slowly, quietly, gently until I could hear someone screaming my name from down the hallway. "I'm being summoned."

"I'm not done," Ari groaned, kissing me harder.

I laughed, kissing her back twice more before pulling away. "Tonight, I'm all yours. I promise."

She pouted but was smiling as she playfully swatted me on the ass. "I'm holding you to that."

"I hope you do." I wiggled my brows at her and opened the laundry room door to head out.

"Mmm, look at her go," Ari said in a low voice as I walked away.

I shook my ass for her viewing pleasure and offered her a wink before I was back in the kitchen and staring down at my mother holding my daughter completely covered in what appeared to be ketchup.

"What the heck happened?" I asked, taking Gracie from her. "Guests are going to be here in like fifteen minutes!"

Chicky shrugged. "I gave her some chicken nuggets and she wanted to dip them in ketchup. She likes to finger paint, you know. She might be an artist one day. We should really foster her gift. Creativity is soul food."

"That's fine, except now I need to get her cleaned and in a new outfit before the party starts." I was trying not to sound annoyed, but I was. I kissed Gracie on her tomato-covered cheek and walked her back to her bedroom.

She grabbed at my earrings, and I gently tugged one out of her hands. "Gracie, girl, do you remember what today is? You're one year old. A whole year old!"

I held up one finger to her as I placed her on the changing table and began using eighty-seven baby wipes to control the ketchup massacre. She giggled and squirmed, and I carefully removed her clothes so as to avoid even more ketchup spreading. Finally, after she was all clean, I dressed her again in something fit for her party and held her in my arms.

Even at one year old, she still had that baby smell when I sniffed at her head, and I pulled her against my body with a fierceness I never knew I possessed before her. It was like I loved her so much, I wished I could just absorb her back into my body so we never had to be apart, ever. I kissed her pudgy cheeks and tickled her belly, and she laughed and threw her body around as I made my way back out into the hallway.

"Hey, baby girl." Ari found us, stretching out her arms to our daughter. I had placed both of our names on the birth certificate, and Ari had taken to motherhood in a way that I had not expected. But maybe I should have. She was loving and warm and clearly the *fun mom* out of the two of us. Gracie absolutely adored her, and I still found myself in moments like this, wondering how it was all possible. How had this become my life?

Thank God, they had become my life.

Gracie waved her arms at Ari, and I handed her over. "Say hi to Mommy!"

Ari kissed Gracie's cheek and took her in her arms.

"Yasmeen says she needs help with the cupcakes," Ari told me. "Something about the flavor being wrong."

My brow furrowed. "What? I didn't order any cupcakes."

"Maybe that's the problem?" Ari laughed, bouncing Gracie on her hip. "Oh, also, you left your phone in the laundry room and it's blowing up."

She handed it to me, and I glanced down at the screen. Two missed calls from my agent and a text message that just said: *You got the part. See you in Los Angeles on Monday.*

I turned my phone screen to Ari so she could read it. "Holy shit."

She grinned. "We're going to Hollywood, baby."

"Are we ready for this? I mean, I know we talked about it before I auditioned, but this is...this is *real*." I had been auditioning for the lead in a queer sitcom that was exactly the type of work I wanted to be doing. Not that I'd ever expected acting to be in my future, but it was kind of a natural progression from comedy, and I found that as long as the storyline was funny, I enjoyed being in it.

"Mila, we've been talking about this for six months," Ari reminded me. "We're ready for this. We will follow you anywhere. Right, Gracie?"

Gracie held out her hands to me and I gave her a big kiss.

"Happy Birthday, baby girl," I cooed at her. "Your mommies love you so much."

"And your mommy loves your mommy so much," Ari added, kissing me this time. "Come on. We've got a lot to celebrate today."

I grinned and took her hand as we walked down the hallway toward the living room feeling so incredibly full and happy in a way that I'd never even known to dream for.

"Hey, do you think your brother would give us more sperm so Gracie can have a sibling?" I casually tossed out the question to Ari.

She whirled her head toward me. "You want to do this again?"

"I mean, it went so well the first time." I grinned, squeezing her hand in mine.

Ari laughed and shook her head. "You are wild, woman. I'm not saying no, but let's just adjust to Hollywood before we expand even further. That's a lot of change at once."

"That's fair," I agreed, but in the back of my mind, I was already thinking about what a family of four might look like a few years down the road.

BONUS SCENE

"How is that *not* a crocheting hook?" I asked, my eyes widening as I stared down at Dr. Allen in the labor and delivery room.

Yep, I never did end up switching to a new obstetrician and I was now paying the price for my decision born out of pure laziness.

"It's not a crocheting hook," he assured me. "It's to break your water. Pop that sucker open."

Ari grimaced and squeezed my hand. "I thought it did that on its own. Every movie with a pregnant person has their water gushing out all over a restaurant floor or something."

"Well, this isn't the movies, and the only food we serve here is cafeteria quality," he reminded the both of us, and I swallowed hard. "But you're still not allowed to eat until after delivery."

I was fully aware of that fact already, despite many complaints. The growling in my stomach was only dull because of the labor pains distracting me from it.

"You've been having contractions for ten hours now," he continued. "You are three centimeters dilated, and your water is still intact. If we want to get this show going, we're going to need to help it along. Otherwise, we're going to have to start some Pitocin."

"I heard that back in the day, they used to just put women to sleep until the baby was out. Can we go back to that?" I asked.

Dr. Allen gave me a hard look over his surgical mask and then lifted the not-a-crocheting-hook up in the air. "Are you ready?"

I turned to Ari and squeezed my eyes shut. "Ari, can you watch for me?"

"What?" She balked. "Why can't I close my eyes, too?"

"Because I have to close my eyes, and I still want someone to tell me about it!" I insisted. "Either that or take a video."

"No videos in here," the nurse next to Dr. Allen commented.

Ari groaned and stepped closer to the doctor, not letting go of my hand once. "Fine. I'll watch."

"All done!" Dr. Allen popped back up and smiled at me as Ari scurried back to me, white as a sheet, like she'd just witnessed a crime. "We're going to have you straddle a peanut ball now for a bit, and then I'll check back in about an hour."

"A what?" Christ, why were balls such a prominent part of my pregnancy and birthing story? Why couldn't I scissor sit on a taco or something?

One of the multiple nurses buzzing about walked into the room with a giant blue inflatable ball that looked like a cross between an exercise ball and a giant peanut-shaped ball sack. "Here it is. We're just going to put it between your legs to help you dilate a bit quicker."

"Sitting on this ball sack is going to make her give birth quicker?" Ari asked, and then I heard her mumble *goddamn patriarchy* under her breath.

I tried not to laugh but miserably failed. "Between this or the crochet needle, this feels like the smaller concession."

"Fair," Ari agreed.

The nurse helped place the peanut ball between my legs carefully—which took some serious adjustments since I mostly couldn't feel or move my legs at all. *Sweet, sweet drugs, baby.* I'd demanded the full epidural as soon as they'd give it to me, and despite the fact that a giant needle hooked around my spine (only Ari saw it, and she nearly passed out) and then my entire back felt like it was on blazing fire for ten seconds, it was the best decision I'd made all day. My labor contractions had gone from a fifteen out of ten to maybe a one point five.

When the nurse finally left us alone, Ari pushed a folding chair closer to the edge of the bed I lay on and took a seat.

"What do you think she'll look like?" I asked, my last contraction behind me as I spent a little time basking in sentimentalism.

"I kind of hope she has Aston's cleft in her chin." Ari rubbed a finger against her own chin. "I always loved that on him when he was a baby. It was so freaking cute."

I smiled at the thought. "I hope she has my eyes. Chicky says that's the first thing she noticed about me. Has she messaged anything new?"

Ari pulled her phone out of her pocket and showed me the screen, which was just an unending list of notifications of text messages Ari had received from Chicky and other members of our family, plus friends. I'd left my phone in my bag and told everyone that if they wanted updates throughout this whole thing, Ari would be in charge of that. *It's called boundaries, damn it.*

"I'll send a mass text to the group of them in a few minutes with the most recent update because I can't keep up with all the individual messages," Ari said. "Chicky alone has sent over thirty texts—and half of them are links to birthing positions."

"Mute her." I chuckled and shook my head. "She'll find out soon enough."

Ari pushed the phone back in her pocket and smiled at me, but something about it didn't reach her eyes. She averted her gaze like she was hoping I wouldn't notice, but I knew her well enough at this point to see that something was wrong.

"You okay?" I asked, reaching out for her hand again.

She let me. "Yeah, it's just..." Her voice faltered for a moment, but I didn't say anything, waiting for her to continue when she was ready. "I'm scared. What if something happens to you?"

I knew where her triggers were coming from, and I completely understood why she was feeling that way. Truth was, I wasn't entirely *not* nervous either. Despite the fact that I was at one of the best hospitals in the area and in a time and age where mothers were often fine...maternal deaths during child-birth still happened. I'd just watched a documentary last week called Aftershock that I absolutely should not have watched a week before giving birth, and now the minority Latinx in me was freaking the fuck out about racial disparities in maternal deaths in the United States.

But enough of my soapbox for the moment.

"Ari, I'm scared, too," I admitted. "It's honestly just, I mean...anything could happen. And I know you've seen that firsthand."

I could see her visibly swallow hard, looking out the window now.

"But I also know that whatever happens, it's going to be okay," I continued. "You're going to be listed on the birth certificate right next to me. This is your child as much as she is mine. All the paperwork is already done and filed with the lawyer if the worst-case scenario happens. You're going to be an incredible mother."

"*With* you," Ari clarified. "We're going to be incredible mothers together."

I squeezed her hand again, smiling now. "I mean, they're going to write books about us. That's how amazing we'll be."

She laughed and shook her head. "That would be a really boring book."

"Eh." I shrugged. "Maybe we'd include a few spicy scenes and that would bring in the folks."

"Yes, because fetishizing female relationships is the only way to make something like that actually popular with the masses." Ari tilted her head to the side, gazing at me. "I love you, Mila. I really fucking love you."

My smile was wider than hers now and I tugged her toward me because there was zero chance I could sit up more than the hospital bed was already propping me up. Her lips reached mine and we kissed.

"All right! Time to check on your progress," Dr. Allen announced as he walked back into the room as if he hadn't just ruined our perfect moment.

Nerves tingled across my skin. "Has it been an hour already?"

"Forty-five minutes," he replied, snapping gloves on with the help of a nurse. "But I'm about to take a lunch break, so I wanted to check before I go."

Not surprised. The nurse removed the peanut ball from between my legs, and Dr. Allen shoved his whole fist where the sun didn't shine, fingering my cervix to see how dilated I was. And, yes, I could absolutely feel all of this, but thanks to the drugs, it was more like a heavy pressure and mental discomfort, rather than physically painful or specific.

"Well, there goes my lunchtime," Dr. Allen said wistfully, removing his hand. "Mila, you're ten centimeters already. It's go-time."

"What?" I squawked out the word like I didn't believe him. "Are you serious?"

"You want to check for yourself?" he asked, lifting one brow and staring at me over the sheet across my knees.

"Uh..." I shook my head. "What do we do then? Like...what happens now?"

Ari was on her feet and looking more than a little panicked, but she was doing a great job keeping it to herself. "What should I do?"

"Here, Mom," the nurse said to Ari. "Hold her leg like this and I'll hold the other."

I saw the flicker of a smile cross Ari's face at being called Mom, and she followed the nurse's instructions on how to hold my leg out at an angle, knee bent. I couldn't even feel her holding it, to be honest.

"You're going to push on the count of three," Dr. Allen began his instructions. "We'll do that three times in a row, then take a break. Then three more pushes, then break. Got it? Three on three."

I nodded my head, feeling a surge of adrenaline push through me as he began counting off. I pushed when commanded, took breaks when I could, and felt the sweat dripping down my face as each moment passed. It felt like seconds were going by, but I could see the clock on the wall, indicating a much longer time span.

This entire experience was wild and so...feral. Like, I felt this primal sense of self take over my body as I was pushing and then when that final push came, I screamed as I exited her from my body.

"You did it, Mama!" Dr. Allen lifted a gray-skinned, bloody, white-cheesy-looking-substance-coated, cone-headed alien up for me to see.

I gasped. "Oh my God, what's wrong with her?"

Ari laughed. "I think that's normal, Mila."

"That's our baby." It was both a question and a statement as I tried to process everything I was seeing right now—this new person I had just created. She was here. She was alive. She was *mine*.

"Hey, and you didn't poop the table," Ari added, grinning at me. "I love that for you."

Small miracles. I laughed, but it probably came out more like a strangled, sweaty cry.

"You cutting the cord, Mom?" Dr. Allen asked Ari, handing her a pair of giant, sterile scissors.

She nodded and did the snip snip without passing out—even when the umbilical cord shot out some blood like someone letting go of a hose still turned on—and I couldn't help but feel incredibly proud of her.

"We'll get the baby cleaned up," Dr. Allen assured me, passing the baby off to a team of nurses who were doing God knows what at a little medical bassinet setup. "The skin color will be normal in about twelve hours—same with the head shape. The vaginal canal just squishes it a bit. You ready to push again?"

"What? Why?" I looked over to where the baby was, desperately wanting to hold her in my arms.

"The placenta has to come out. Ready, on three again." Dr. Allen went back under the curtain, and I cursed every Hollywood movie that didn't prepare me for this part at all.

A few more pushes later and Dr. Allen lifted up a giant red-and-purple organ-looking sac for me to see before dropping it into a white medical bucket. "Look at that sucker. You have a healthy placenta there, Mama. Make sure to tell the nurses what you want us to do with it once you're cleaned up."

"Okay," I said weakly, still trying to peer over the doctor's shoulder at the baby station. "Can I hold her yet?"

"As soon as I'm done stitching you up," he confirmed. "You've got at least three internal stitches and maybe one or two external ones. Don't worry, you didn't rip to your anus."

"Well, that's just great." I let my head fall back onto the mattress as he finished stitching me up—thankfully, I could barely feel that at all, and my only focus was on Gracie.

The nurse carried her over to me, wrapped in a small, soft blanket and placed her on my chest. I maneuvered out of their way as they moved the fabric between us so Gracie was skin to skin on my chest.

Ari leaned in next to us, squeezing my arm as we both looked down at the little baby's squishy face.

"Hi, Gracie...welcome to the world," I whispered. "It's a terrible place to be, but we're going to do everything in our power to make it the best thing you've ever experienced."

"God, she's really beautiful." Tears were in Ari's eyes, and although I didn't yet see what she saw—hello, the creature still looked part alien—I loved that she saw it.

I didn't feel that insta-love in that moment that some moms

say they feel. I thought I would, and I was kind of sad that it wasn't there. Instead, I felt an insta-protectiveness. This bond or attachment that was like I would fiercely defend and protect this little alien creature, no matter what. The love part...that would come as I got to know her. That would come as we got to know each other over the coming weeks and months, and I had no doubt that she'd be one of the greatest loves of my life.

I placed a gentle, soft kiss against Gracie's head and then looked up at Ari. She smiled, tears already flowing down her cheeks and then she kissed Gracie's head next.

"Welcome to the family, Gracie," Ari said. "This is forever. The three of us—we're forever."

"Forever," I agreed.

Bonus Scene

The Story of Gracie's Birth

"How is that *not* a crocheting hook?" I asked, my eyes widening as I stared down at Dr. Allen in the labor and delivery room.

Yep, I never did end up switching to a new obstetrician and I was now paying the price for my decision born out of pure laziness.

"It's not a crocheting hook," he assured me. "It's to break your water. Pop that sucker open."

Ari grimaced and squeezed my hand. "I thought it did that on its own. Every movie with a pregnant person has their water gushing out all over a restaurant floor or something."

"Well, this isn't the movies, and the only food we serve here is cafeteria quality," he reminded the both of us, and I swallowed hard. "But you're still not allowed to eat until after delivery."

I was fully aware of that fact already, despite many complaints. The growling in my stomach was only dull because of the labor pains distracting me from it.

"You've been having contractions for ten hours now," he

continued. "You are three centimeters dilated, and your water is still intact. If we want to get this show going, we're going to need to help it along. Otherwise, we're going to have to start some Pitocin."

"I heard that back in the day, they used to just put women to sleep until the baby was out. Can we go back to that?" I asked.

Dr. Allen gave me a hard look over his surgical mask and then lifted the not-a-crocheting-hook up in the air. "Are you ready?"

I turned to Ari and squeezed my eyes shut. "Ari, can you watch for me?"

"What?" She balked. "Why can't I close my eyes, too?"

"Because I have to close my eyes, and I still want someone to tell me about it!" I insisted. "Either that or take a video."

"No videos in here," the nurse next to Dr. Allen commented.

Ari groaned and stepped closer to the doctor, not letting go of my hand once. "Fine. I'll watch."

"All done!" Dr. Allen popped back up and smiled at me as Ari scurried back to me, white as a sheet, like she'd just witnessed a crime. "We're going to have you straddle a peanut ball now for a bit, and then I'll check back in about an hour."

"A what?" Christ, why were balls such a prominent part of my pregnancy and birthing story? Why couldn't I scissor sit on a taco or something?

One of the multiple nurses buzzing about walked into the room with a giant blue inflatable ball that looked like a cross between an exercise ball and a giant peanut-shaped ball sack. "Here it is. We're just going to put it between your legs to help you dilate a bit quicker."

"Sitting on this ball sack is going to make her give birth

quicker?" Ari asked, and then I heard her mumble *goddamn patriarchy* under her breath.

I tried not to laugh but miserably failed. "Between this or the crochet needle, this feels like the smaller concession."

"Fair," Ari agreed.

The nurse helped place the peanut ball between my legs carefully—which took some serious adjustments since I mostly couldn't feel or move my legs at all. *Sweet, sweet drugs, baby.* I'd demanded the full epidural as soon as they'd give it to me, and despite the fact that a giant needle hooked around my spine (only Ari saw it, and she nearly passed out) and then my entire back felt like it was on blazing fire for ten seconds, it was the best decision I'd made all day. My labor contractions had gone from a fifteen out of ten to maybe a one point five.

When the nurse finally left us alone, Ari pushed a folding chair closer to the edge of the bed I lay on and took a seat.

"What do you think she'll look like?" I asked, my last contraction behind me as I spent a little time basking in sentimentalism.

"I kind of hope she has Aston's cleft in her chin." Ari rubbed a finger against her own chin. "I always loved that on him when he was a baby. It was so freaking cute."

I smiled at the thought. "I hope she has my eyes. Chicky says that's the first thing she noticed about me. Has she messaged anything new?"

Ari pulled her phone out of her pocket and showed me the screen, which was just an unending list of notifications of text messages Ari had received from Chicky and other members of our family, plus friends. I'd left my phone in my bag and told everyone that if they wanted updates throughout this whole thing, Ari would be in charge of that. *It's called boundaries, damn it.*

"I'll send a mass text to the group of them in a few minutes with the most recent update because I can't keep up with all the individual messages," Ari said. "Chicky alone has sent over thirty texts—and half of them are links to birthing positions."

"Mute her." I chuckled and shook my head. "She'll find out soon enough."

Ari pushed the phone back in her pocket and smiled at me, but something about it didn't reach her eyes. She averted her gaze like she was hoping I wouldn't notice, but I knew her well enough at this point to see that something was wrong.

"You okay?" I asked, reaching out for her hand again.

She let me. "Yeah, it's just..." Her voice faltered for a moment, but I didn't say anything, waiting for her to continue when she was ready. "I'm scared. What if something happens to you?"

I knew where her triggers were coming from, and I completely understood why she was feeling that way. Truth was, I wasn't entirely *not* nervous either. Despite the fact that I was at one of the best hospitals in the area and in a time and age where mothers were often fine...maternal deaths during child-birth still happened. I'd just watched a documentary last week called Aftershock that I absolutely should not have watched a week before giving birth, and now the minority Latinx in me was freaking the fuck out about racial disparities in maternal deaths in the United States.

But enough of my soapbox for the moment.

"Ari, I'm scared, too," I admitted. "It's honestly just, I mean...anything could happen. And I know you've seen that firsthand."

I could see her visibly swallow hard, looking out the window now.

"But I also know that whatever happens, it's going to be okay," I continued. "You're going to be listed on the birth certifi-cate right next to me. This is your child as much as she is mine.

All the paperwork is already done and filed with the lawyer if the worst-case scenario happens. You're going to be an incredible mother."

"*With* you," Ari clarified. "We're going to be incredible mothers together."

I squeezed her hand again, smiling now. "I mean, they're going to write books about us. That's how amazing we'll be."

She laughed and shook her head. "That would be a really boring book."

"Eh." I shrugged. "Maybe we'd include a few spicy scenes and that would bring in the folks."

"Yes, because fetishizing female relationships is the only way to make something like that actually popular with the masses." Ari tilted her head to the side, gazing at me. "I love you, Mila. I really fucking love you."

My smile was wider than hers now and I tugged her toward me because there was zero chance I could sit up more than the hospital bed was already propping me up. Her lips reached mine and we kissed.

"All right! Time to check on your progress," Dr. Allen announced as he walked back into the room as if he hadn't just ruined our perfect moment.

Nerves tingled across my skin. "Has it been an hour already?"

"Forty-five minutes," he replied, snapping gloves on with the help of a nurse. "But I'm about to take a lunch break, so I wanted to check before I go."

Not surprised. The nurse removed the peanut ball from between my legs, and Dr. Allen shoved his whole fist where the sun didn't shine, fingering my cervix to see how dilated I was. And, yes, I could absolutely feel all of this, but thanks to the drugs, it was more like a heavy pressure and mental discomfort, rather than physically painful or specific.

"Well, there goes my lunchtime," Dr. Allen said wistfully, removing his hand. "Mila, you're ten centimeters already. It's go-time."

"What?" I squawked out the word like I didn't believe him. "Are you serious?"

"You want to check for yourself?" he asked, lifting one brow and staring at me over the sheet across my knees.

"Uh..." I shook my head. "What do we do then? Like...what happens now?"

Ari was on her feet and looking more than a little panicked, but she was doing a great job keeping it to herself. "What should I do?"

"Here, Mom," the nurse said to Ari. "Hold her leg like this and I'll hold the other."

I saw the flicker of a smile cross Ari's face at being called Mom, and she followed the nurse's instructions on how to hold my leg out at an angle, knee bent. I couldn't even feel her holding it, to be honest.

"You're going to push on the count of three," Dr. Allen began his instructions. "We'll do that three times in a row, then take a break. Then three more pushes, then break. Got it? Three on three."

I nodded my head, feeling a surge of adrenaline push through me as he began counting off. I pushed when commanded, took breaks when I could, and felt the sweat dripping down my face as each moment passed. It felt like seconds were going by, but I could see the clock on the wall, indicating a much longer time span.

This entire experience was wild and so...feral. Like, I felt this primal sense of self take over my body as I was pushing and then when that final push came, I screamed as I exited her from my body.

"You did it, Mama!" Dr. Allen lifted a gray-skinned,

bloody, white-cheesy-looking-substance-coated, cone-headed alien up for me to see.

I gasped. "Oh my God, what's wrong with her?"

Ari laughed. "I think that's normal, Mila."

"That's our baby." It was both a question and a statement as I tried to process everything I was seeing right now—this new person I had just created. She was here. She was alive. She was *mine*.

"Hey, and you didn't poop the table," Ari added, grinning at me. "I love that for you."

Small miracles. I laughed, but it probably came out more like a strangled, sweaty cry.

"You cutting the cord, Mom?" Dr. Allen asked Ari, handing her a pair of giant, sterile scissors.

She nodded and did the snip snip without passing out—even when the umbilical cord shot out some blood like someone letting go of a hose still turned on—and I couldn't help but feel incredibly proud of her.

"We'll get the baby cleaned up," Dr. Allen assured me, passing the baby off to a team of nurses who were doing God knows what at a little medical bassinet setup. "The skin color will be normal in about twelve hours—same with the head shape. The vaginal canal just squishes it a bit. You ready to push again?"

"What? Why?" I looked over to where the baby was, desperately wanting to hold her in my arms.

"The placenta has to come out. Ready, on three again." Dr. Allen went back under the curtain, and I cursed every Hollywood movie that didn't prepare me for this part at all.

A few more pushes later and Dr. Allen lifted up a giant red-and-purple organ-looking sac for me to see before dropping it into a white medical bucket. "Look at that sucker. You have a healthy placenta there, Mama. Make sure to tell the nurses what you want us to do with it once you're cleaned up."

"Okay," I said weakly, still trying to peer over the doctor's shoulder at the baby station. "Can I hold her yet?"

"As soon as I'm done stitching you up," he confirmed. "You've got at least three internal stitches and maybe one or two external ones. Don't worry, you didn't rip to your anus."

"Well, that's just great." I let my head fall back onto the mattress as he finished stitching me up—thankfully, I could barely feel that at all, and my only focus was on Gracie.

The nurse carried her over to me, wrapped in a small, soft blanket and placed her on my chest. I maneuvered out of their way as they moved the fabric between us so Gracie was skin to skin on my chest.

Ari leaned in next to us, squeezing my arm as we both looked down at the little baby's squishy face.

"Hi, Gracie...welcome to the world," I whispered. "It's a terrible place to be, but we're going to do everything in our power to make it the best thing you've ever experienced."

"God, she's really beautiful." Tears were in Ari's eyes, and although I didn't yet see what she saw—hello, the creature still looked part alien—I loved that she saw it.

I didn't feel that insta-love in that moment that some moms say they feel. I thought I would, and I was kind of sad that it wasn't there. Instead, I felt an insta-protectiveness. This bond or attachment that was like I would fiercely defend and protect this little alien creature, no matter what. The love part...that would come as I got to know her. That would come as we got to know each other over the coming weeks and months, and I had no doubt that she'd be one of the greatest loves of my life.

I placed a gentle, soft kiss against Gracie's head and then looked up at Ari. She smiled, tears already flowing down her cheeks and then she kissed Gracie's head next.

"Welcome to the family, Gracie," Ari said. "This is forever. The three of us—we're forever."

"Forever," I agreed.

Interested in reading more in this universe?

The next two books, LES BE HONEST and DOPPEL BANGER, are coming soon! Check the author's website for updates.

Acknowledgments

Before I dive in, I'm going to answer a few of the most common questions I get from readers about this book!

Is this book real? No, it's a fictionalized story based on real-life queer families and different journeys to creating family.

Is there an app like this? Yes, it absolutely exists and helps people of all backgrounds. It isn't called Baby Bank, though.

Do sperm donors like that exist? Yep. Good people are out there. Every scenario in this book is based on real-life examples and situations, including situations like the Baby Mama Mingle.

Are there families like Mila and Ari's? Yep. Family is what you decide it is. It can look however you want it to look.

Why do you call this a lesbian romance? This book has all kinds of characters including pansexual main character, lesbian main character, and varying other sexualities throughout. Some people might choose to put the label "sapphic romance" on this, but I personally don't like to use the term sapphic, which is generally used for romances between non-men and non-men. However, we don't give another vague term for gay male romance to refer to non-women loving non-women. It gives me patriarchy vibes, and I don't like it. Lesbian can mean whatever you want it to mean, and I'm not going to gatekeep the term.

Why was it so easy for Mila to get pregnant? It's common feedback that I should "show more struggle" with Mila's fertility journey, but I made a choice not to. Mila's pregnancy journey is directly based on my own, and I was blessed to get pregnant both times the first time I tried. My heart aches for those who don't have an easy experience like that, and I know it's a very real reality for many. However, this book has pieces of myself in it, and this is my story.

Why wasn't there more trauma and conflict? Because there are an unending number of books out there to fill that need, but so few books that demonstrate happy, healthy queer people and relationships. Happy, healthy queer people who are out and proud, and go to therapy and have resolved past wounds...exist. Period.

* * *

All questions aside, I want to give a little history about how this book came to be and how hard I fought to make it something you're readying right now.

I originally wrote the first draft of Baby Bank in 2021 before ever getting pregnant with my second child and before Roe v. Wade was overturned. It was a wildly different world back then, and I had to go back and make quite a few changes over the years as the laws started rapidly changing.

After writing, I sent it to my agent who loved it and got it out to everyone in the publishing industry immediately. It was read by over 50+ different editors at every big traditional publisher and film agents and other professionals as I spent nearly two years trying to get someone to get behind this book with me.

No one did. The responses I got were along the lines of "America isn't ready for this" or "Jane Doe in So-So State wouldn't like this" or "it just seems so far fetched" or "there needs to be more conflict and trauma." I received rejection after rejection after rejection.

All of the responses just reiterated the message that living a happy, normal queer life is still considered...abnormal.

The reality is that queer people create families in dozens of ways, and live happy, healthy lives doing so. Or at least, have the potential to do so when they're not targeted by others or the government.

Finally, after years of being rejected and told my experience as a queer person wasn't palatable for the public, I decided to self-publish. And here we are.

I hope you enjoy reading this story as much as I enjoyed writing it.

An incredibly large thank you to my literary agent, Nicole Resciniti, who championed this book for years and continues to do so. Also, thank you to my developmental and diversity editors, Kay Springsteen, Renita McKinney, and Ellie McLove. Thank you to One Night Stand Studios for your hard work on the audio version of this book, and Karla Serrato for narrating it so perfectly. Thank you to Murphy Rae and Ashley Ranae for the beautiful cover and artwork.

Writing a book is a solo project, but publishing is a group effort and I couldn't have done any of this without all of you and everyone else who helped along the way.

Last, but not least, thank you to my beautiful little family who embraces my queerness in every way.

Excerpt from the Next Book in the Queerly Devoted Series

Les Be Honest, Coming February 2024

Please note that this excerpt is subject to change and currently unedited as the book is still being written by the author.

Chapter One

"I honestly don't understand how the edible panties didn't take off," I said to my best friend and former roommate for the last decade, Rachel Blumenthal. "It was a one in a million idea—if Shark Tank hadn't turned down my application..."

Rachel shot me a look as she placed the last box down on top of the stack of other moving boxes stacked against one wall of what would soon be my living room. "There was zero chance Mark Cuban was going to invest in that, Yas. He's vegan."

I sighed and plopped down on the sectional couch pushed against the opposite wall in pieces. Eventually I'd put the entire thing back together, but moving day had been exhausting enough just getting all my things from our former home in Washington, DC to this new, larger apartment in Arlington, VA.

I'd crossed the bridge and become a Northern Virginia girl.

The irony wasn't lost on me given how often I make fun of people who can't stick it out in the big city—not that Washington, DC was that big of a city to begin with. But still, it wasn't

Virginia. *Shudder.* Despite the location, I had to admit...the price was right and the size was even righter. Real estate on this side of the bridge was significantly cheaper than in the city, and, frankly, that's what I needed right now.

That, plus a new idea for a business that would actually take off this time. The thought reminded me of the unreturned voicemail from my father on my cell phone about joining the family business, but I quickly squirreled that away to the area of my brain where childhood guilt permanently resides.

"I can't believe we're not going to be roommates anymore," I sighed, my voice stretching out like a whine. "And Mila's gone and started her own family. You and me are just...here."

"Speak for yourself, Yasmeen," Rachel replied as she dropped onto another unconnected part of the sectional couch and tossed her feet up on an spare ottoman. "At least I'm still in D.C."

I shot her a look, my eyes rolling back as far into my head as I could without getting them stuck. Was that even a thing? My grandmother had been insistent that it was, and I'd never tempted to test her wisdom—may she rest in peace.

"Okay, but you got stuck with Macavity, so..." I gave her an evil grin, referring to Mila's cat who had refused to move with our former roommate Mila thanks to her frenemies bond with Rachel.

"The world's worst consolation prize," Rachel joked, though there was absolutely truth to it.

I still couldn't believe that the three of us had gone separate ways after almost a decade sharing the same roof.

Rachel had that environmental lawyer money and so she'd gotten her own place near Barrack's Row in Washington, D.C. when we'd all split. She'd offered for me to move in with her, but it felt like time to start fresh. We were in our mid-thirties now, and I couldn't still have a roommate when I hit forty. Not that that was anytime soon since I'd just turned thirty-one last spring.

Please God, let time slow the fuck down.

Our other roommate, Mila, now lived on the east coast half the year, splitting her time between D.C. and New York City, and then spent the other half of the year filming her television pilot in Los Angeles. Fancy as fuck, but I'm not jealous at all. Nope, not even a little...but maybe the smallest smudge. Plus, Mila also had a wife and a baby girl who kept her pretty busy, so I was trying to be understanding of the lessened communication from her and that it wasn't just about her going all Hollywood on us.

Still, I missed her and the life we'd had together.

"Have you heard from Mila lately?" I asked Rachel.

Rachel shrugged loosely. "Last time I FaceTimed her, she was breastfeeding Gracie while taking a shit on the toilet. I love boobs, but even that was a lot for me."

I grinned and shook my head. "Have you ever been with a mom before?"

Rachel shook her head. "Naked Becky was my last try for a MILF, but you know how that went."

Our former next door neighbor and her messy divorce was a story for another day.

"I think I'd make a great mom one day, but I don't want to be the one who carries it. I'll let my wife do that," I commented, musing at the idea of my potential future partner. "It's super hard to find Black sperm donors though, and I'd want a kid who looks like me a little bit at least."

Not that I blamed black men even in the slightest for not trusting volunteering their DNA over to organizations. Still, it was a frustrating dichotomy for us Black lesbians.

"Hey—" I began.

The quiet room suddenly felt like it was split in two by the loud and low bass roaring of what could only be described as the Lord Jesus Christ returning and smiting half of Washington, DC.

"They have sonic jets out here in Virginia, too?" I placed both hands over my ears and groaned.

"What?" Rachel raised her voice to a near-yell.

"SONIC JETS IN VIRGINIA?" I screamed back, but the sound had passed by the time I got to Virginia so now I was just screaming into the void. "Oh. I mean, I didn't know they could hear them in Virginia, too."

"You're like less than a quarter mile from the Pentagon, and maybe three miles from the White House. You're going to hear sonic jets, babe." Rachel laughed and shook her head, but I just frowned. "Speaking of our beloved city, I should get home. I need to shower before my date tonight."

"Is this person from the kickball team, too?" I lifted one brow, because Rachel's hobby of intramural kickball had become more of a dating game show than an actual sport. "You know you're going to have to find a new team soon enough."

Rachel waved her hand as she stood and wove her way around the maze of boxes and scattered furniture. "No, this is one of my teammate's exes. She's not *on* the actual team, so it's fine."

I sucked my lips in between my teeth and shook my head. "Yeah, somehow I don't see that going the way you hope it does."

Rachel just shrugged, and I loved that she was naturally fearless in everything she did. "Maybe, but she's taking me indoor skydiving, so you know I'll try anything once."

She stood up and grabbed her tote bag that was sitting by the front door with READ QUEER BOOKS in rainbow letters across the side that she'd purchased last time we'd visited Little District Books—a local queer-owned bookstore that only sold books by queer authors or about queer characters. She slung the bag's handle over her shoulder and glanced at her phone in her other hand.

"Thanks for helping me move," I commented again as I walked her over to the front door. "Text me when you get home."

"Will do!" Rachel waved over her shoulder to me, but didn't turn to look back at me.

There was a row of haphazard electric scooters parked at the end of my street and Rachel hopped on one, linked it to her phone, and headed for the metro. I didn't trust those damn scooters as far as I could throw one—which was maybe an inch.

After she was out of sight, I returned inside and stared at all the boxes—seemed like a good day for ordering dinner in. Pulling out my phone, I scanned the options on DoorDash in my new neighborhood. Definitely not as bountiful as D.C., but it wasn't terrible either.

I was about to click on the dessert section when my sister's picture appeared on the screen—her incoming call refusing to be ignored.

"Hey, Nia. What's going on?" I turned the call on speaker and started opening one of the boxes in front of me to keep my hands busy.

"Dad says you haven't returned his call," my older sister spoke into the phone like she was exhaling all the stress she had been holding in to that one sentence. "Why do I have to be the middle man? Can't you just call him back?"

"Absence makes the heart grow fonder." I sidestepped her answer like the skilled baby of the family that I am. "He's a lot happier with me when he doesn't actually know what I'm doing."

"Oh, God..." Nia groaned loudly and I heard her typing on a keyboard in the background. I glanced at the time on my cell phone, noting that she was nearing the end of her work day and there was nothing that was going to distract her from being Type A productive. In fact, I'm pretty sure there has not been a single day at her job that she's even considered clocking out before five o'clock. Typical older sister syndrome. "Does that mean there's something going on with you that would make him unhappy? You realize I'm the target left behind when you're missing in action?"

Maybe it was the oldest daughter gene, but there was nothing Nia wouldn't do for our family and she cared for my parents and my brother and I more than she ever did for herself. Hell, it was basically the story of her entire life, including her career as an executive in the non-profit world making a lot less money than she deserves.

"Why can't Demetrius pick up the slack?" I asked, referring to my older brother, the middle child and golden boy in the Kiani clan. "He's the one working for dad anyway. He gets a paycheck to deal with his bullshit."

"Paycheck—something you really need to know more about," Nia added. "You know dad wants you to come on board at the firm. He said you could start off as an executive assistant, just get your feet wet in the field, you know? You could shadow an investigator and get involved in the security side once you feel ready—no rush."

I rolled my eyes at the very thought of one day working in corporate security for government contractors and rich people Capitol Hill-adjacent. "Nia, the day I walk into a giant conference room full of white men in suits whose girlfriends meal-prepped them bland boiled chicken and unseasoned broccoli for lunch is the day I've given up all hope for happiness."

She let out a low chuckle, and I could imagine her shaking her head. "I mean, they're not *all* white."

"Everyone we contract with is basically a Ted Cruz lookalike," I countered, because while Kiani Security was a Black owned business and made sure to staff BIPOC employees, there was still an abundance of government contracts we bid on that were basically white-washed. I mean, the entire Hill was.

It's not like I wasn't proud of everything my father had built as a single father—another thing I tried not to think about because the guilt itched at me there, too. Not that I could blame myself for our mother passing away shortly after giving birth to me—an unnecessary c-section that led to an infection she just couldn't fight. I should blame the medical system and the disparity in care when it comes to Black mothers.

And yet, still, I can't help but feel like I'm here...and she's not.

It's not unrelated.

My father had been working as a Capitol Police Officer at one of the Senate buildings at the time, but in the aftermath of my mother's death, he'd decided to leave the force and begin his own security consulting company. They'd started with physical security first, but eventually expanded into everything from private investigations, background checks, and, most recently, cyber and IT security.

I felt the familiar weight on my chest and my internal defenses kicked into gear—keep it light, keep it humorous, keep it at a distance where it can't hurt me.

"Plus, Nia, it's not like *you* work for dad," I reminded her with a barely-joking lilt in my tone. "You ran the moment you graduated college. Why do I have to be the scapegoat?"

"Because, first of all, I actually graduated college, and second of all, I *have* a job, Yas," Nia reminded me. "You're living off the family trust and random dead-end jobs."

I bristled at the completely true accusation. "Okay, but I live pretty frugally for someone with a trust fund. It's not like

I'm out here being some sort of Instagram influencer riding private jets all day. I pull my own weight."

"I know that." Nia sighed.

We both were more than aware that that trust fund was an incredibly thoughtful gift our mother put into place before Demetrius was born that she insisted her life insurance pay directly into if anything ever happened. She hadn't known things would turn out the way they did, but that small step had set up all of her children to continue to thrive after she was gone. My father said it was one of the last things she spoke about before she passed—making sure we were all taken care of even when she knew she wasn't going to be here.

Nia's voice sounded heavier when she continued. "Can you at least give him a call back so *I* don't get the calls instead? Do it for me, Yas."

"Fiiiine," I replied, even though I was absolutely not going to do that. "We still down for bottomless brunch this weekend?"

"Absolutely." She said her goodbyes and hung up the phone.

I shoved my phone in the pocket of my lightweight palazzo pants—which, remarkably, actually had pockets. Don't get me started on how women are expected to carry everyone's shit and yet are rarely given pockets in our clothes for just that.

The box I began opening was full of kitchen dishes and bowls, and I immediately lost all motivation to continue unpacking today. Instead, I checked DoorDash again and saw that the Peruvian chicken place I've been eyeing was a quarter mile from me.

Perfect excuse to go for a walk and explore the neighborhood.

A convenience store, a hipster-type coffee bar, and a bank later, I came to the end of the block and crossed over to the other side of the street. On that corner was a sports bar, and there were at least ten mid-twenties former frat boys on the patio section.

Ugh, I immediately missed my old haunts. The main queer-friendly bar in Arlington was a gay bar in Crystal City—admittedly, they have great karaoke—but damn, I missed the lesbians and trans folks from queer bars. There's nothing better than a lesbian bar, which is one of the reasons why it's super irritating that there are only a handful in the entire country. Like, literally less than twenty-five. If you think I'm joking, they made a whole docuseries about it.

The damn patriarchy doesn't stop at pockets or sexuality.

Two more blocks down and I was almost at the Peruvian chicken place when I came across a storefront with a "for lease" sign in the front window. My steps slowed for a moment and I peered through the darkened window—the inside looked like a former hair salon with mirrors and spinning chairs and a shampoo station in the back.

I stepped back from the window for a moment, but my brain was already beginning to spin its gears. The front door to the empty shop opened and I jumped back even farther, not expecting someone to have been inside. A woman with dark brown hair that reached past her shoulder blades and hung in a heavy curtain across her back stepped onto the sidewalk and then turned to lock the door behind her.

"Excuse me, miss?" I called out.

When she turned to face me, I tried not to notice how deeply blue her eyes were but failed almost immediately. I wondered if they were colored contacts, because I had never seen eyes that shade of blue before that somehow perfectly meshed with the spray of brown freckles across the tops of her pale pink cheeks and nose.

"Yes?" She straightened as she looked at me, and I didn't

miss the way she swallowed hard when her eyes found mine. *Interesting.* "Can I help you?"

"Are you the property owner for this place?" I asked, pointing to the "for lease" sign in the window.

She glanced in the direction I was pointing. "Uh, I'm the property manager."

"It's still available?" I asked—and why the hell was I even asking that? The idea was forming in my head quicker than my inhibition could shove it down.

She nodded. "Technically, yes. We've had quite a few inquiries lately, so I think it won't be long. Were you looking for retail space?"

"I'm Yasmeen," I replied, sticking a hand out toward her. "And I think I have the perfect idea for this space."

The woman looked hesitant, but shook my hand in return. "I'm Tyler, and I'm all ears."

I was still stuck on her eyes, but if she wanted me to look at her ears, too, I don't think I'd say no.

Want to read more? Preorder Yasmeen's story, Les Be Honest, coming in February 2024!

About the Author

Contemporary Romances Across the Rainbow

Sarah Robinson first started her writing career as a published poet in high school, and then continued in college, winning several poetry awards and being published in multiple local literary journals.

Never expecting to make a career of it, a freelance writing Craigslist job accidentally introduced her to the world of book publishing. Lengthening her writing from poetry to novels, Robinson published her first book through a small press publisher, before moving into self-publishing, and then finally accepting a contract from Penguin Random House two years later. She continues to publish both traditionally and indie with over 25+ novels to her name with publishers like Penguin, Waterhouse Press, Hachette, and more. She has achieved awards and accolades including 2021 Vivian Award Finalist, Top 10 iBooks Bestseller, Top 25 Amazon Kindle Bestseller, Top 5 Barnes & Noble Bestseller, and sold successfully in digital, print, and mass market paperback. She has been published in three languages.

In her personal life, Sarah Robinson is happily in a mixed-orientation marriage with a gentle giant and they have two beautiful daughters. Their home is full of love and snuggly pets in Arlington, Virginia.

Follow the Author on Social Media

booksbysarahrobinson.com
subscribepage.com/sarahrobinsonnewsletter
facebook.com/booksbysarahrobinson
twitter.com/booksby_sarah
goodreads.com/booksbysarahrobinson
instagram.com/booksbysarahrobinson

Also by Sarah Robinson

Queerly Devoted Series
(*Romantic Comedy*)
Baby Bank
Les Be Honest
Doppel Banger
(and more!)

Heart Lake Series
(*Small Town Romances*)
Dreaming of a Heart Lake Christmas
The Little Bookstore on Heart Lake Lane
A Heart Lake Summer

Women's Fiction
Every Last Drop

Nudes Series
(*Hollywood Standalone Romances*)
NUDES
BARE
SHEER

At the Mall Series
(*Romantic Comedy Shorts*)

Mall I Want for Christmas is You

Mall You Need is Love

Mall Out of Luck

Mall American Girl

Mall-O-Ween Mischief

Mall Year Long: The Box Set

The Photographer Trilogy

(Romantic Suspense)

Tainted Bodies

Tainted Pictures

Untainted

Forbidden Rockers Series

(Rockstar Romances)

Logan's Story: A Prequel Novella

Her Forbidden Rockstar

Rocker Christmas: A Logan & Caroline Holiday Novella

Kavanagh Legends Series

(MMA Fighter Standalone Romances)

Breaking a Legend

Saving a Legend

Becoming a Legend

Chasing a Legend

Kavanagh Christmas

Standalone Novels